ELIZABETH BRUNDAGE is a graduate of the Iowa Writers' Workshop and the NYU Film School, as well as a former screenwriting fellow at the American Film Institute. She lives with her family in New York.

Praise for *A Stranger Like You*

"*A Stranger Like You* operates at the highest tension point. . . . For each of these well-drawn figures, life is most definitely not a movie—and yet, none of them are able to depart from a script beyond their control."   —*Los Angeles Times*

"Brundage is an astonishing writer—some passages are as claustrophobic as Chase's imprisonment. This is the best novel I've read about the underbelly of Hollywood since *The Day of the Locust*."   —*The Cleveland Plain Dealer*

"In this intense, provocative thriller about power, war, and the portrayal of women in film . . . Brundage brilliantly shifts back and forth between Hugh, Hedda, and Denny, an injured Iraq war veteran, who plays a key role in Hedda's fate. The action culminates in illuminating revelations about the intersection of theater with reality."
—*Publishers Weekly* (starred review)

"Elizabeth Brundage is a wonderful storyteller who digs into those secret little corners of lives and personalities and lays bare the thoughts and emotions that reside therein. . . . *A Stranger Like You* so perfectly captures the modern vacuum of the soul of Southern California that it is worth rereading this work just to take notes on how she does it. I was reminded by turns of John Barth, Raymond Chandler, and Walker Percy."
—Bookreporter

"Brundage's novel is a brilliant surprise, the plot a perfect combination of pulp thriller and literary suspense."   —Curled Up With a Good Book

"Quirky, dark, full of unexpected surprises, and oh yes, a wonderful, thorny portrait of Hollywood."

—CarolineLeavittville

"[Brundage] continues to examine the way women are depicted in media and what sort of consequences that has in daily life. . . . There are no answers in *A Stranger Like You*, but there are certainly timely questions, sharp observations, and great writing. . . . Her prose is delightful, every word precise."

—My Friend Amy

"The intense character profiles and the disturbing intimate lives we glimpse through Brundage's unique approach [are] riveting. The characters—all who move masterfully through their arcs of development—will haunt you long after you finish."

—Booklovers

"*A Stranger Like You* could not be better written; it is a showcase of clever plotting, memorable characters, and dialogue that reads as if it were overheard."

—Head Butler

"A brilliant story that indeed grabbed my attention in the first two pages and didn't let go until the last."

—Bookin' with Bingo

"Brundage excels at pushing her characters to their limits and then reflecting on the consequences of their behavior."

—*Booklist*

"'People are ugly and cruel. They are relentless. They will stop at nothing to get what they want.' Like *The Player*, *A Stranger Like You* tests this hard-boiled lemma against the beautiful, nasty backdrop of Hollywood. Elizabeth Brundage delivers a pithy, ironic L.A. noir full of broken dreams and snappy repartee."

—Stewart O'Nan, author of *Songs for the Missing*

"Truly wonderful, stay-up-all-night reading . . . Brundage delivers a story that . . . is not just believable and unclichéd, but also emotionally moving and thought-provoking— without sacrificing the thriller pacing Hollywood relies so heavily upon."

—Meg Waite Clayton, bestselling author of *The Wednesday Sisters*

"Elizabeth Brundage is the real thing—an ambitious, serious novelist. Not for her, small bites. She uses Dickensian coincidence and the Russians' sense of tragic destiny, all while observing modern life with a biting acuity and a throwaway humor, and she dares you to care for characters whose self-contempt, earnest longings, and sad ingratiation are uncomfortably unalloyed. Brundage imbues Hollywood with a mystical super-reality, and scrubs it of anything stock. I couldn't stop turning the pages of this action-packed, poetic, large-souled novel. And I closed it with a pounding heart."

—Sheila Weller, bestselling author of *Girls Like Us*

"*A Stranger Like You* is a disturbingly believable thriller that catches you in a spider web of blind ambition, karma, and cinema dreams. Elizabeth Brundage perfectly captures the laid-back perniciousness of L.A. and the dark heart of the movie biz. It's a twenty-first-century 'noir' that takes you on a journey that leaves you fearful for yourself. Brundage is a singular talent."

—Dirk Wittenborn, author of *Pharmakon, or The Story of a Happy Family*

Praise for *Somebody Else's Daughter*

"Brundage has a penchant for turning topical subjects into gripping novels."

—*The Washington Post*

"A well-turned thriller . . . Brundage writes with startling clarity."

— *St. Louis Post-Dispatch*

"A deft balancing act of taut plot and richly drawn characters . . . Brundage is a storyteller supreme."   —Wally Lamb, author of *She's Come Undone*

"Riveting . . . very moving and completely involving . . . Brundage is a brilliant novelist."

—Richard Bausch, author of *Peace*

"A taut tale of suspense rounded out with sharp observations on parenting, adoption, and the fraught business of keeping up appearances."   —*The New York Observer*

"A terrific fast-paced summer read."   —*The Library Journal*

"Marvelous . . . This second finely crafted novel is superior in its superbly balanced character development. . . . *Somebody Else's Daughter* is topical and relevant."

—Mostly Fiction

"A dark, disturbing novel that was difficult to put down."   —Blog Literarily

Praise for *The Doctor's Wife*

"Appearances are deceiving in this psychological thriller . . . a compelling read."

—*The Boston Globe*

"A well-crafted work . . . From the very first paragraph of Elizabeth Brundage's debut novel, it is evident that things will not end neatly. No character inhabiting this story will escape unscathed from the choices they've made."   —*Ms. Magazine*

"An examination of what happens [to us] when we are drawn to the very thing that promises to destroy us."   —*Publishers Weekly*

"*The Doctor's Wife* is certainly a tense and compelling psychological thriller, but it's more than just a page-turner. In her dark depiction of small-town intolerance, Brundage invites us to question . . . our engagement with the world."

—Ruth Ozeki, author of *My Year of Meats*

"Elizabeth Brundage has captured the tension that resides at the crossroads of self and society. *The Doctor's Wife* encapsulates not only our uncertain, conflicted times but the maddening, endearing, fascinating contradictions of the American moral construct. This novel is as politically pertinent as it is a page-turner."

—Meghan Daum, author of *Life Would Be Perfect If I Lived in That House*

A STRANGER LIKE YOU

ELIZABETH BRUNDAGE

A PLUME BOOK

PLUME
Published by the Penguin Group
Penguin Group (USA) Inc., 375 Hudson Street, New York, New York 10014, U.S.A. • Penguin Group (Canada), 90 Eglinton Avenue East, Suite 700, Toronto, Ontario, Canada M4P 2Y3 (a division of Pearson Penguin Canada Inc.) • Penguin Books Ltd., 80 Strand, London WC2R 0RL, England • Penguin Ireland, 25 St. Stephen's Green, Dublin 2, Ireland (a division of Penguin Books Ltd.) • Penguin Group (Australia), 250 Camberwell Road, Camberwell, Victoria 3124, Australia (a division of Pearson Australia Group Pty. Ltd.) • Penguin Books India Pvt. Ltd., 11 Community Centre, Panchsheel Park, New Delhi – 110 017, India • Penguin Group (NZ), 67 Apollo Drive, Rosedale, Auckland 0632, New Zealand (a division of Pearson New Zealand Ltd.) • Penguin Books (South Africa) (Pty.) Ltd., 24 Sturdee Avenue, Rosebank, Johannesburg 2196, South Africa

Penguin Books Ltd., Registered Offices: 80 Strand, London WC2R 0RL, England

Published by Plume, a member of Penguin Group (USA) Inc. Previously published in a Viking edition.

First Plume Printing, July 2011

10 9 8 7 6 5 4 3 2 1

℗ REGISTERED TRADEMARK—MARCA REGISTRADA

The Library of Congress has catalogued the Viking edition as follows:
Brundage, Elizabeth.
   A stranger like you : a novel / Elizabeth Brundage.
      p.   cm.
   ISBN 978-0-670-02200-7 (hc.)
   ISBN 978-0-452-29709-8 (pbk.)
   1. Women executives—Fiction.   2. Motion picture industry—Fiction.   3. Screenwriters—Fiction.   4. Psychological fiction.   I. Title.
   PS3602.R84577 2010
   813'.6—dc22   2010003979

Printed in the United States of America
Original hardcover design by Carla Bolte

PUBLISHER'S NOTE
This is a work of fiction. Names, characters, places, and incidents are either the product of the author's imagination or are used fictitiously, and any resemblance to actual persons, living or dead, business establishments, events, or locales is entirely coincidental.

FOR SCOTT

How far we all come. How far we all come away from ourselves. . . .
You can never go home again.

—JAMES AGEE, *A Death in the Family*

For everything to be consummated, for me to feel less alone, I had only to
wish that there be a large crowd of spectators the day of my execution and
that they greet me with cries of hate.

—ALBERT CAMUS, *The Stranger*

GREED LEADS TO DESTRUCTION; BETRAYAL LEADS TO SEPARATION; LUST LEADS TO OBSESSION; ADULTERY LEADS TO DIVORCE; POVERTY LEADS TO ISOLATION; TRICKERY LEADS TO DECEPTION; DECEPTION LEADS TO CHAOS; LOVE LEADS TO HAPPINESS; AVARICE LEADS TO DESTRUCTION; COMPASSION LEADS TO RESOLUTION; WAR LEADS TO DESTRUCTION; OBSESSION LEADS TO DESTRUCTION; INTELLIGENCE LEADS TO REVELATION; EDUCATION LEADS TO PROSPERITY; EDUCATION LEADS TO ENLIGHTENMENT; KNOWLEDGE LEADS TO PROSPERITY; INDULGENCE LEADS TO DECADENCE; DECADENCE LEADS TO RUIN; GREED LEADS TO DESTRUCTION; BETRAYAL LEADS TO SEPARATION; LUST LEADS TO OBSESSION; ADULTERY LEADS TO DIVORCE; POVERTY LEADS TO ISOLATION; TRICKERY LEADS TO DECEPTION; DECEPTION LEADS TO CHAOS; LOVE LEADS TO HAPPINESS; AVARICE LEADS TO DESTRUCTION; COMPASSION LEADS TO RESOLUTION; WAR LEADS TO DESTRUCTION; OBSESSION LEADS TO DESTRUCTION; INTELLIGENCE LEADS TO REVELATION; EDUCATION LEADS TO PROSPERITY; EDUCATION LEADS TO ENLIGHTENMENT; KNOWLEDGE LEADS TO PROSPERITY; INDULGENCE LEADS TO DECADENCE; DECADENCE LEADS TO RUIN; GREED LEADS TO DESTRUCTION; BETRAYAL LEADS TO SEPARATION; LUST LEADS TO OBSESSION; ADULTERY LEADS TO DIVORCE; POVERTY LEADS TO ISOLATION; TRICKERY LEADS TO DECEPTION; DECEPTION LEADS TO CHAOS; LOVE LEADS TO HAPPINESS; AVARICE LEADS TO DESTRUCTION; COMPASSION LEADS TO RESOLUTION; WAR LEADS TO DESTRUCTION; OBSESSION LEADS TO DESTRUCTION; INTELLIGENCE LEADS TO REVELATION; EDUCATION LEADS TO PROSPERITY; EDUCATION LEADS TO ENLIGHTENMENT; KNOWLEDGE LEADS TO PROSPERITY; INDULGENCE LEADS TO DECADENCE; DECADENCE LEADS TO RUIN; GREED LEADS TO DESTRUCTION; BETRAYAL LEADS TO SEPARATION; LUST LEADS TO OBSESSION; ADULTERY LEADS TO DIVORCE; POVERTY LEADS TO ISOLATION; TRICKERY LEADS TO DECEPTION; DECEPTION LEADS TO CHAOS; LOVE LEADS TO HAPPINESS; AVARICE LEADS TO DESTRUCTION; COMPASSION LEADS TO RESOLUTION; WAR LEADS TO DESTRUCTION; OBSESSION LEADS TO DESTRUCTION; INTELLIGENCE LEADS TO REVELATION; EDUCATION LEADS TO PROSPERITY; EDUCATION LEADS TO ENLIGHTENMENT; KNOWLEDGE LEADS TO PROSPERITY; INDULGENCE LEADS TO DECADENCE; DECADENCE LEADS TO RUIN

PART ONE

THE PREMISE

1

He had been watching her for days. Methodically, he'd researched her background on the Internet. She'd been raised in New Jersey and had gone to Yale—according to *Variety* she was on *the fast track* and Harold Unger, her boss at Gladiator Films, was paying her six figures for it.

Surprisingly, Hedda Chase was not attractive. A photograph revealed the calamity of her looks, a gangly, unsmiling woman in somber clothing, with a bent nose that should have been fixed and a distracting little mole on her cheek that beckoned a dermatologist. It was a face you might have seen in a history book, chronicling some anonymous woman's plight in the Dust Bowl, and Hugh could only assume that, in a town like Hollywood, where most of the women insisted on being perfect, her indifference to her appearance was deliberate and may have accounted for the attitude she exuded, a kind of forlorn complacency. She lived in a bungalow in Los Feliz, on Lomita Avenue. It was a one-story Spanish style cottage, circa 1920s, hidden behind tall hedges, with a single garage in the rear. A small toolshed supplied an ideal hiding place, and it was from inside its sweltering quarters that he'd witnessed her for the first time. At half past six on a Wednesday evening in late spring a vintage blue BMW pulled into the driveway and parked in the garage, its flanks buffed to a shine. Chase emerged from the dark garage into the golden haze of sunset, pulling her sunglasses onto her head. She was talking to someone on a cell phone, a stack of scripts under her arm. Just the sight of her made him sweat. In truth, Hugh was accustomed to feeling inferior around certain women, his wife being one of the few exceptions—it was something he'd been working on with his therapist. Even his boss at Equitable Life, a consummate barracuda, liked to remind him of his pitiable status on the corporate food chain. As Chase passed the shed, he caught a whiff of her perfume, a jackhammer jasmine, and felt the prickly little hairs on his neck go stiff. She paused in the driveway, listening with contempt to whoever was on the other end of the conversation. She was dressed in a droopy ensemble, a scarf tied around her head in a failed attempt at bohemian flair. It was no outfit for a studio executive, he thought. A plane flew overhead, roaring over the orange rooftops. She shut the phone irritably and went up the steps of the small porch, unlocked the door and disappeared inside. A light came on in the foyer and then another in what he predicted was her bedroom.

It was almost dark. Through the small window of the shed he could see the last of the sun sinking into the brown horizon. The air began to cool. A car pulled into the adjacent garage and a moment later a man emerged, Chase's neighbor, and disappeared inside the house next door. The air smelled good, someone grilling a steak. Hugh slid out of the shed and walked down the concrete driveway. A shoulder-high cement wall ran along the edge of the property, over which Hugh could see the neighboring yards, the lights just coming on in windows, a trio of children being called indoors for supper. It seemed like Hedda Chase lived a nearly ideal life, he thought idly, one that he would intentionally disrupt, just as she had disrupted his.

He grabbed a metal green chair, the sort of chair his grandmother would put out on her porch in summertime, and brought it around to the side of the house where the lights from the kitchen window streamed out onto the driveway. He climbed up onto it, wobbly as a surfer, and looked inside. There she stood at the sink—they were facing each other, the thin glass of the window between them—opening a jar of herring. Gingerly, as if involved in a scientific experiment, she forked the fish onto a cracker, hors d'oeuvres style, and ate it then took a glass from the cupboard and filled it with vodka.

Sipping her drink, she turned on the radio. The phone rang and she answered it, frowning. He heard her say: "No, *Mother!* I've told you before, I can't *do* that, I *can't* and I *won't.*"

Another plane flew overhead, so low he could nearly make out its passengers. It was exceptionally loud. Peering up through the leafy branches of an avocado tree he concluded that Chase's home was under the flight path of LAX. Under the circumstances, he couldn't help appreciating the irony of the situation.

A car pulled up out front and a moment later a man entered the house and came into the kitchen. They kissed unhurriedly. The man was tall, with hunched shoulders and an oppressed demeanor. He wore a long leather coat with bulging pockets and carried two camera bags, which he gently set down onto the floor. He removed a disc from his pocket and slid it into her DVD player. Images filled the flat-screen TV on the wall. They stood there looking at it. The film appeared to be a documentary. Street people milled about a parking lot. A bearded man in a woman's pink raincoat was pulling an empty refrigerator box, straining with the effort. Closeups on his unruly beard, his vigorous squint.

Hedda handed the man a drink and Hugh heard her say, "You're brilliant, Tom. Congratulations." They toasted each other and drank their drinks and within seconds they were kissing again, stumbling out of the room in the direction of her bedroom. Hugh stepped down from the chair—he wasn't a pervert. He'd parked his car down the block, a rented Taurus. It sat waiting for him in the darkness. He walked along the crooked sidewalk. The air carried fragments of deciduous noise. In the car, he sat in the silence. Thoughts of his wife, Marion, floated through his head. An hour or so passed. And then he saw them coming out of the house.

The man drove an old Ford Bronco. It was mustard-colored, in perfect condition, the sort of jeep you could drive in the desert. Everyone drove a splendid car in Los Angeles. People were on the move, going places. They had interesting lives, they'd been lucky. He thought of Marion, driving around in her new Subaru with her little bag of wool beside her on the seat, the woolly shape like a beloved pet.

Hugh decided to follow them. The Bronco was dirty, mud-splattered, covered with bumper stickers about kite surfing. Hugh didn't know anything about kite surfing, but it conjured in his mind images of men in wetsuits on the beach. They stopped at a light. Two cars behind, he watched their heads moving through the windshield of the convertible in between. A car pulled up in the lane beside him, full of rowdy Mexican girls wearing masks of Marilyn Monroe. The masks were strange, they frightened him, and he was relieved when the light changed and the cars began to move. The Bronco turned up Laurel Canyon and wound up to a plateau. The street was lined with Spanish-style houses with orange roofs. They pulled over on a high ridge overlooking the lights of the city. Parked cars lined the curb below a party in one of the houses. The house seemed to be embedded in rock, spilling over with purple flowers, bougainvillea they called it. The Bronco slid into a tight spot and the couple got out and climbed the long narrow walkway up to the brightly lit house. People roamed in and out. Some were carrying drinks or bottles of beer. Hugh found a spot down the street and got out and walked to the party smoking a cigarette. There didn't seem to be any point in rushing or feeling nervous. He felt a pang of longing for his wife. He couldn't remember the last time they'd gone out together. On weekends, they mostly stayed at home. She'd sit at the kitchen table playing solitaire while he practiced piano. Playing the piano was the single thing he did particularly well and it pleased Marion to hear it, but he thought of his ability as a skill more than a talent, the result of years of diligent practice. The piano in their living room had been his mother's and whenever he played it he imagined her sitting there beside him on the bench, nodding her head thoughtfully the way she'd done when he was a boy, the cross she wore around her neck swinging gently as she moved.

He flicked his cigarette and climbed the stairs. The house was crowded, music simmered inside the dimly lit rooms; Coltrane. Chase abandoned her boyfriend, who sulked on the sidelines making calls on his cell phone while she meandered through the living room, kissing people on both cheeks, laughing, squawking, throwing her head back with a kind of self-possessed joy. He had to admit she was something to watch. She was like a version of Tweety Bird, the yellow feathers of her hair, the hooked nose, her birdlike stature, and yet there was nothing timid about her. She had a certain power, an edge that cut into you and made you want to be cut. It wasn't beauty that made them look; rather it was her lack of it, the indifferent eyes, the dissatisfied pout. As he watched her it came to him that her entire demeanor, down to the slightest off-putting glance, was designed to inspire doubt and awe in her underlings, losers like him who ended up working for people like her.

"Hello, there," a woman said, touching his shoulder. "What a nice surprise."

He turned around. "Hello."

"You don't remember me." She was short and compact, with freckles and pushy little breasts. Obviously, she had him confused with someone else.

"Of course I do."

"How've you been?"

"Fine. It's good to see you."

Squinting as if in pain she said, "Forgive me. I'm terrible with names."

"Hugh. Hugh Waters."

"Ida Kent, hello again." She shook his hand; hers was warm and damp.

"I'm trying to remember where we met," he said, trying not to look at her breasts.

"Something at the Writer's Guild," she ventured. "Although I haven't gone to anything in a while."

"Working on anything good?"

"Of course not. But I'm getting paid, which is apparently all that matters."

"Lucky you."

"God bless indecisive directors." She raised her glass. "Uncertainty can be very lucrative—of course nothing I write ever gets made. I suppose my work has become a very tedious habit," she said dramatically. "What about you?"

"I'm writing something on spec," he said, because he'd heard other writers say it and it sounded good. "A thriller."

"Nice," she said. "I love a good thriller."

The little group in the center of the room burst into laughter. It was the exclusive sort of laughter he remembered from his youth, the kind that made his stomach churn. Hedda Chase seemed to be at the center of it, her arms around a man in a white linen suit and fisherman's sandals. Meanwhile, the man who had come to her house was standing off to himself, talking on a cell phone.

Ida said, "That's Hedda Chase, from Gladiator—do you know her?"

"Yes," Hugh said. "I know her very well."

"Bruno is *such* an asshole." She nodded at the man in the white suit. "I don't know why I came, I can't stand him."

"Nor can I," he agreed.

"I got so screwed by him."

"Join the club."

She looked at him, her forehead tight. "I just wish things were different, don't you?"

"Of course I do."

"Some of the things that happen," she said. "It's just not right."

"I know." He held up his empty glass. "Do you want another?"

"I would, thanks."

He took her empty glass and tried to find the bar. It was loud, hot. The music stopped and a moment later something else came on, sitars and drums. Hugh overheard someone saying it was the sound track for Bruno's new movie. Parties with insurance people were much different, he thought. Hugh and Marion would sit politely on somebody's sofa, sipping weak martinis and saying very little to anyone, and on the ride home they said even less to each other. At home, they'd undress in their dim bedroom to the nightly chorus of the neighborhood dogs. It occurred to Hugh that back home he was different—a different sort of person—and people thought of him differently.

They probably thought he was boring, a real nerd. At this party, people looked at him with curiosity, as if they were wondering who he was or what he did or what he'd done, and, because there was always the possibility that he was someone important—more important, perhaps, than a few of the other guests, in fact—they smiled at him with interest, as if knowing *him* might be good for *them*. He felt pumped up; he filled his lungs with the good, sweet air of possibility, for that was what they all shared in this place, the thrilling idea that, under the right circumstances, anything was possible—it kept people going, it kept you in the game, whether you had the goods or not, and it was what most of the people in this town subsisted on.

Many of the women were beautiful. They were like rare and unusual birds. They were not available to him, he knew. And yet, he was happy just to be near them. Unlike the sourpuss women from work who smirked at him with the superior knowledge of some inexcusable personal embarrassment that he had yet to discover, the women at the party simply smiled. It occurred to him that he was not the sort of person who usually encountered a smile. Rather, expressions of dismay or distrust seemed to be the norm. At work, especially, crammed inside the elevator with an assortment of familiar strangers, many of whose expressions at half past eight in the morning seemed terribly, terribly complicated, the nonnegotiable smile was a complete anomaly.

He found the bar and fixed himself a drink and one for his new friend: Ida. Turning back into the living room, he saw Hedda Chase walking off with the host, hopping as she took off her heels while hanging onto his shoulder in what he imagined was an uncharacteristically delicate gesture, because Hugh was absolutely fucking certain that a woman like her, a woman in her position, had very few delicate qualities. He watched her narrow heels as the two of them descended the stairs like a pair of teenagers in search of recreational oblivion. Hugh brought the drinks back into the living room and handed Ida her martini while she completely ignored him. Of course he understood, in the way all subordinates understand these things, that Ida was talking to Someone Important, her face over-bright and buzzing like an almost-dead lightbulb. He excused himself and walked in the direction of the stairs. She wasn't really his type and, anyway, he'd lost track of his subject. The house was interesting, all cartoon angles and Starburst colors. People were dancing. Most of them had taken off their shoes. Watching them, it occurred to Hugh that they were like some jiggling religious cult—they all knew the steps by heart; the nonbelievers watched forlornly from the sidelines. Downstairs, the air smelled like those candles they gave you when your pet died, tinged with cherry and cinnamon. It was not a good smell. He found himself in a dim hallway and overheard Chase and their host talking in a nearby room. Gently, he pushed open the door and the motion seemed to startle them. Abruptly, the room went silent. They stood there looking at him without expectation, blank-faced. In the moments that transpired a story not without scandal erupted among all three of them, and then their faces changed subtly as if to affirm the possibility, the speculation. Hugh said nothing and then Bruno cleared his throat with purpose and said, "Down the hall on the left."

Driving back to his motel, he thought about his conversation with the other writer, Ida. As he was leaving the party, she'd pushed a piece of paper into his hand and mouthed over the noise *call me*. She'd said she'd gotten screwed. It was something that happened to writers, he thought, it had happened to him. He'd been back in Montclair, waiting for his check, when the phone call had come. His agent's whiney-voiced secretary had explained that his producer, Cory Rogers, the veritable *founder* of Gladiator Films—who'd begun his career making B movies on shoestring budgets *and was proud of it*—had dropped dead of a heart attack—a sudden and unfortunate turn of events—"he was in his seventies, you know," the secretary offered sympatheti-cally, "his *late* seventies, actually." Now this other person—this *wench*—had stepped in and dumped his movie. "It's not unusual for projects to go into turnaround," was how the secretary had put it. "Especially in situations like these." Hugh pictured his script turning through a meat grinder—and now the project, which had been slated for production in late September, was a heap of shredded papers in the trash. Exactly why it had gotten trashed was unclear to him. After a bit of coaxing, Beck's secretary admitted that Ms. Chase had hated the script. "She didn't like the premise."

"No." He tried to recollect what the word premise actually meant.

"I'll fax you her letter if you want."

In his tiny office at Equitable Life, where he'd unwittingly entrenched himself as an underwriter—something to hold him over, he'd explain to people, until his real career kicked in—he'd watched the white page emerge from the squealing grin of the fax machine. Hedda Chase had written it herself, on studio letterhead, in the inflated syntax of an Ivy League brat: *an idiotic premise, inane characterizations, a thoroughly implausible ending!* Frankly, she'd said, the experience of reading the script was akin to passing a kidney stone. *And let's not forget the misogynistic overtones!*

In fact, the letter went on to complain that the script's entire premise was anti-female. The violence he'd so precisely conveyed was, in her opinion, *over the top*. His agent, Miles Beck, had told Hugh not to take Chase's letter too seriously, things like this happened all the time in the business, he'd said. "You just have to suck it up and move on." Beck assured Waters that he'd try to set it up somewhere else—but after several months of "trying" nobody else wanted it and the agent admitted that Chase had a big mouth. "These are uncertain times," he'd muttered, sheepishly. "Word spreads pretty fast in this town. For some godawful reason, people trust her opinion."

Hugh couldn't help thinking that Beck did too; he'd discerned a twang of pity in the agent's tone as he'd rushed Hugh off the phone.

Hugh knew he shouldn't take it personally, but he couldn't seem to help it. The disappointment festered in his mind.

"I guess we won't be moving to Hollywood after all," Marion had said, almost gratefully.

It had taken Hugh five years to finish the screenplay, squeezing in an hour or two at the computer after work. Unlike some of his writer friends, he hadn't gone to film school, but had taken night courses at the local community college. Hugh had fond memories of the cement block building with its submarinelike corridors, the fast-food-bright room where the class met around a Formica table that pretended to be wood. His classmates were an assortment of misanthropes: the disenchanted housewife; the fledgling private investigator; the bored tax attorney; the cancer survivor; the bitter widower—and him. When they had gone around the table at their first meeting, he had described himself—with pride—as being an underwriter with untapped ambitions. And it was true, wasn't it? The instructor, a balding ex-hippie with sideburns that looked like Band-Aids, had a disarming stutter that made him speak very slowly. As a result, his words had surprising weight and meaning and at the end of each class Hugh experienced small and powerful revelations, as if he had just been to church. He would walk to his car, heady with optimism.

At home, he'd watch movies late into the night in his basement, long after his wife had gone to bed, sucking hits from a bong he'd had since college. He had an extensive collection of film classics. There was *Dersu Uzala; The Passenger;* Visconti's *The Leopard.* He had watched *The Passenger* numerous times; it was his favorite film. He could watch it again and again, marveling at the elegant pans of the African desert, the swells of emptiness, the persistent wind. He knew the dialogue by heart; the actor's gestures. He could almost taste their cigarettes, their gin. Watching Jack Nicholson in that stifling hotel room—Hugh would give anything to be there now—he could almost feel the sweat rolling down his back. The bleach-white walls disrupted only by the occasional spider—it was how Hugh felt about life—that the real dangers were the slippery interlopers that went unnoticed, the subtle influences that were like termites of the soul, before you knew it there was nothing left. And then later, with Maria Schneider, her understated hips, her breasts, her almost boyish swagger. *What are you running away from?*—and Nicholson's answer—*turn your back to the front seat.* She turns, watching the road spill away—letting the past go—letting freedom overtake her—the seduction of the unknown—as the camera rises up into the shimmering trees. Always at the end of the movie, Hugh felt a sense of loss. As he climbed the two flights up from the basement, he'd question his existence. Lying awake beside his sleeping wife, he'd study the web of shadows on the ceiling of their suburban bedroom, as though trying to crack some obscure, divine code.

He knew plenty about film, he studied carefully, but no one would ever guess. At work, his colleagues baited him, "How's that screenplay of yours coming? Any calls from Hollyweird yet?" Or, derisively, at a cocktail party, "So, tell me, Waters, are you *still* writing that script?" Hugh was the first to admit that finishing it had been nothing short of a miracle. With discreet pride, he'd presented the script to his screenwriting instructor, offering the stack of pages like the white sheet cake his wife had baked on his fortieth birthday. His instructor liked the script and offered to give it to his agent, Miles Beck, who, remarkably, succeeded in selling it. Cory Rogers, Hedda Chase's unfortunate predecessor, had paid him an enormous sum, which had helped Hugh and his wife immeasurably after years of sacrifice—they'd moved out of their cramped apartment in the city and bought a house in Montclair; his wife had bought a Subaru. That had been the last Hugh had heard, and then Beck's secretary had called to give him the news. Hugh had tried to call Chase, but she was always out at meetings. "I'll leave word," the male assistant assured Hugh in a bored, irritable voice, but Hugh doubted she ever got the messages because she never called him back.

He parked in the motel parking lot and wandered out to the street. It was nearly midnight and he was hungry. He didn't like Los Angeles, really. It was a sprawling, complicated city, unlike New York, which seemed straightforward by comparison. It had been his wife's idea to move out of the city, blaming it on his paltry salary when in fact she'd never liked the city and had wanted a house just like the one she'd grown up in, with a driveway and a garage and a front lawn and a bird feeder that attracted more squirrels than it did birds, and cheerful, suspicious neighbors. Mornings, he rode the train into Hoboken with all the other commuters. He didn't mind it, really. He would look out the train window with interest at the row houses in East Orange, slim buildings adorned with cheesy facades or painted in hues of gelato— pistachio or peppermint stick or lemon—and he would think: *What is it like to live there?* Or the dilapidated motel in Newark where people seemed to be living, the large, movie-screen-sized windows, the pus-yellow water in the once lovely pool, someone's skeletal dog tied to the fence. In truth, Hugh found the mystery of those rooms compelling, and he'd find himself daydreaming about the possibilities of life inside them. Eventually, the train pulled into Hoboken, a sluggish caterpillar crawling to its destination. He'd look out across the wide V of tracks and see the workers in their plaid coats at the breakfast wagon, hunched over paper cups of coffee, their cigarettes, then follow the parade of suits and overcoats down into the tubes and the subterranean journey across the river to the city, a jagged, squealing ride through flashes of darkness that always reminded him of death, after which, climbing unhurriedly out of the subway into the bright, powdered-sugar daylight that signified his arrival, he felt little relief. Somehow, in life, he felt misinterpreted. His colleagues at work, their greedy eyes in the boardroom, their handy disdain tersely dispensed like the slang of some foreign language he could not understand. Even his wife, when he'd look at her from time to time, seemed like a stranger to him and he sometimes wondered what he was doing there in that house on Rollins Avenue. Completing some ordinary and necessary task like taking out the trash, he would say to himself: *What am I doing here?* Sometimes, when he woke in their bed, he felt disoriented, the way he'd felt as a sickly child waking from a fever, the strangeness of staying home from school, his bedroom brimming with sunshine, the sense he'd had of being left out, kept apart. Separate. He felt it now, as an adult. He'd felt it all along.

He came to an all-night coffee shop and went in and sat down at one of the tables. He didn't know what he wanted. A girl was sitting alone in an adjacent booth having a hot fudge sundae. "I'll take one of those," he told the waitress. "And coffee."

"I'm making a fresh pot. It'll be just a minute."

The girl in the booth looked over at him. She was maybe thirteen or fourteen, he didn't know. Hugh and Marion didn't have children. They had tried, of course—didn't everyone? They'd been to specialists; they'd done all the tests. Finally they'd given up. The experience had changed his wife somehow.

They did not discuss it. But there it was at the dinner table. There it was in the bowl of peas, the loaf of bread, the bottle of wine, the roasted chicken. There it was on the beige carpet as they climbed the stairs night after night. And there it was in the empty room beside their own, empty like an open mouth, screaming.

The girl in the booth had a hard look. Her hair was blond, tied up in pigtails. She had a pencil case on the table; it had a picture of a unicorn on it. There was something moving around in her pocket, a disconcerting jumble, and then he saw the flash of a thin white tail.

"You've got something in your pocket," he said to her.

"I know."

"What is it?"

Frowning, she put her finger over her lips as if to shush him.

His ice cream sundae came. It looked exactly like the picture on the menu. For a while he just studied it. It occurred to him that he didn't want it now. The girl had already finished hers and was clanking the spoon against the parfait glass.

"Do you want this?" he said. "I haven't touched it."

"You don't want it?"

He handed it to her. "I want you to have it."

The girl didn't hesitate. He watched her eat, sucking the chocolate off the spoon. The waitress brought his coffee and the check. The coffee tasted bitter. It did not taste like a fresh pot. Outside, it had begun to rain. The bell on the glass door jingled as stragglers came in to wait it out. He put his money out on the table.

The girl touched his arm. "Hey, mister? You got a car?"

The question caught him off guard. "What?"

"You're not a pervert, are you?"

He blurted a laugh. "No, I'm not a pervert."

"I'm staying on Argyle. It's not far."

They ran through the rain to the motel parking lot where he'd left his car. The girl wore only a light jacket; he thought she must be cold. In the car he noticed that her eyes were glassy and her nose was running. He turned on the heat and she put her wet hands up to the vent. Her fingernails were green with dirt. She took a white rat out of her pocket, shifting it from hand to hand like a ball of dough. "This is my friend."

Hugh was not fond of rodents. The rat was alarmingly fat. He tried to concentrate on the road.

"He keeps me company," the girl said.

"What's his name?"

"Snowball. Snowy for short. He looks like a snowball, doesn't he?"

"Yes, he does." Hugh wondered where the girl had gotten it.

"I'm not from around here," she said, grimly.

"No?"

"South Dakota."

"Where do you live now?"

She shrugged, playing with the rat. "Nowhere special."

Argyle Avenue wasn't far and she pointed to a building on the corner that had a sign out front: Transients Welcome. The cement blocks of the building had been painted mint green. A single tube of florescent light hung over the door, attracting moths. A few people were hanging around out front, shielding their heads from the rain with newspapers.

"What's it like in there?" he asked her.

"It stinks." She sat there. She didn't seem to want to get out.

"Look, don't take this the wrong way, but I've got a room you could stay in. It has two beds."

"You said you weren't a pervert," she said with a hint of provocation that seemed beyond her years. *"Liar."*

"It's just an extra bed," he explained. "It's just a better place for you to stay."

She looked at him, sizing him up. "Okay, Mister Daddy. If you say so."

He drove back to the parking lot of the motel and returned his car to the same space they'd left only minutes before. His stomach ached slightly; he'd been foolish not to eat. They walked over to the motel, up the stairs, down the long corridor to the room. He took out the key and opened the door. The room smelled like insecticide. The rain made a gentle sound against the window. "Help yourself."

She went into the bathroom and put the shower on. He heard the plastic curtain sliding across the rod. He sat on the bed, waiting. She took her time. Then she came out dressed in her clothes again and got into one of the beds.

"Where did you put your little friend?" he asked.

"In my sock." She held it up for him to see. The rat's little pink nose was sticking out, its whiskers twitching. "Don't worry, he won't bother you."

"What's your name?"

"Daisy."

"Like the flower."

She turned away from him. After a moment his cell phone rang. He knew it was his wife. He let the phone ring. He looked over at the girl and saw that she had fallen asleep. For a long while he sat on the edge of his bed, watching her. She made noises in her sleep, a wheezing sound rushing up her throat. It troubled him, and he worried that she might be sick. His stomach went tight as he watched her. She shouldn't be living like this, he thought. It was wrong. It was an awful thing to see.

He slept fitfully, and was awakened at dawn by the elephantine wail of a garbage truck. The girl was still in the bed, sleeping. She had turned on her side and was sucking her thumb. It alarmed him, seeing her like that, with her thumb in her mouth. It gave him a feeling inside. It made his eyes water.

He dressed quietly, then left the room and drove to the beach. He parked and took off his shoes and socks and walked barefoot down to the shore. The sand was damp, cool. He couldn't remember the last time he'd seen the ocean. As a boy, he'd gone to the Jersey shore in summertime, but this was the Pacific. There was something about this ocean. In the distance, the air looked brown, like an old-fashioned sepia print, the water copper in the sunlight. The sea was calm, the air smelled of fish. Savage birds dove and fought. He watched them for a while, then walked back up the beach to his car.

———

At half past eleven Hedda Chase emerged from her house in work clothes, holding a cup of coffee, her hair swept up in a white turban. Morbidly, he thought of Norma Desmond. Apparently late, Chase rushed toward her car, coffee splashing over the rim of her cup, onto her hand, the hunk of keys. Hugh emerged from the darkness of her detached garage. "Good morning, Ms. Chase," he said.

She looked perplexed. "What?"

"I wondered if I could have a moment."

"I'm late," she said. "Whatever you're selling—"

"I'm not selling anything, Ms. Chase. I just want to talk."

"What about?"

"I'm Hugh Waters."

She shook her head vacantly like someone coming up out of the water in a swimming pool. She coughed.

"You don't remember me?"

"We weren't," she hesitated, squinting at him with distaste, "intimate, were we?" She looked at him. "Because if we were you were entirely forgettable."

For a moment he couldn't seem to speak. "I'm Hugh Waters." His voice sounded weak. *The Adjuster?*

"The what?"

"I wrote it."

"Oh, *that*," she said softly. She shook her head as if the memory was giving her a headache. "You're a writer? You're a *fucking* writer?" Her voice nearly shouted the revelation.

"I don't need a lot of your time," he said. "I just thought you might be able to explain some things."

"I don't conduct meetings with writers in my driveway, Mr. Waters. You'll have to make an appointment like everyone else."

"You didn't return any of my calls," he said.

"Look, call my office. I'll make sure to fit you in."

"I read that letter you wrote. You said some horrible things about me." She looked confused.

"I just want to talk."

"It's not possible," she said, opening the door of her car, but he grabbed her arm.

"Look, I've come all this way."

She began to struggle, trying to free herself, but was quickly subdued under his grip, ascertaining, perhaps, that the knot of pressure in the small of her back was the tip of his .45. "We'll go inside and have our meeting. And then I'll go." It was a lie, of course; he had no intention of going.

She nodded, her face glossy, her lips wet. It occurred to him how exhilarated he felt by the unanticipated shift in his plan. He had not imagined that he would have to touch her—not yet anyway. He had not fully anticipated what might occur between them that morning and was only beginning to realize how his fantasy of their encounter had been far more innocent than the reality of what was unfolding between them now.

Ushering her across the driveway, up the stairs to her porch, it occurred to him that she was smaller than his wife, almost frail. Her shoulders were knobby like the small stones he had fondled earlier that morning on the beach. Under his fingertips he discerned that she was shaking and he confirmed in his mind that nothing quite made an impression on a person like physical contact. He had once read an article about it, suggesting that if you wanted to leave someone with a lasting impression on a job interview you might gently touch their arm while looking at them with a sense of intensity. Your eyes should say, *I want this job,* while your gentle touch implied, *I'm your friend, you can trust me.*

"Give me your keys," he said.

"This is ridiculous," she said. "This isn't happening."

It's happening all right, he thought. *It's happening to you.*

He unlocked her door and they went inside and he dropped the keys into his pocket. The house was disappointing, not what he would expect from a movie executive. The furnishings were ordinary; uninspired, as if the room were part of a hotel suite and not a person's private home. Hedda Chase was not a housekeeper. There were heaping piles of dirty clothes, dirty plates scattered around the room, ashtrays full of cigarettes, lipstick-stained glasses with day-old booze. Stacks and stacks of screenplays. Screenplays strewn across the floor or left half-read on the coffee table like fallen birds at a skeet shoot. He pressed the gun into her back and shuffled behind her into the kitchen. "Pour us some coffee," he said, noticing the leftover pot on the counter.

He stood behind her, like a puppeteer, and watched as she took down two cups from the shelf and set them on the counter and poured the coffee.

Outside, two men were arguing in Spanish, and shortly afterward they heard the neighbor's car pulling down the driveway. Hedda glimpsed through the window, longingly, he thought, squinting in the bright sun. For a moment he imagined they were a couple, that he lived here with her, instead of back in Montclair with his wife. He indulged in the fantasy, briefly. Pictures and colors flared up in his head.

"Bring the coffee," he said, motioning to the table with the pistol.

She took the two cups in her shaking hands, the coffee spilling on her fingers. Then she set them down and looked at him as if for instruction.

"Sit." He pointed to the chair with his gun. He thought of Jean-Paul Belmondo in *Breathless*. Early in the film the actor had aimed his gun in jest—later it was the very thing that caused his demise. But in Hugh's case, the gun was only a prop; he had no intention of using it and, for that matter, had not even loaded it. He found it pathetic, of course, and very sad, that it was the only way he could get this woman to meet with him.

Just now he had the producer's full attention.

"Look," she said. "I'm sorry about what happened, all right? It's not like it's a big deal, it happens all the time. Rogers and I had different ideas," she tried to explain. "We had different ideas about things. Anyway, he's dead."

"And you're in charge."

"That's right."

"We had a deal," he said. "We had a green light."

"We're not doing those sorts of pictures anymore, Mr. Waters. We have a different philosophy now. I'm sure you understand."

"I don't think I do."

"Violence, for one thing. I think the American people have had enough of it."

"You sound like a politician."

"I read all these scripts—the stuff that goes on, the things people write . . ." She looked at him. "All the incredibly sick things people come up with—people like you, Mr. Waters." She gave him a cold look. "It's very disturbing."

"It's what people want," he said. "It's what people want to see."

"I'm not so sure." She pulled herself up dramatically like a woman about to break into song. "To be brutally honest, Mr. Waters, your script—it just wasn't any good. I didn't buy it for a minute. The ending in particular. That business about the kidnapping, parking the car at the airport. I had a hard time believing that nobody *heard* her."

"She was in the trunk," he stated in his underwriter's voice.

"Screaming!"

"Your point?"

She shook her head as if he were too stupid to understand her. "The device of the trunk—it's been done. It's a gangster cliché."

"It works, that's why people use it. It's convenient."

"Convenient?"

"Everyone has one. It's a good place to put someone." He looked at her carefully. "There's a certain irony in that."

She squinted at him as if the sight of him was hurting her eyes. "Irony is such a cheap writer's trick. I didn't buy it. I didn't buy it for a fucking minute. And they weren't going to buy it in Toledo, either!"

He could feel the sweat on his back, dampening his shirt. He swallowed. His throat felt a little sore. He could feel his feet inside his shoes, heavy as doorstops. He could feel his legs, their weight, and his large hands on his thighs.

The phone rang.

They sat there listening to it. It rang and rang.

"That's my boss," she said. "I have to go. I have to get to work."

At last her machine picked up. Hugh recognized the voice of Chase's assistant, a man with a British accent. "Harold's been waiting over an hour, Hedda. He's leaving for the airport in fifteen minutes. He's really getting pissed."

"I'm afraid you've kept Harold waiting."

"He's going to fire me."

"And then what will you do?"

She looked up at him almost hopefully then seemed to catch herself. "He's not going to fucking fire me," she said, as if it were the most obvious thing in the world.

"It doesn't matter now. It's better not to think about it."

"What?"

"I don't want you to get your hopes up."

"I don't understand."

He got up and took the phone off the hook. There was something intensely menacing about the sound it made and he could see it registering in her mind.

"You don't understand my boss. He gets insulted if I'm even a second late. He takes it personally." Her cell phone began to vibrate inside her pocketbook. "Look, I really need to get to work."

"You're not going to work today."

"What?" she said. "What?"

"By law you're entitled to a sick day."

"But I'm not sick."

"You're looking very agitated."

"Well, I *am* agitated."

"I have some medication for that."

"You what—I don't understand."

He took the pills out of his pocket and showed them to her. "You seem very anxious."

"Look," she said. "You need to go. We've had our meeting. There's nothing more to say. You said you would go."

"I know what I said. But I've changed my mind."

"What? Are you *crazy*?"

He didn't like the question. "I thought we'd try an experiment. I thought it might be fun."

"Fun? Did you say *fun*?"

"I thought it might be fun to do a little test. To see who's right."

"You're crazy. You're fucking insane."

"You have a very nasty mouth," he said. "Why can't you be nice?"

"What? *Nice*?"

He picked up the gun. Again, he showed her the pills. "It's just some Valium," he lied, "to calm you down."

"I don't want to be calm," she shouted and stood up and started for the door. He was quick—he grabbed her. He wrestled her to the ground, her little chest heaving. It was odd being on top of her. Her breath smelled of coffee. She looked at him; she refused to look.

"You're going to have to calm down." He pulled her up and pushed her back into the chair. "Take the pills."

She shook her head.

"Look," he spoke as if to a toddler. "Either you take the pills, or I shoot you. You decide."

"You're going to shoot me over *this*?"

"I'm not myself," he admitted. "I'm feeling very," he hesitated, "unbalanced."

"You're not going to kill me," she said in a patronizing tone. "Even I know that."

Just like the scene he'd written in his script, he pressed the gun into her temple and cocked it. "Are you sure?"

"I don't know what you want," she said, her voice quavering. "I don't understand what you want from me."

"Make me happy." He smiled like a banker.

She looked at him.

"Take these." He opened his hand. The pills sat in his palm like snowflakes. He handed her a glass of water. She just sat there. "Don't make me shoot you," he said, "because I will."

Maybe she saw something in his eyes, something that he didn't know he had, some menacing affect, because her fingers crawled into his palm and grasped the pills and then she took them and drank all the water and put down the glass and glanced at him with contempt. That was all right; he didn't care. "I'll get you back for this," she said. "Don't think I won't."

"We'll see."

"You're dead. You'll never work in this town."

"All right. If you say so."

He sat back down in his chair and watched her. Now her face was pale, almost beautiful. If she tried harder she could be beautiful, he thought. He didn't understand why some women who could be perfectly decent looking didn't make more of their looks.

At length he said, "That wasn't so bad, was it?"

Her eyes were glassy, vividly blue. "I'm not afraid of you."

"I'm glad." He smiled. "I'm not a very scary person." He laughed.

"You realize this is a mistake."

"Perhaps." He tilted his head and smiled, thinking of his therapist back in Montclair, the way they'd sit together on adjacent couches in her office while the tops of the birch trees swayed outside the second-story window. They were such solemn trees, he thought. Looking at them always made him melancholy. His therapist had a tender smile and yet she was the sort of woman who would smile even if you'd told her she'd just swallowed a cockroach. When all was said and done she gave him very little advice. Sometimes, when they sat there in the quiet room he'd try to smell her; he'd try very hard. But she had no scent. No scent at all, he thought it was strange. He'd wonder what she was thinking—whether or not she was actually listening to him, or whether she was reviewing a grocery list in her head or her schedule of errands after work. Once, he'd followed her home after their session, taking care to drive several cars behind. In her backyard, he'd stood in the bushes and spied on her through the window of her white Cape, eating supper out of a bowl in front of her Facebook page.

"You think you know me," Chase said bitterly. "You've made assumptions about me. You think I'm this horrible person, right? But you don't know me. You don't know anything about me."

He shrugged. "I know enough." He looked at her. "I know that you're very sad." It was something his therapist had said to him.

Her eyes flashed, but she said nothing. Then she said, "You writers are all the same. You come into my office, trying to butter me up. And you know what I've learned? Ideas? Everybody's got one—they drop out of the sky like bird shit. The truth is, you can turn any idea—and I mean *any* idea—into a movie. You can work a screenplay like tailoring a suit. It's not fucking brain surgery. We could have made your movie. And, yeah, *somebody* would have liked it. But after a week or two, it would have disappeared—collecting dust in some video store." She looked at him hard. "To be perfectly honest, Mr. Waters, I'm tired of making films that make women look like idiots or Barbie warriors—I've tried some of those moves and they're impossible, I couldn't get out of bed for a week. Then one afternoon I'm sitting with my friend's sons, they're twins, fourteen, and it occurs to me that they've witnessed rape and murder in gruesome detail more times than I like to think about. I'm wondering how they process it. I used to be okay with it, but I've changed; I'm not that person anymore. You might say I experienced an epiphany."

Hugh remembered the word from an English class back in college, but just now the meaning escaped him. He tried to think of something clever to say, but the look on her face, her eyes glassy as a dictator's, rendered him speechless.

"I want to tell meaningful stories," she said. "I want to make people feel better about things, not worse. . . . I want to make people feel . . ." Her voice drifted off.

"Feel what, Ms. Chase?"

"Feel—" But her eyelids began to flutter and a moment later she went limp and dropped to the floor. When he'd bought the pills on the street, they'd told him this would happen—they'd told him not to panic. Eventually, the drug would wear off and she'd be fine. He stood over her, looking down at her motionless body. It was strange because her eyes were open. It worried him; he felt a little desperate. He got up and gripped her under the arms and shuffled backward as he dragged her into the living room and pulled her up on the couch. "Are you all right?" he said, fixing the pillows, but of course she couldn't answer. Her eyes seemed to scream *what have you done?* He sat down gingerly, the way one sits at the bedside of a very ill patient. He held on to the arms of the chair as if something was about to happen—an earthquake—a nuclear bomb. But of course nothing did. He watched her closely, the rise and fall of her chest, grateful to see that she was breathing.

There is the dream of something and it is a beautiful dream, he thought. And then there's what's real.

He was beginning to feel bad and he didn't want to feel bad. He stood up, looking down at her. He could leave now, he thought. Just walk away. Go home to his wife. But when Hedda Chase woke up she would call the police. They'd come after him, he'd be arrested. He imagined the look on Marion's face as they put the cuffs on him. His life would be over.

No. He couldn't take that chance.

He had started this; he had to finish it.

It occurred to him that he hadn't eaten for a very long time. His stomach grumbled and he felt dangerously light-headed. He went into the kitchen and opened the refrigerator. It was empty save for a loaf of white bread and a jar of green olives with beady red eyes. He took out the bread and a tub of margarine and found a knife in one of the drawers. He brought the food back into the living room and laid it out on the coffee table. He ate a butter sandwich and washed it down with the quart of milk only to realize after he'd drunk down half of it that it was sour. He spat some of it out onto the floor, making a puddle. "For *fuck's* sake," he said.

Hedda Chase did not move.

He went to the kitchen sink to wash out his mouth then washed his hands thoroughly, using the soap on the windowsill. He didn't know why he was washing his hands, but he felt it was necessary. The soap was green and had a strong, masculine scent. The sun came bright at the window. He heard the sound of a chain saw and looked out and saw the neighbor trimming the lilac hedges on the other side of the concrete wall. The man was Mexican, shouting in Spanish to someone inside the house, whose hands could be seen in the window. They were the gnarled hands of an old woman, presumably the man's mother, and they were gesturing sharply at the areas of the hedge she wanted him to trim. The man seemed angry. The woman shut the window and the lace curtains fell back into place.

Hugh dried his hands on a dishtowel. The clock on the oven seemed to be broken, with the big hand stuck upon the little hand. In Hedda Chase's kitchen time had stopped. Time was irrelevant. He went back into the living room and looked at her again and looked away. He glanced into her bedroom and saw the unmade bed. An ashtray full of cigarette butts on a pillow. Trapped under the same pillow was a little stuffed teddy bear, its fluffy legs sticking out. Instinctively, he reached under the pillow and pulled it out and set it gently into place. Now that it could breathe, the bear seemed to smile at him. A photograph on the nightstand caught his eye. It was of Chase as a small child, wearing a little plaid jumper. Perhaps it had been taken on her first day of school. She had chubby thighs, a barrette in her hair. She was not smiling. The photograph made him feel sad. For a moment, he considered lying down on her bed. He thought of closing the door and staying in her room and never coming out, but of course that wasn't realistic.

Instead, he packed a small bag for her, gently tugging open her drawers, selecting items that she might choose for a short trip including a variety of strappy undergarments that made his fingertips burn. In the bathroom, Hugh selected the toiletries that looked used—a bar of black soap that resembled a cube of tarmac, a toothbrush with its crusty handle, a finger-poked jar of moisture cream, and a slimy tube of makeup. When he was through, he brought the bag to the door and set it down, alongside her pocketbook.

There were voices outside. Hugh could see the neighbor and his friends walking toward his garage. The neighbor had slicked-back hair. He was wearing a suit. The women were in dresses. They were laughing. They were laughing and laughing. What could possibly be that funny? he wondered. Hugh watched as they disappeared inside the garage. A moment later, the car backed down the driveway. The afternoon sunlight flashed off the car like a staccato melody. For a moment he stood there watching the neighbor's house. The window shades were pulled. The house seemed indifferent, mute.

He sat down in the chair. He looked at the woman on the couch, who was suddenly a stranger to him. It made him think about life and death. How they said your spirit left you when you died and people could tell the difference when they looked at a dead body. He'd once seen a dead body in the subway and, thinking about it now, he would have to agree—the body did look different. Hedda Chase was alive, but looked dead, and that was worse somehow, it was much worse.

It was a drowsy time of day. In places like Spain people took naps at this hour, but not here in America. People worked. They worked around the clock. If he was at work right now he'd be drifting over his desk, trying to keep his eyes open. There were sheets and ledgers and lists and statistics. Numbers, a language of abstraction that made perfect sense. There was the muffled sound of progress.

The house was not quiet. There was the whir of the refrigerator, the dripping faucet, the pulsing radio of a passing car. Time passed, an hour, maybe two, and the house began to fill with shadows. He felt a little better, pretending not to be there, pretending that it was an empty house with nobody home.

Hugh took the airport exit off the freeway. The car was an older model with leather seats and a wood steering wheel. It didn't have the usual conveniences of a modern car. There was no latch to open the trunk from the inside, for example, you had to get out of the car in order to open it, and it had a separate key. The keys were attached to a rabbit's foot. Hugh fondled the bony tendons with his fingertips. The car had the smell of old leather which he rather liked, but it didn't handle as well as the car he had rented, a cheap American economy car, but then this car was old and most old things didn't handle the way you wanted them to. He went through the long-term parking gate, passing the lighted gatehouses with their sleepy, change-making clerks, and found a spot under one of the streetlamps. People generally tried to park near the lights, thinking it kept their cars safer. For his purposes, it would illuminate the interior of the car. He cut the engine and got out, leaving the keys in the ignition. The night air was cool and he pulled on his sport jacket. There were a few people getting out of a car down the row, laughing over some joke. Struggling with their luggage, they headed toward the terminal. He opened the back door and took his bag out of the backseat, moving with the jocular ease of a tourist, then removed the parking ticket from his shirt pocket and placed it out on the dashboard where anyone walking by might see it. It would be there, in plain sight, in the morning.

The scream of a jet filled the sky. Thick black smoke trailed the plane. The sound of it was even louder than he had imagined when he'd written the scene in his script. Before leaving the car, he ran his gloved hand over the top of the trunk in a gesture of apology. Of course he hoped that she'd been right about his ending. He hoped in the deepest part of him that she'd been right and standing there he whispered a prayer to the heavens that, come morning, someone would hear her muffled cries and save her.

That all depended on fate, of course.

On the other hand, it was entirely possible that someone would steal the car and drive away.

He didn't know what fate had in store for Hedda Chase, and he didn't care.

He walked into the terminal and checked in at the airline's counter. The woman took his bag and he watched it disappear on the conveyor belt. He stood there watching it vanish. The bag contained nothing he would miss. "Mr. Waters?" The woman smiled at him with her orange lipstick the way people smile too much when they think you're crazy and handed him his ticket and directed him toward the gate. Walking across the slick floors toward the escalator in the distance it occurred to him how disinterested he was in going home. He tried to picture Marion's face. She was a mirage, he thought. The sounds around him seemed to fade. It became very quiet, almost as quiet as the African desert. He was thinking about the famous last shot in *The Passenger,* the camera framed on an open window through which the world beyond continued, despite Nicholson's unfortunate death.

It made him think of poor Hedda Chase.

It made him think of her gentle weight as he'd carried her out through the darkness to the garage, her head pressed against his chest like a child's, tufts of breath escaping from her mouth. He'd set her down into the trunk with the utmost care.

A car horn went off outside the glass doors. Headlights glared. It occurred to him that getting on the plane was the last thing he wanted to do. On an impulse, he turned around and headed for the Hertz kiosk. He rented a car; a Mercedes. He had never driven a Mercedes before. It handled smoothly, he thought; it was a terrific car. He sat back and pulled onto the freeway. There was traffic; he didn't mind. He was glad to have time to think. He sensed that something important had occurred. Something profound. He thought about what he wanted to do with the rest of his life. He was fairly certain it didn't have anything to do with Equitable Life. In fact, he was glad his promotion hadn't come through. They could take their promotion and shove it, that's what they could do. He was tired of waiting in line for things he didn't even want. Tired of being manipulated by false promises. He wanted to change the way things were. He wasn't sure how, exactly, but change seemed inevitable. And whether or not his wife would be part of it, well, he didn't know that either.

He thought of the girl in his motel room and wondered if she'd found the money he'd left for her. A girl like that was at a tremendous disadvantage, he realized. Leaving the money had been the right thing to do. He hoped she would use it wisely.

A feeling of happiness flooded his body. So what if it was a lousy script, he thought. It wasn't the worst thing.

He leaned back against the seat and looked out the window at all the cars and the people in them. How strange the world was, he thought. How strange and marvelous. And how blessed he felt to be part of it.

2

Hugh drove along Hollywood Boulevard past the brightly lit windows of vacant stores. The store fronts reminded him of the animal displays at the natural history museum, depicting the habitat of a particular species. The manikins stared out at the darkness with passive confusion. The pursuit of fashion had taken precedence over the hunt for food. Food had become the predator, the evil sad thing in a box.

It was after midnight. A few stragglers drifted on the sidewalks. Consciously or unconsciously he was looking for the girl from his motel room. He entertained the possibility that she was still in the room where he'd left her, waiting for him, but of course that was unrealistic—he knew she'd left the room hours ago. Her name was Daisy, he remembered. She may have gone to that awful hostel, he thought, and considered going there to check. It wasn't right that a girl like her, a girl of her age, was wandering around the streets at night. Just thinking about it made his chest burn.

He parked in the motel parking lot and went into the motel office with its green fluorescent light and tapped the bell and the manager came out of a darkened room. It was a place to stay, Hugh told himself. It was the only place he knew.

The manager looked pleased to see him. "You came back," he said.

"Yes."

"No luggage?"

"Not tonight."

The manager was an obsequious Pakistani who should have been working in a better hotel, not a place like this, where the guests were slippery incarnations of some alien presence, and when he walked down the corridor past the battered anonymous doors, he sensed that something was going on, something amorphous and strange—*out there*—that no one could ever fully appreciate, and he could almost feel the earth shifting under his feet, his sense of balance compromised by the tilting planet, the topple of a wayward globe.

This room was a little better than the first, he thought, one flight up, and it smelled a little better. Instead of looking out on the parking lot, the room looked out on a side street crammed with stucco houses, the surfaces of which resembled thickly spread cake frosting. Small yards were enclosed by chain-link fences. One house in particular caught his interest. It had a large picture window, lit up by a crystal chandelier. A little white dog was barking out one of the windows. It was rude to let a dog go on barking like that; it wasn't nice. Hugh didn't like little dogs like that.

For a moment, he sat on the bed and did nothing. The room seemed dim and depressing and he suddenly longed for his wife. Not *her* exactly, but the idea of her. He felt a little afraid. He knew he should call her, but instead he turned his cell phone over in his hands like some found artifact, as if he were oblivious to its purpose. His life back in Montclair was like an old episode of some TV melodrama. He supposed he had switched the channel long ago, at least in his own mind. He lay down for a few minutes and watched the shadows on the ceiling, the gliding light of passing cars. A helicopter crossed the sky, its spotlight grazing his windows, and he felt as if he were in a foreign place, where dangers beyond his comprehension were routine. When he woke hours later, still in his clothes, the room was light. His body felt weak, hungry. He stood at the open window looking out. The sun was bright, he could feel it on his hands. He went into the bathroom and pulled open the shower curtain just as a cockroach scurried down the drain. His body shuddered as he turned on the water and took off his clothes and stepped under the stream of tepid water.

Hugh dressed and went down to the café and sat at the counter and ordered eggs and flapjacks and white toast. The waitress behind the counter wore a uniform, the fabric of which was the color of cantaloupe. Around her waist was a frilly apron. It occurred to him that everyone in Hollywood looked like an extra in some movie. There was something about the place—different from back home—maybe it was the sunlight that painted everyone a bit too bright. The waitress was frowning and Hugh could tell that she wasn't in a good mood even though it was a Friday. Most people were in a good mood on Fridays, that was one of the things he had always liked about work, the way people loosened up on Friday afternoons and let you in a little bit—but not her, and she was not impressed with his patience as he waited for his coffee, the expression on his face passive as an idiot's. Half way through his meal he broke down and reminded her and her face singed like she'd been burnt. When she poured the coffee, it spilled over the side of the cup onto the saucer, but she was too busy talking with another customer to notice, and when he got up to pay the check she swiped it from his hand as if he'd stolen something.

Back at the motel, he called Ida Kent, the writer. She sounded happy to hear from him and agreed to meet him later that afternoon in Santa Monica. She suggested a restaurant near the pier, an oyster bar named Sullivan's.

In a men's shop around the corner Hugh bought two pair of trousers and two fresh white shirts. The little man who took care of him had an accent he couldn't place and while he was pinning up the trousers Hugh saw that he was missing a thumb. The man promised they'd be ready in an hour. Killing time, Hugh walked up the boulevard, across the Walk of Fame, stepping on the stars of famous people. He wondered what it was like to be a person who had a star. A throng of tourists were filing into a bus outside Grauman's Chinese Theatre. Many were snapping pictures. They were like chattering penguins, he thought. Affecting an air of superiority, he walked swiftly past them. Already he felt a rich contempt for them.

Abruptly, he called his wife. After several rings she answered. "Where are you, Hughie," she cried, her voice wavering. "Why haven't you called me? I've been worried, I've been worried sick."

"I know, I'm sorry, I feel terrible."

"What are you doing? Where are you?"

"It's just I've been talking to some people."

"What people? Who have you been talking to?"

"Film people," his voice lurched. "Producers. Things are looking very promising."

"Oh, I see."

"I need more time out here."

He could hear her sniffling into a tissue and it made his blood race.

"I'm too boring for you," she muttered. "I've always known it."

"Marion."

"It's true."

"Don't make this into something it's not."

She had started to cry.

"I'll call you in a few days." He hung up.

The little man with the missing thumb had been telling the truth; the pants were hemmed within the hour. Hugh paid and brought the parcel back to the motel, where he changed into the new shirt and trousers and took care to clip his fingernails and comb his hair. His date with Ida wasn't for several hours; he decided to take a drive. He went down to the parking lot and found his car and drove along the boulevard with the sun in his eyes. Again a helicopter appeared overhead like some mammoth creature. He glanced at himself in the rearview mirror, his nickel-plated guilt, the cold line of his mouth, and tried not to think about what he'd done to Hedda Chase.

The beach was crowded. In his street clothes he began to sweat. He watched the people. Everyone seemed to be moving. Some were on Rollerblades. Some girls were playing volleyball in their bikinis. The sun was bright. He bought a baseball cap from a vendor who spoke no English; perhaps he was an Arab. The hat had an American flag on it. It was the cheapest one. Hugh put it on and rolled up his pants and walked down to the shore. Two teenaged girls looked at him and laughed—maybe they didn't like the hat.

Maybe they thought he was patriotic. Some children were dashing in and out of the waves, laughing. As he approached, they looked at him and he looked away. He had no business looking at small children. You never knew what people could say about you. They could say you were looking at them with interest, and that could imply something strange. Stories could build from nothing, he thought. The ocean was choppy and when the waves broke the water sprayed his face. He found himself thinking about the ancient Greeks, their sophistication, their ingenuity. That had been the beginning; this was nearly the end. He couldn't help feeling shame—the shame of being a stupid American—and now he regretted buying the hat. The beach was not clean. Trash undulated in the sand, just enough to stir up his anger. People didn't care; not really they didn't.

For an hour or two, he lay in the sand and thought. He tried not to think about the producer in that dark trunk. When he could not stand it another minute, he returned to his car and drove out to LAX. He took the airport exit and entered the labyrinth that wound around to long-term parking, taking a ticket at the gate as though he had planned a trip. For a moment he contemplated getting on a plane, going somewhere, Europe perhaps. That would be the smart thing to do, he told himself. The lot was crowded—he had left her car in section H, near the tall fence. The car was still there. He felt a mixture of emotions, both relief and dread. He rolled past its dirty rump, the tidy, German box of the trunk, and thought: *She's in there.*

His heart began to beat very fast as he put his window down. His chest began to hurt. Sweat spread across his back, the tops of his hands. He sat there a moment, listening to the lull of traffic beyond the fence, the expectant quiet of the parking lot, the screaming jets filling the sky, and thought: *What if she's dead?*

He thought: *Get out and open the trunk.*

A car beeped behind him. Hugh glanced in the rearview mirror and saw a woman gesturing for him to move, cursing him. The horn had alerted the gate attendant, who was coming toward him. Hugh signaled his apology and pulled away. When he went through the gate, the attendant noted his ticket and said, "Change of plans?"

Hugh nodded. "Would you believe I forgot my luggage?

The attendant needed a shave and wore a strained expression like he was in a little bit of pain, but could do nothing about it. He looked at Hugh doubtfully. "No charge." The gate opened and Hugh drove through it.

The restaurant was a seedy place on a side street near the pier. It took him a while to find a parking space and then he had to search for quarters. You could smell the ocean and the late, damp sunlight. The beach was nearly empty. He saw an old couple shuffling through the sand, lugging their beach chairs, their shoulders hunched, their faces preoccupied and complex.

Ida was waiting at the bar in a sleeveless dress and sandals. Her shoulders were pretty. Her face was like one of those women in the laundry detergent commercials, he thought, a wife who could keep house like nobody's business. When they kissed hello she smelled lemon-fresh. "Hey."

"Hey, yourself," she said. She stood there looking at him. "I took the liberty of ordering. You like oysters, don't you?"

He told her he did and took the leather stool next to hers and ordered a beer. Ida was drinking something pretty.

"If you're good I'll give you the cherry," she told him.

"Oh, I'll be good."

"She's got you well trained."

He grunted a laugh. "Is it that obvious?"

"On second thought, you don't get the cherry."

"We're separated," he told her, and it occurred to him how easy it was to say it. "We're in transition."

"Well, *good* for you. Transition is an interesting place to be."

"Speaking from experience?"

"Oh, yeah. Experience is something I happen to have a lot of. Or, as my mother would say, *source material*. My mother has a way of looking at things. She tweaks everything. Like my ex-husband. Instead of admitting he was a cheap fucking bastard, she'd say it's the thought that counts. Well, you know what? It's *not* the thought that counts. Cheap is cheap, *period*." She swallowed the last of her drink and shook the ice around in her glass like a rattle. "I've been divorced twice."

"Ouch," he said.

She made a face like it hurt. She twisted her torso to catch the bar tender's attention and seesawed her glass. "I guess I'm not the marrying kind, whatever *that* means."

"I'm not sure I want to know, actually."

She laughed, showing her little white teeth.

"Maybe it's not important," he said.

She looked at him as if the idea had never occurred to her, and then said, "But of course it's important. It's the most important thing in the world. And I happen to suck at it."

"Maybe you just haven't met the right guy."

She tilted her head. "Maybe."

The bartender brought her drink.

"Took you long enough."

The bartender winked. "Now you really want it."

"Wanting it's the least of my problems."

The bartender looked at Hugh. "You want another?"

"Sure."

"Here," she said, fishing her cherry out of the glass, holding it by the stem. "I want you to have it after all."

"Why the change of heart?"

"Something tells me you've been deprived." She dangled the cherry over his mouth. Feeling foolish, he caught the slippery thing in his teeth. When he bit into it the sweet pulp prickled his cheeks.

"They've been exploited, of course, like everything else."

"Cherries?"

"But they're symbolic."

"How do you mean?"

"When you're a kid you always get the cherry. It's like a kid-bonus. And then you grow up and you're not supposed to want it anymore."

"You're starting to sound like my shrink."

She smiled. "Cheap philosophy from a second-rate writer."

"I doubt that." He looked at her. She was both charming and pathetic. "Why do you say that?"

She shrugged. "I don't know. Because it's true."

"What sort of stuff do you write?"

"Crap," she said. "I'm the first to admit it. I've actually made my peace with it." Her modesty seemed genuine; a little too genuine.

"I don't believe you."

She looked down at her hands, shrugged.

"Let me read something. I'll tell you if it's crap."

She gave him a coy smile. She had a look about her that he couldn't quite figure.

"We can act out the scenes," he suggested. "I'll play the hero."

"Who says there's a hero?"

"This is America. There's gotta be a hero. You want to sell tickets, don't you?"

"All right, if you insist. But you're not exactly who I pictured for the part."

"I clean up good."

"Who said anything about clean?"

"Now I'm getting curious."

"Dirty interests me."

"Really?"

"Still interested?"

"I'm a very convincing actor."

"I'll bet you are."

They ate oysters, noisily sucking the shells. They drank all afternoon, then stepped out into the dwindling light, blinking. They ran to the beach, kicking off their shoes. The water was cold and very blue. The sky was violet. He could not remember seeing a more beautiful night. Ida looked like a kid, running in the surf. She had short, pale legs, full thighs. He knew he could kiss her if he wanted to. He could feel her thinking about it, wondering if he would. Maybe he would, later. Still, he sensed there was something fragile about her. Maybe she was broken. She had a history. He wasn't sure he could deal with it.

"I'll tell you my life story," she had whispered in his ear at the bar, "if you'll tell me yours." Under the circumstances, the way she'd said it with her warm oyster breath had turned him on. She'd been born and raised in Iowa. He tried to imagine her as a girl there with her knock-knees and flat feet and precocious breasts and slightly swayed back. He pictured a tire swing on a big oak tree, somebody's pickup in the driveway. A clapboard house with a porch. A big red tractor out in the field. She could twirl a baton, she'd said, and he imagined her festooned with pom-poms in the Fourth of July parade. The images seemed familiar to him, selected from his mental archives— visual scraps from old Budweiser commercials—and he realized they were not his own.

Ida was looking out at the ocean, squinting with such earnestness that he thought she must be drunk.

"Hey," he said, and touched her back. "You look sad."

"I'm not. Not really, I'm not."

"What are you looking at? What's out there?"

"Everything," she said. "And a whole lot of nothing."

Holding hands, they walked over to the pier. It was strange holding hands with her and he found himself wondering how to break apart without insulting her. He imagined what Marion might think of it. They walked on the pier, toward the lights of a carnival. Ida wanted to ride the Ferris wheel. The air smelled of popcorn, a buttery rancid smell—maybe it was puke. He had never liked rides and now, whirling up backward after drinking so much, made his stomach turn. "Scaredy cat," she accused him, as he gripped the handlebar and closed his eyes. She took his hand in her sweaty palm and held it very tight and whispered into his ear, "Don't be afraid."

Later, they lay on the beach in the cool sand, looking up at the stars. For a while they didn't speak. You could hear the ocean, the breaking waves, people screaming on the rides. As he lay there beside her, he thought about the variations of terror that existed in the dark.

He turned onto his side and looked at her. She had put her hair into two braids and looked wholesome as the next Midwestern girl, and yet he was pretty certain that she was not. On the one hand, she was sturdy and resilient and resourceful. She seemed dependable too, like if she said she would do something you could count on her to do it. On the other, she had a kind of wounded beauty that came from being let down. She was like a pressed flower in somebody's scrapbook, he thought, signifying some important event, the memory of which left something to be desired.

"About my script," she said. "I'm realizing how awful it is."

"It's not awful. I know it's not."

"You don't know that."

"I know you. At least I'm getting to know you."

"You don't know me," she said disdainfully.

"I want to. I want to know you."

"Maybe you just want to fuck me."

The comment startled him and he said nothing because there was a possibility that it was true.

"You're still married."

"I know. I have to figure that out."

"I've been through a lot," she said. "I've been hurt."

"I promise not to hurt you," he said, touching her arm gently, and he meant it.

"Men suck."

"Not all men."

She nodded. "All men. Men can be brutal."

"Not all men."

"Most."

"I don't think that's true."

"That's because you're one of them. I could provoke you, if I wanted to."

"Why would you do that?"

She looked away. In a strange way, the conversation was turning him on. "Go ahead, provoke me."

"You asked for it." She rolled on top of him and started tickling him all over and he laughed even though he hated being tickled and then she pummeled him wickedly all over his chest. He got a little angry and rolled her onto her back and climbed on top of her and held down her wrists and she strained against him and her face changed slightly and for a moment he imagined being inside her. He could feel her squirming, the bones of her hips, her belly, her thighs. He seemed to come out of a haze and released her and rolled back onto the sand. Side by side, they were breathing hard.

"You provoked me," he said.

"I know. It's okay. Maybe I liked it." Her eyes were shining, her face flushed.

He didn't know what to say to her, so he said nothing.

He lay back down and looked up at the stars. At length he asked, "What are your plans?"

"My plans?"

"What do you want?"

She repeated his question without answering.

"In life," he clarified.

"I have no idea what I want. I don't know." Then, like it was a joke, she said, "I want a husband and a little house in the country with a picket fence and a whole gaggle of kids." He watched her, trying to figure out if she was serious. "I want a high-paying job where I get to be nasty to people." Then she added, "I want a flat in Paris."

None of those things seemed to fit her destiny.

"I suppose I want what most women want."

"Which is what?"

"Tranquillity."

"Sounds like a perfume."

"I want to feel at peace. In here," she tapped her heart. "I want to stop feeling like I'm second rate."

"You always say that. It's not true."

"I don't know why I say it; I *feel* it."

"Maybe you should get out of L.A."

She shrugged. "I like it here. I like the sunshine."

"Maybe you've gotten used to being second rate."

"Maybe it's another one of my bad habits." She turned onto her side and looked at him. "What about you? What do you want?"

He had never really thought about it— not really—at least not nearly enough. The truth was he didn't have a clue. Instead of prolonging the conversation he leaned over and kissed her. He pushed his tongue deep into her mouth as if the words he needed to answer the question might be inside of it somewhere, waiting for him to fish them out.

3

Back in his motel room, he lay on the bed watching TV with the sound turned off, drinking warm whiskey. The bedspread was gold and shiny, with a design that reminded him of something you'd find under a microscope. It frightened him to think that bugs might crawl on him while he slept. He watched the television, the onslaught of images, one after another. On the way home from Santa Monica he'd stopped at a package store and when he'd come out he'd caught someone pissing on his car. For the next half hour, he'd driven around looking for a car wash, the smell of urine filling his nostrils, but none of the car washes were open. He'd showered, but he could still smell it. The incident had upset him. The world outside his window seemed too loud. The barking dog across the street. The crowds down on the sidewalk. Strange laughter coming from one of the rooms. He dozed off and woke to the sound of something banging against the wall in the room next door. It came to him, in his drowsy state, that his neighbors were having sex. It was a sound that you knew when you heard it, he thought. When he could no longer stand it, he left the room and went down to the street. He considered calling Ida, but thought better of it. She hadn't invited him over after their date. Instead, he had kissed her leisurely and helped her into her car. He walked down to Hollywood Boulevard and watched the people on the sidewalks. Kids walking in groups. Sunburned girls with long straight hair, smelling of shampoo. Boys in baggy jeans, dripping chains, their underwear sticking out. Tourists; people from faraway lands, speaking languages he could not understand.

The freeway out to the airport was thick with traffic. It was only eleven o'clock, people were still going out. The night was young. He realized he was in a desperate frame of mind. He had to concentrate very hard on the road. His mouth was very dry and had the sour aftertaste of the whiskey. Drinking had been a mistake, he thought. His evening with Ida, too, had been an error of judgment, for he was in no position to be in any sort of a relationship with any woman other than his wife.

His cell phone rang. Hugh glanced at his watch. It was half past eleven, three hours later in Montclair.

"I need to know what's going on," his wife said.

"Marion, what are you doing up so late?"

"I can't sleep. I want you to come home."

He didn't say anything.

"Hugh?"

"Look," he said. "I can't."

"Why not?"

"I don't know how to say this—I mean—I wanted to tell you in person."

"Tell me what?"

"Look, it's not working out."

"What are you talking about?"

"Us. Our marriage."

"What are you saying, Hughie? What are you *saying*?"

"I don't know. I don't know what I'm saying."

"It's because of me, isn't it? It's because I can't—"

"It's not because of that," he cut her off. "It has nothing to do with that."

"I don't know what to do," she said.

"Do what you always do." He pictured her twirling stem-tape on roses, watering all the plants in the greenhouse where she worked. Sometimes she came home with her fingertips pricked. When things were better between them, he would take her hands and kiss the tiny wounds.

"They called from work," she said. "I told them you were sick."

I am sick, he thought. *I'm very ill.*

"Why didn't you tell me about the promotion? They think it's why you're not there. They think you're upset."

"She was more qualified for the job," he said. "I've come to terms with it."

"But you've been there longer, Hughie. It wasn't fair."

Marion didn't know the whole truth about why he hadn't gotten the promotion. He'd made the mistake of making a pass at his competitor, a neatly wrapped blonde in a JCPenney suit. It had been a foolish thing to do, he understood that fully now, and yet at the time, after drinking half a dozen martinis at the annual Christmas party, he'd felt pretty certain that their interest in each other was mutual. In retrospect, putting his hand on her ass under the festering gazes of his superiors probably wasn't a great idea. He'd forced himself on her later in the coatroom, among the guileless hunkering overcoats of his coworkers. He'd had her pressed against the wall, fragrant and ripe—and then she'd come to her senses. She'd slapped him across the face and walked out, threatening to sue him for sexual harassment. Obviously, she'd used the mishap to her advantage.

"She has her MBA. Look, it's out of my hands." The traffic came to a sudden halt; he had to slam on his brakes. He watched the people in the car behind him take the jolt. The lights of an ambulance flared in his rearview mirror. The promotion would have meant a lot more money, a better office on a better floor. More vacation time. His own assistant. "I didn't want it anyway," he lied.

His wife didn't say anything and for a moment he wondered if he'd lost her.

"Marion? Are you there?"

"I feel like I'm disappearing. You don't see me anymore."

"Don't be so dramatic."

"We used to be fine. We were fine before you left."

We were not fine. "Look, Marion, I have to go."

"Hughie, *please.*"

"I'll call you tomorrow." He closed his phone, disconnecting the call. It wasn't nice, he knew, to hang up on his wife. As a result, she would be up all night, and yet he didn't care. He was glad he wasn't with her—glad he would never return to their stilted little house with its singing Disney birds and garbage cans or to his cubicle on the thirtieth floor of the tower of immutable suffering otherwise known as the Equitable Life Insurance Company. The truth of it was he didn't give a good goddamn about the promotion.

An ambulance reeled past. The cars inched along. Finally, he passed the accident. A car had smashed into the divider. Luckily, his was the next exit. Once off the freeway, the road was clear. He pulled into the airport and wound up to long-term parking, just as he had done earlier that afternoon. The alcohol had given him a headache, and he felt slightly disoriented as he passed through the gate. He drove over to section II. Some of the street-lights were blinking and when he put his window down he could hear the buzzing of electricity and it made him consider how small he was in the scope of things. There were people out there who controlled things—things like lights and traffic. He was just a small part of the great epic drama called humanity, he thought.

The lot seemed eerily quiet. There didn't seem to be any planes taking off. No people around either. It was the weekend; you'd think it would be crowded, but it wasn't crowded at all. He had decided that, this time, he was going to save her. He was going to open the trunk and get her out. But as he drove around the lot again, retracing his steps, it occurred to him that the car wasn't there. He drove around a second time. There was no mistake. The car had moved. It was gone.

Perhaps she had actually gotten out, he thought. Perhaps, by some stroke of incredible luck, she'd freed her hands and pulled the tape off her mouth. Perhaps someone had heard her cries and been determined to save her. It had been one of her complaints with the scene—the woman screaming in a crowded parking lot without being saved—she'd said she didn't buy it, but now that her mouth was taped there would be no crying for help. There would be no chance of anyone hearing her. And the car would be stolen by some unassuming thief. Problem solved, he thought. With a few simple modifications, he had addressed her complaints. He had to admit, she'd been right; the scene was far more convincing now.

Still, strange things happened. Everyday miracles like the ones in those supermarket newspapers.

This time he got a woman at the gate. More interested in her cell phone conversation than in his strangely brief visit to the long-term parking lot, she let him through without even looking at him. Hugh drove back to Los Feliz, foolishly challenging the speed limits, and turned onto Lomita Avenue. The street was quiet, lit with the old gas lamps. He parked at the curb across the street from her house. To his surprise, a light burned in the tall arched window. Was it *possible*? His heart began to beat—perhaps it was true—he felt almost giddy with relief. She had survived his cruel joke—that's what it had been—a joke—no real harm intended! The gun hadn't even been loaded! He had only wanted to teach her a lesson. And she'd been victorious after all—miraculously, someone had heard her cries and freed her—kind soul!

And yet, as he crossed the street and approached the house, he grew increasingly uncertain. He saw a man inside her living room, his shadow looming monstrously on the wall. It was Chase's boyfriend—the filmmaker—pacing and shouting into a cell phone. Hugh dropped back into the shadows and walked down the driveway, hearing a rattling salsa in the house next door. Through a gap in the curtains he could see the neighbor dancing with one of his lady friends in his undershorts, the woman in her bra and panties.

The boyfriend's jeep was parked in the garage. Chase's car was nowhere in sight.

Hugh deliberated his options. It was possible that she was there—that perhaps the car had been left somewhere. Perhaps she hadn't been able to drive, he thought. He pictured her tucked into bed, recovering from her ordeal, a cup of tea at her side. The boyfriend on the phone with the police. And yet her bedroom was dark. It seemed unlikely that she was there.

"Who is it?" the man said from behind the door.

"I must have the wrong address," Hugh said.

The door opened and the boyfriend stood there, taller than Hugh had anticipated, and bigger, but he did not really look like a fighter, his eyes were too kind. "Who do you want?"

"I'm looking for Hedda Chase."

The man just stood there.

"I know it's late. Forgive me, is this —" Hugh took an old receipt out of his pocket and glanced at it. "Thirty-one Lomita?"

"You got the right address." The man had a slight Southern accent. "And you're right, it's late. Very late, in fact. What do you want?"

"She told me to stop by tonight."

"Really? When did you speak to her?"

"This morning."

The man looked surprised. "You spoke to her this morning?"

"She called my hotel and left a message. We've been playing phone tag."

"That's one of Hedda's favorite games. Who are you?"

Hugh considered giving a false name, but then thought better of it. The man looked smart, intuitive; he might sense Hugh was lying. "My name's Hugh. Hugh Waters." Saying it aloud felt like an accomplishment and he felt himself blushing. He extended his hand; they shook. The man looked over Hugh's shoulder at the Mercedes across the street. "I'm from New York. We knew each other a long time ago. I'm here on business."

"She's never mentioned you. Not that it matters, there are lots of things she doesn't tell me."

"I'm only in town a few days," Hugh said. "I was having dinner near here with some friends." He mentioned the name of a Japanese restaurant he had passed on Vermont Avenue, one with a bold neon sign. "I was driving by and saw the lights. I figured I'd give it a shot."

"She's not here. I'm waiting for her myself."

"I'm sorry I missed her."

"I don't know where she is."

"Tell her I stopped by." Hugh turned to leave.

"I was just about to have a drink if you want to join me. Maybe she'll show up."

"No, I don't want to trouble you."

"It's no trouble." The man opened the door wider, inviting him in. "Whiskey all right?"

It wasn't a good idea, but Hugh said, "All right. Sure, why not?" He stepped inside.

"New York, huh? Circa when?"

"Just after college. We worked for the same company," he said, retrieving the information he'd found on Wikipedia. For a brief period of time Chase had worked in an advertising agency. "Rollins and Beck. It was a long time ago."

The man led him into the living room. "I seem to remember something about that. What was she like back then?"

"Popular," Hugh said meaningfully, and smiled.

"She does have that talent for celebrity."

Hugh nodded and tried to swallow. "You haven't told me your name."

"It's Tom. Tom Foster." He glanced at Hugh to see if he recognized it.

"Why does that sound familiar?" Hugh said, even though it didn't.

"I make documentaries."

"Sounds interesting."

"Used to be interesting. Now it's complicated and expensive."

Hugh was suddenly desperate for that drink.

"Hedda calls it my *Sullivan's Travels* phase." He looked at Hugh to see if he understood.

"Preston Sturges," Hugh said. "He was a genius."

"I suppose, after three films, it's no longer a phase."

The liquor was set up on a little cart. While Tom fixed him a drink, Hugh began to wonder if perhaps it was a trick—he scanned the room, the dark rectangle of her bedroom doorway, but saw nothing, and when Tom turned with the whiskey he smiled at Hugh and the smile seemed genuine. Hugh tried to relax. He took the glass with his left hand, knowing that the presence of his wedding ring might suggest some aspect of normalcy and stability, when in reality it was more a symbol, at least to Hugh, of everything that was wrong in his life.

"Thanks," Hugh said.

"Cheers."

Hugh raised his glass in a silent toast and took a sip. The whiskey was bitter; it burned his throat.

"Have a seat."

"Thanks." Hugh sat down on Chase's couch, in the same spot where she had lain the night before. It was hard not to picture her there, the way she'd looked after the pills kicked in, totally motionless, her eyes stuck on the ceiling. At one point he had touched her forehead to make sure she was warm, the way you're supposed to be when you're alive.

"What are you working on now?"

Tom poured himself a drink and took a seat across from him. "I just finished a film about a shelter in Hollywood. In fact," he reached into his pocket and produced a postcard, "there's a screening tomorrow night if you're still around."

"Thanks. I'll try to make it." Hugh put the postcard into his pocket.

They sat there a moment, drinking. There was the possibility that she'd show up, he thought, although it seemed unlikely. The car was gone; someone had taken it.

"Where do you suppose she is?" Hugh asked.

"I don't really know. It's not unusual, really, she's done this before."

"Done what?"

"Disappears for a few days. Usually means she's pissed off. Mature, huh? Probably gone off to Sparta for a few days to brush up on her ashtanga. It's out in the desert, no cell phones—I tried calling her office, but everybody was already gone for the weekend and Harold's on his way to Cannes."

"Harold?"

"Her boss. Where are you staying?"

"In Beverly Hills," Hugh managed to lie. "At the Hilton. I live in New York," he emphasized. "I'm a writer."

"Ah," Tom said. "Good for you." Apparently satisfied with Hugh's biography, he stretched out his legs on the coffee table and relaxed. He had the expansive body language of a king or a rock star. At the moment, Hugh was playing the loyal servant.

"What do you write?"

"Screenplays," he said. "I'm afraid I'm not very good at it."

Tom laughed. "Well, then, you've come to the right place." He raised his glass. "May you be paid handsomely for your humble efforts," he said in a King Arthur voice.

"I guess it's not all crap," Hugh said, thinking of Ida. "Some of it's pretty good."

"You're starting to sound like Hedda. She's unbearably optimistic." Tom finished his drink and got up and brought the bottle over and poured more whiskey into their glasses then set the bottle down on the coffee table.

They drank intently. Tom was sitting on a wood chair that had been covered in cowhide. It didn't look very comfortable, too small for his long, lanky build. His loose trousers and wrinkled blazer made him look as though he had suffered a lengthy illness. The dark circles around his eyes were those of a chronic insomniac's. He lit a cigarette and tossed down the pack, then leaned back and again stretched out his legs on the coffee table.

"This is a nice place," Hugh said.

"This? It's a dump. It's only temporary, of course."

"What do you mean?"

"Until the house is ready." Tom looked at Hugh. "She told you about the villa?"

"Oh, yes, right," Hugh said. "The villa."

"Although I sometimes get the feeling that she has second thoughts. Buyer's remorse."

"I had that with my house."

"I thought you were in the city?"

"My wife wanted a house in New Jersey. It was a mistake to move out of the city," he said, suddenly clear on what had happened to his marriage over the several months inside that house. "It destroyed our marriage."

"Wives have a knack for sabotage. It's Freudian, actually." Tom dragged on his cigarette with obvious pleasure. "They can't help themselves."

The house in Montclair was blue clapboard with plastic shutters upon which a horse and carriage had been replicated. When they'd gone to look at it for the first time, there were plastic pansies in the window box. The fake flowers had dared Marion, the purist, to save the pathetic Colonial from terminal kitsch. After they'd moved in, she'd replaced the plastic pansies with real geraniums and pulled out the colossal shrubs and lilac bushes surrounding the house. Hugh had tried to be happy about moving out of New York, but it wasn't easy for him. Unlike the suburbs, the city presented small opportunities for escape. He could get out for a walk, or run a suddenly essential errand, grateful for a few minutes to himself. He found Marion's silence oppressive. "And we had squirrels in our attic."

"Suburbia plus," Tom said knowingly. "All the comforts of home."

It occurred to Hugh that, at the moment, sitting there in Hedda Chase's living room with Tom Foster felt like the most natural thing in the world, as if they were old friends, as if what he'd done to her last night had been nothing more than a bizarre fabrication in his mind. Now he wished it had been. He didn't want to think about what would happen if she walked in here.

"It's getting late." Hugh stood up. "Look, I should go. Say hello to Hedda for me."

Tom glanced at his watch. "Here, let me try to call her again." He opened his cell phone and pressed send. He shook his head. "She's not picking up. I've been calling her all day. It's pretty obvious she doesn't want to talk to me. For a woman with such big balls she's pretty goddamn histrionic."

Hugh held up his hand as if he didn't need to hear it—it wasn't any of his business.

But Tom confided, "She wants me to leave my wife."

Hugh tried to hide his surprise. "You're married?"

"Of course I'm married."

"Does your wife know?"

"Of course she knows. This isn't a town where people are particularly skilled at keeping secrets. Discretion isn't exactly a virtue here."

"Oh. Well. I'm sorry."

Tom shook his head. "It's my own fault. Lucia is very emotional."

"Your wife?"

"Here, you try. Let's have your phone."

It wasn't smart to take out his cell phone, but Hugh handed it to Tom and watched him punch in the number. He put on the speakerphone. They sat there listening to it ring. Just minutes after putting her in the trunk, Hugh had set her pocketbook on the front seat of the car. The phone had continued to vibrate and, out of frustration, he'd dug it out and tossed it into the glove box. He pictured it there now, vibrating. Stupidly, he hadn't turned it off, but perhaps it had been deliberate. He had thought, perhaps, that someone might be able to locate her; an open door that invited in the world.

Sweat prickled his skin as he waited in anticipation of Hedda's agitated voice, but it was someone else who picked up—a man. "Yeah?" The voice gritty, tentative. "What?"

"Who the fuck is this?" Tom shouted.

"Who the fuck is *this*?"

"Where is she?"

"She's not here," the stranger said.

"Look, I know she's fucking there."

"Nobody here but me," the man said.

"You put her on the phone—right fucking now!"

"Hey, go fuck yourself." The line went dead.

Tom checked the phone to make sure he'd dialed right. He hit the send button again, but this time her voice mail picked up. Now they heard the voice of Hedda Chase identifying herself, the characteristic inflections of condescension as it requested the caller to leave a message—she'd call you back, her tone seemed to suggest, if you were important enough.

Tom sat there shaking his head and muttered, "I don't fucking believe this."

"What? Who was that?"

"I don't have a clue."

The queasy feeling Hugh had had before came back. A sour taste coated his tongue. He washed it down with some more scotch. Tom sat there with his head in his hands. He looked at Hugh. "Could she be fucking somebody?"

Hugh shrugged.

"I didn't recognize his voice." Again, he looked at Hugh as if waiting for his answer. "This is her getting back at me. I guess it really is over." He shook his head and conceded, "She should be with someone else; I can't give her what she wants."

"What does she want?"

"What do any of them fucking want?"

Hugh thought about Marion. Before they were married, she'd been livelier, more convincing about her love for him. Once they'd gotten married, she'd become secretive, remote. It occurred to him now that he didn't have the slightest idea what she wanted.

"Truth is, I've never had much luck with women and I've had no shortage of opportunities, I can tell you that. But with Hedda it was different. It makes me feel *hollow* to admit it, but I'm in love with her—and I've never had the decency to tell her. I think about her and I get a stomachache. It's not the same with my wife. There's something about Hedda that makes me—" He stopped himself and shrugged it off.

"What?"

He shook his head. He looked upset. "Whole, I guess."

"Whole?"

Tom nodded. Hugh had been in love only once. The girl had worked in the billing department. Once they'd ridden up on the elevator together. She'd been crying over something, her face turned away. Her lips were pale, chapped—it was winter—and her cheeks were rosy, burned by the wind. Around her neck was a scarf the color of cornflowers. If she were a painting, he had thought, her surface would be cracked and yet it was exactly the damaged nature of her features that intrigued him. He'd put his hand on her shoulder and said, "It's going to be all right." She'd smiled, briefly, her eyes glassy, and nodded appreciatively, and then the elevator doors opened and she walked out. He never saw her again because she never came back to Equitable Life. He tracked down her address, a walk-up apartment on 43rd Street, but the apartment was empty and the superintendent would not supply her forwarding address. Still, for a period of time, the memory of that day in the elevator remained fresh in his mind, and he would think of her from time to time, grieving over the life they'd never had together.

"She makes me feel complete," Tom added.

"My wife is just the opposite," Hugh admitted. "I'm like rejected merchandise. I think if she could she'd return me with a whole list of complaints. Not only would she want her money back, she'd want to speak to the store manager."

"Sounds to me like you need to get back on the shelf." Tom stood up and staggered into the bathroom to take a piss. The sound of his urine hitting the toilet seemed alarmingly loud. When he came out he was holding something—an empty soap dish. His face was pale, and his hand trembled slightly. "May it please the court," he said gravely, presenting the empty soap dish to an imaginary jury. "Apart from me, she has one single obsession: her skin. It's one of her few vanities—uses this terribly expensive black soap— never goes anywhere without it—it's a soap for fucking witches, looks like charcoal, never misses a night, and where is it?"

It wasn't there because Hugh had thrown it into her bag, attempting to produce, in the minds of the police, the possibility that she had left on her own accord. "Look," Hugh said, scrambling for some clarity. "I'm sure there's a perfectly good explanation, Tom." Saying his new friend's name aloud made him feel important. "Maybe something happened to her. Something bad."

But Tom shook his head. "Bad things don't happen to Hedda Chase. She's with *him*," he pointed to the cell phone. "The fucking tart," he muttered.

"Couldn't it be . . . couldn't you be jumping to conclusions?" Hugh attempted to speak clearly. "What if something happened? You never know these days. There are lots of bad people out there."

"Let me tell you something about that woman," Tom said, his voice lit with spite. "Nothing happens by chance—it may appear that way—but trust me. She's strategic. She's got all the moves planned out way before anyone else has even sat down at the table."

Hugh felt a fresh surge of hatred for Hedda Chase—almost to the point where he could rationalize what he'd done—like maybe even he'd done Tom a favor. He swallowed the rest of his drink. "I hope, for her sake, you're right."

Like a pair of drunken comrades they took the Bronco and stopped at a package store on Franklin for some beer. It was nearly two a.m., but the city was alive. All the creeps had crawled out of their dark little corners. The extras, he thought, the filthy, ugly, stinking people you rarely saw in daylight. They were nocturnal, like all the other unpleasant creatures that came out at night—*including me,* he thought.

They drove up to the snake, a circuitous road that ran along the canyon, the city of Los Angeles twinkling below. They were unlikely brothers, Hugh thought, at once awkward and intimate. Tom parked the jeep in an overlook and lit up a joint. The moon was fat and dirty. It was a big fat bundt cake of a moon, he thought. The lights of the city winked like the lattice wings of dragonflies. They passed the joint back and forth. The pot was good. It made him languid, amphibious. His skin stippled with goose bumps. His face hot, and yet cool and damp too, as if he'd just stepped out of a sauna. He could hear everything. The sound their bodies made, taking in air. Swallowing; sniffling; moving. The sudden wind. The branches of trees like magic wands, casting spells.

He focused on his own breathing, the sound of his beating heart. He had this same feeling when he'd gone to court to contest a speeding ticket. Sitting there with all the other infracted people, waiting to speak to the judge. Some of them had serious problems. For one reason or another, they had all been caught.

Hugh thought: *What have I done?* He thought of his wife, alone in their house. He imagined that she had fallen asleep watching television, as she often did. He'd find her there in the morning lying on the brown couch they'd inherited from her parents, under a crocheted blanket some distant aunt had made, surrounded by crumpled tissues. Marion didn't get high, she didn't approve of it, and he rarely smoked in front of her. Pot had saved him from the ravages of suburban blight, all the hours he'd spent alone in his basement getting stoned and watching movies. He hadn't been ready to leave her, he supposed, but he was ready now. For months, she had been a vacant presence in their house; they were roommates, sharing a place. Even on the rare occasion when they'd make love it was a silent, absorbing act, akin to some sudden physical drama that they didn't discuss. They had met at Keene State in a behavioral science class and started dating, he a freshman, she a sophomore. He'd lost his virginity to her on the narrow bed in his dorm. He could remember feeling a certain terror when he'd entered her for the first time. Her touch had been tentative. Light and abrupt as the sudden, deadly appearance of a praying mantis, the iron smell afterward, of one crushed bug. He didn't really know why he'd decided to marry her. He supposed it was because he hadn't met anyone else. No one who showed any interest in him, anyway—not because he wasn't good-looking—he fancied himself a rather attractive man and even his mother had told him he was—she'd described him as having aristocratic good looks—clean and well-groomed with neatly trimmed fingernails and fine clothes that she'd find on sale at Lord & Taylor's—but he was and always had been exceptionally shy, a gentle, unassuming manner, his mother called it, and always polite. His parents had encouraged their marriage, wanting him out on his own, wanting some other woman to wash his dishes and do his laundry and iron his shirts—relieved, perhaps, that it was a woman he'd chosen after all. Shortly after their marriage, they lived in a studio apartment on the fourth floor of a walk-up on Cornelia Street. It was a lively neighborhood, and the city was a good distraction, the restaurants and theater, the cinema. Marion worked in a small flower shop and was often busy on weekends, doing weddings and bar mitzvahs and funerals. Aside from an occasional blowjob from a male prostitute—something he spoke of to no one—he'd remained faithful to Marion for six years and then, quite by chance, about a month after they'd moved out of the city, he met a woman named Jolene in a Hoboken bar. She lived in Newark, in city housing. She brought him to her apartment complaining of the noise, the slow elevator, the spotted orange carpet. The corridors smelled of cumin and cloves, turmeric and cinnamon. The apartment was nicer than he'd expected. Jolene was an unemployed graphic artist who worked as a temp at a printing company in Hoboken. She wore long skirts and g-strings and bright scarves. They would smoke pot and make love, her skin the impenitent green of old bay leaves, her nipples like the smudged rubber thimbles of a bookkeeper, and then she'd make him tea with mint that she grew on her windowsill. Compared to his wife, Jolene was easily satisfied, uninhibited about her nakedness, her smells, her moody breath. She moved with the unhindered heft of a wrestler, whereas Marion moved very little, as though the weight of Hugh's body upon hers was too much to bear. He knew he could not satisfy her—nor did he feel he could discuss it with her. She was not willing to be open to him, he thought. For him, he supposed, she endured sex, but she did not enjoy even a second of it. It made him feel bad, like he had no right. With Jolene, he could be himself or some closer version of himself. She would grip his shoulders and throw back her head, her breasts swaying, her flesh rumpled and damp. After sex, he would lie on her mattress naked, his penis soft, and she would feed him slices of apple. She'd stand at the mirror and fix her hair, using a pungent wintergreen oil that he carried home on his clothes. His affair with Jolene didn't last; she'd gotten a job in Cincinnati and moved away. Eventually, she'd married and they'd lost touch, but whenever he'd open the closet he could smell her there on his coat.

The pot had finally dulled his guilt. For a few minutes he had forgotten about Hedda Chase; he was able to suspend, in a dark little bubble inside his brain, the truth about what he'd done to her and what might become of him as a result.

"Tell me about this wife of yours," Tom said.

There were many nice things he could have said about Marion, but for some reason the only thing that came to his mind was, "My wife is a mouse."

Tom laughed. "You married a mouse?"

"I'm leaving her," Hugh said. "I don't love her anymore."

"That's a good reason to leave. Love is a strange thing," Tom said. "It can be fickle. It can disappear."

"She doesn't know it yet. When I get home—" His voice faltered and somehow he couldn't finish the sentence.

Tom took him to a nightclub where strippers pranced around deerlike on a stage to canned music. Hugh found it depressing but acted like he was having fun. Tom was traipsing all over the place in his baggy suit, spilling his drink, kissing strangers on the mouth, and then wandered off somewhere into the back of the club. Hugh sat there, waiting for him to return. It was three o'clock in the morning; he was getting tired. For a split second, he found himself wishing he were at home, in bed beside his wife.

Those days are over, he thought.

When Tom came back he tossed something at Hugh—a little square ticket that said PAID on it. "Go for it, Tiger. She's waiting for you."

"What?"

Tom nodded toward the back. "Room sixteen."

Hugh sat there.

"Go on, man. You deserve it." Tom waved over a waitress and ordered another round and started talking to someone he knew, a man with a shaved head in a black suit.

Hugh got up and shuffled down the carpeted incline toward the stage. You deserve it, he told himself. There was an odor—of sweat and perfume and something else—wet money. The woman in room sixteen didn't speak any English. Her yellow skin turned green under the strange blue lights. "You like?" she said. "You like me?"

He told her he did, but he didn't, not really. He didn't like her at all. Still, he was curious. The room was very small, windowless. She put his ticket in a jar. He watched as she took off her clothes. He noticed a tiny snag in her stocking. He could hear her wheezing a little as she danced and he thought she must be a smoker. There were sounds all around, the kinds of sounds you hear at night, walking outdoors, sounds you cannot place. The woman, too, was like some kind of nocturnal creature, something you might catch in your headlights that gave you the willies.

When he got back to the table Tom was gone. Hugh looked around the club then went outside. There was no sign of his friend. It had gotten cool and he shivered. The night had been long and he suddenly felt lost—betrayed by the fact that Tom had left him there. In the cab back to Hedda Chase's neighborhood, he began to cry. The driver glanced at him uneasily in the rearview mirror. Hugh had not cried for many years. Bad thoughts crowded his mind. He had the driver stop on Los Feliz Boulevard, several blocks from Chase's street, and got out. He walked on the crooked sidewalks, hearing the insects, the keening of the overhead lamps. Her house was dark; there was nobody home. He stood there for a moment, looking at it. A car came down the road. As it passed, he stepped into the darkness, its headlights brimming across his back. When it had disappeared, he continued down the sidewalk to find his car.

In the motel, he showered, scrubbing himself raw. Hugh had never been to one of those places before. His dancer had been a woman of uncertain descent. While she shimmied in the tight space, her face seemed disengaged, as if the batteries in her head had worn out, while the batteries in her body were still good. Her sweat had sprinkled his skin like sea spray. He dried himself off and got into bed and lay there listening to the night. In high school, he had been abused. It had been a teacher he admired, a short little man in a bow tie with a prodigious command of the romance languages. Hugh had had difficulty with languages. One afternoon it had simply happened. He wasn't even sure if it fell into the category of abuse. He didn't know, really. It had been a strange incident, a fluke. The teacher's fingers had smelled of tobacco. The file cabinet shook. It wasn't something he liked to think about. He'd never told anyone. Sometimes it came back to him and he had to try to shut it out. It wasn't fair. It wasn't fair some of the things you had to deal with in life, things you didn't ask for.

Through the open window, he could hear people on the street, a drunken crowd outside of a bar. A car alarm went off. He got out of bed to have a look. The men outside the bar had begun to fight, one man shoving the other against the car. A helicopter erupted overhead and they scattered. Another man came out of the bar to check his car and silenced the alarm. He stood there, cursing, looking left and right, then spit into the gutter and went back inside.

Hugh lay awake thinking about Hedda Chase—trying to picture her inside the trunk in a fetal position, her hands tied behind her back. When he had tied her up he had felt something real, something like hate. Reflecting on it now, he felt worried; ashamed. Who was the man on her cell phone? he wondered. And where were they now? Had he opened the trunk and discovered her yet? And if he had, what had he done next?

Ever since that night Hugh had tried to convince himself that what he'd done to her had only been a joke that had gone awry—he'd never intended for her to disappear, really—perhaps he hadn't thought it through—perhaps he'd been in some kind of a mental state—yes, a deranged state at that—but he was better now, he'd come out of it. He wasn't a bad person, he *wasn't*!

Somebody else had her now. That man who'd answered her phone. It was his crime now. He was the real criminal.

PART TWO

SUSPENSION OF DISBELIFF

4

It begins in late September, when you first see the car. It is raining and you are happy for the rain because you have grown irritable with so much sun and the rain soothes you somehow and reinforces the fact that you were not born in this sun-bleached emotional wasteland, but back east where people are moodier and unapologetically disenchanted. The sky is grim, the air cool, and you are driving home from the studio as on most afternoons around this time, only today is different because of the rain, the long line of traffic down Los Feliz Boulevard. The car is parked on a grassy corner, adjacent to one of those prehistoric mansions, an enormous, mushroom-colored Spanish Colonial entrapped in vines. It is a blue BMW, an older model, a For Sale sign taped on the windshield. You think of stopping, but in truth you are not the sort of person who buys things from strangers—you have come to rely on the expertise of people you trust for getting you what you need, when you need it, and you are not really comfortable pursuing things on your own. For the several weeks that follow, you notice the car as you pass by, as the grass grows up around it, dappled with fluffy dandelions, and you begin to dream about owning it, driving home in it, showing it to your colleagues at the studio, your small collection of important friends.

Then, days later, again on your way home from work, you happen to notice a van parked in the driveway. It is raining again, the clouds hauntingly black, a yellow fluorescence to the light as if the sky, the air, is sick. The driveway runs up off of Delacroix Avenue, a side street off the boulevard. The van is black with gold lettering: COUNTY CORONER. Instinctively, you take your foot off the accelerator and turn onto Delacroix, pulling up alongside the curb with the car idling. They are bringing a body out. It is covered with a black water-repellent sheet. It is an eerie thing to witness and you watch with apologetic fascination as they load it into the van. You have felt the same uncertain empathy whenever you pass an accident on the freeway—that morbid anticipation—you can't help thinking of the famous scene in *Weekend*, the Godard film, a ten-minute tracking shot of a traffic jam caused by an accident—or when you are behind an ambulance and can see inside, the EMT's diligent face, his solemn concentration as he works on the patient. It is an expression reserved for the saving of a life, and it is rare, and fine. As a filmmaker, you have come to know about expressions and there are certain expressions that are not for everyone and that are difficult to duplicate for the camera. You have come to realize that both saviors and executioners wear the same expression and there is, of course, a heady irony in that.

The rain begins to fall harder and you see a woman come outside with an umbrella. She is Mexican, in a housekeeping dress, holding the umbrella over the coroner's head. At one point he takes her hand and guides the umbrella over her head, and she smiles gratefully. It is a brief and touching exchange and you make a mental note to work it into a movie. Thinking about the car, the strange dark house, the alarming appearance of the body, you drive home to your rented bungalow. Death is something you fear and you can never gauge its proximity. Sometimes you sense it encroaching upon you like some thief in the night, looking into your windows. Sometimes you lay in bed, brittle, waiting for evil to find you. Images sprawl through your mind, arbitrary scraps of terror that have become all too ordinary. To some degree, you have been nurtured on fear.

Stopped at a traffic light you review the facts of your life: You have achieved so much, and yet your heart is empty. It is the truth; it is something you know. You have come to a point in your life—success has garnered certain privileges—you are grossly overpaid, and yet you are overworked; you are rarely alone, and yet you are intensely lonesome; you have accomplished what you set out to, and yet you feel your ideals have been compromised. When all is said and done, you feel a weary sense of ambivalence.

You are forty, which in Hollywood is not a good thing. Not that you are actually *old*, because of course you are not, but you have begun to feel slightly invisible at meetings with certain people, the younger directors for example, most of them men, who grow impatient with your lengthy discussions of character and plot—your questions about context and rationale—and your desire to tell stories that resonate in the hearts and minds of the American public—yes, it is true, your ambitions are lofty—and some of them actually rush you through lunch. In a town like this, where passive aggression is something of an art form, you have invented your own special version of subliminal espionage. In order to survive as a female you are forced to behave like someone with a personality disorder, limiting your range of expression to a deadpan grimace. The smile, that old-fashioned symbol of genuine assurance, has become obsolete, replaced by its nasty cousin the smirk which, when coupled with the cruel but effective once-over, conveys to its recipient that he or she is a complete waste of time. The only time people sustain a genuine smile is when they are certain you can make them money. On your way up you had acquired your own battle scars. And even now—even with all your success—you are besieged with doubt. You have not entirely outgrown the need for approval, the lavishing praise of an expert. Doubt is your compass. It prevents you from feeling happy. Your unhappiness is a strategic part of the mechanism that drives you, the feverish self-loathing that shoves you forward, toward that shimmering light of your destiny.

Most of the people you know are married, either married with kids or gay with kids. Even Harold is more married than you—you have caught yourself envying his lover, Mitchell, whom he showers with love and attention—and you get the sense that people, your friends and acquaintances, have begun to pity you for being unattached—you can see it in their eyes as they evaluate your rather gaunt frame, your jaded eyes, your inexcusably hooked nose— unlike many of the girls you grew up with in Short Hills, you don't believe in nose jobs—and when they have you to their homes, making excuses for their disagreeable children at whom you smile too much until your cheeks hurt, and their cluttered family rooms, you always leave feeling somewhat bereft, as if, somehow, you have profoundly missed out. The truth is, you're not interested in having kids—you don't really even like babies—and you don't really see the need for having a husband. If it weren't for Harold inviting you out to things, insisting you make an appearance, pushing you like an old Jewish mother to meet someone, someone *available,* you would rarely even date. You are a Hollywood anomaly and people resent you for it—and yet, you are one of the most powerful women in town. They resent you for having secured a place as one of the industry's elite, without even fucking anyone for it. Still, your power is subject to conditions. You have few real friends. Your success has created a certain dynamic in your relationships and everything that comes your way is contingent upon something else— you carry other people's destinies around in your pockets like loose change. You think of yourself as a kind of emperor. They would tell you anything if they thought it might get them a deal, and you have witnessed the continual mental jostling that occurs every time you meet with somebody, you can see it in their eyes as they attempt to calculate what you want to hear, what need they might fill, and how, ultimately, you can benefit their career.

Admittedly, your experiences with men have been limited and you realize that there is a part of you that is still a fat little freshman at Yale and yet, when you think about it, you were lucky to be ugly and fat, because it informed your sensitivity, it taught you lessons about life, about communication, that other people—your beautiful colleagues for example—have never had to learn. It helped you in your business dealings, because you understand that making deals is less about the money, the project, the actors, than it is about the machinations of the human heart. What you have come to understand during your Hollywood tenure is that every deal you make is personal. In the rooms where deals are made, a thousand things are going on at once. There are the lurking ghosts of broken dreams. There are the pressures of trying to maintain an existence in a town that is not a real town but only pretends to be real, and where certainty is an ambiguous concept. A town that pretends to be exclusive and yet, in truth, it is open to everyone. It is a hard-working company town and yet, unlike the production of steel or chocolate, the manufacturing of ideas, those fragile little creations, is time consuming and costly. Vulnerable to the elements, ideas must be carefully nurtured. Unfortunately, they cannot be mass-produced. (And yet if they could, you're sure that the studio head would have done it by now). On second thought, they have come pretty close.

In college, you found your way into film by accident when a scheduling mishap landed you in a film theory class. Almost immediately, you became transfixed by the luminous black and white films on the big screen—Bergman in particular, whose dense, analytical explorations were like the discussions you'd grown up on at your own kitchen table, sandwiched between your psychiatrist parents, who would discuss the dilemmas of their patients over dinner. One afternoon, sitting in the dark theater watching *Breathless*, your professor's hand rounded your shoulder—three hours later you were up in his apartment on Everit Street rolling around on his filthy sarouk. On the outside, your professor was like some gloomy storybook creature with greenish flesh and spiky hair and teeth like caramel corn—all the girls in his class made fun of him—and yet he needed you so desperately that he was infinitely giving and generous. Making love on his lumpy futon, you learned one of the most important lessons of your life, that there were benefits to fucking smart men who were losers in the looks department—he had dark, serious eyes and elegant manners and a very efficient penis. So grateful was he for your affection that he did whatever it took to please you and although you were not beautiful he made you feel as if you were. Over suppers of greasy pad Thai he taught you everything he knew about film and you would go to the movies together, to the art cinema, and eat buttery popcorn, your hands mingling inside the bucket. You would whisper throughout the film, critically and admiringly, and then dissect it on your way home. You didn't know it then, but you were learning a language that would be useful to you later, and would convey the deepest aspects of your being. What you realize now is that you are still learning this language, and you are not yet fluent. You are still only dreaming about the films you want to make—dare you admit it—films that have the power to change lives. Your affair with the professor ended abruptly when you graduated, but you still think about him from time to time, one of the few men who ever truly satisfied you. Through the grapevine you have heard he's still in New Haven, married to an art historian. Of course you know it is impossible to ever meet again. You are a Famous Hollywood Producer; you do not socialize with people from your past.

Several days later, when you return to the house on Los Feliz Boulevard, the car has been moved. Now it is parked in the driveway; perhaps it has been sold. A familiar churning grips your belly, part pain, part desire—the same sort of ache you get when you hear a pitch you like—and the car becomes something you have to have—what you fondly characterize as *a must-have item*. The Mexican woman answers the door. Perhaps it is because of what you do, your experience with images, your ability to make an instant assessment, that you understand that she is a woman who is at once magnificently beautiful and yet accustomed to being ignored. Her dark hair frames her face, her black eyes, her full lips. *"¿Sí?"*

"I've come about the car? Is it still for sale?"

She shakes her head, *"No es un buen momento,"* and gestures to the old man, who is slumped in a wheelchair in the living room, gazing out the window at the boulevard. *"Su esposa murió recientemente."*

"Let her in," he says.

"Ella quiere información sobre el automóvil."

"Déjala entrar."

The woman shakes her head again, as though she is disappointed, but lets you in, waving her dishtowel after you like a bullfighter. The house is grand and yet there is something sad and forgotten about it. For a moment you just stand there, taking it in. You guess that it was built in the twenties. The ceilings are impossibly high, painted with cherubs like the Sistine Chapel. As you stand there under a crystal chandelier you feel a sudden chill, as if someone is running their fingers through your hair.

"Please." The woman ushers you into the living room. *"¿Señor?"*

The old man does not turn, only waves you near with his withered hand. The room is large, cluttered with beautiful old things. The large picture window is framed in green and yellow glass, filling the room with colored shadows. Blocks of light scatter the room as if you are inside a kaleidoscope. The corners of the window are cloudy with condensation, blurring the monstrous trees outside. The effect is like an old dream you cannot fully remember, one that supplied a revelation at the time that you could not fully grasp. The rain falls hard, you can hear it running through the gutters, and it occurs to you that the house is weeping.

"Please," the woman shows you to the couch, a green velvet loveseat that is like the beard of an ogre, with horsehairs poking through the cushions.

The old man turns and reaches out for your hand. His is cold and thin.

"My wife," he says, shaking his head. He takes out a handkerchief and blots his eyes.

"Maybe I should go," you say.

The housekeeper scolds, "¡Quizás es demasiado pronto!"

"No, it's not too soon. Make us some tea, my dear Flora."

Again, the man shows you his sad eyes. "She loved the car. It was a birthday present. I bought it for her fortieth birthday."

"I'm so sorry."

He nods appreciatively. "She was spectacular." He hands you a photograph. "I saw her once; that was all it took. I knew."

You study the photograph of the man's wife. "She was very beautiful."

"Have you ever had that feeling?"

"What feeling?"

"When you are completely certain about something. It's like you have finally been roused from sleep."

"I don't know," you admit. "Yes, I think so." If you are certain about anything, it is your own inability to find love—true love—and the idea that there is a person out there who might recognize something in you that he finds undeniably essential seems like a ridiculous dream.

"We are all sleeping," the man says. "Sleeping through life."

"I know. You're right, it's true."

"And then we die." He looks at you and nods. "And there's nothing left."

Dust, you think. You sit for a moment listening to the rain. Flora brings the tea on a tray, the cups trembling on their saucers. She sets the tray down on a coffee table. To be polite, you drink the tea, but really what you'd like is a glass of vodka. The tea is sweet. It tastes of lavender honey.

The old man sips his tea then asks what you do for a living.

"I'm in the film business. I'm a producer."

"Ah," he laughs. "That's a good profession."

"Yes."

"It's a good car for you, then."

"I thought it might be."

"People will be impressed."

"I'm not trying to impress anyone."

"No?"

You shake your head. "I don't care what people think."

The man looks at you curiously. "Are you sure?"

"I just like old cars."

"But this isn't really true, what you say about not caring. I can see many qualities in you and apathy is not one of them. I know about making impressions on people. I was in a similar profession."

"What was it?"

He digs around in his pockets and produces two fat little parakeets, one in each hand. He lets them go and they fly around the room.

"A magician," you say, laughing.

"Yes. But do you want to know the trouble with magic? It is its own worst enemy. And since we are both in the business of making illusions, we can understand each other, yes? An illusion makes the impossible, possible. And yet it is the worst kind of trickery." He smiles as if this is obvious, showing his imperfect teeth. "For example, I could not save my wife with it."

You nod with sympathy, understanding.

"I can make people believe, because it makes them happy to believe. The possibility that there is something else, something larger than ourselves. Something beyond what we can imagine, something inexplicable."

"Like God," you say.

"Or heaven," he says. "Do you believe in heaven?"

You think about it for a moment. "Yes," you say finally. "Because it's better than dirt and worms."

He reaches out for your hand. "Let me hold your hand a moment."

"All right." You give him your hand.

"You are very warm," he says, giving it back. "You have good circulation."

"Do I?"

"You see, there is an explanation behind every phenomenon." He smiles meaningfully.

"*Ella no quiere escuchar un sermón, viejo,*" Flora scolds. "*A ella le gusta el automóvil, déjala manejarlo.*"

"*Pero ella se ve muy triste,*" he says to the woman.

"*Sí, sí, el auto la va a hacer feliz.*"

You don't know what they're talking about and you don't mind not knowing. It's pleasant to be sitting in such a grand room, drinking tea, and you like the sound of the Spanish, a beautiful language. Tea in the afternoon is nice, you think, resenting the fact that you have become an American fool, always rushing from one insipid activity to another. Your life, you conclude, is a series of neurotic solutions to the inevitability of death. Your diets and remedies, your trainers, your amino acids and vitamins, your ineffectual therapist, your personal masseuse.

"Flora says I'm lecturing you. I should let you drive the car. You don't have all day to be sitting around with me. You are busy, an important person."

"Not so important." You suddenly don't like the adjective. It is true that, in the context of your life, you are important; you make enormous decisions; you control millions of dollars; people wait for your calls. But thinking about it now, in relation to your conversation with the old man, you are not so sure.

What good have you really done? Who have you helped? How deeply have you felt about anything? Maybe everything you've accomplished is meaningless. "I'm in no hurry."

"Do you want to drive it?"

"Maybe not today, with the rain."

"You're hesitant. I can see it in your eyes. You're thinking it wasn't smart to come here. You don't usually do things like this."

"Like what?"

"Buy things from strangers."

"That's true, but this is different."

"I am not a stranger, yes?"

You smile at him. "I don't want to trouble you. I'm sorry about your wife."

"We are all strangers to each other." He smiles. *"Flora, dale las llaves del auto."*

Flora disappears for a few minutes and when she returns you hear the tinkling sound of the keys and see them now in Flora's hand. To your surprise there is a rabbit's foot on the keychain. It is a white rabbit's foot and when you hold it in your hand you can feel the tiny bones beneath the fur. The bony foot makes your hand sweat.

"Buena suerte." Flora smiles regretfully, as if she feels badly about whatever she has been saying to the old man and you can tell she's decided to like you.

"We can all use a little luck," the old man says.

"Luck is good," you say.

"Take it for a spin, see what you think."

"Are you sure?"

"You want to try it, don't you? That's why you're here?"

"Yes, of course."

"Jackie O. drove that car, did you know that?"

"No, I didn't."

"Hers was green."

"It's a beautiful car," you say.

Flora walks you to the door. *"Le gusta usted,"* she says, gesturing to the old man. *"No como los demás."*

You shrug, you don't understand.

"The others." She shakes her head. "He don't like. *Pero usted.* He like you."

Now you nod and smile.

"Usted puede conducir alrededor del vecindario." With her hand, she draws a circle in the air to explain, then hands you the keys. "Take your time."

The rain has stopped, but the sky has a greenish tint and you know it will rain some more. The wind is strong. It gusts at your skirt, your hair, deconstructing the image you so carefully assembled this morning and that has now become completely irrelevant. You yank out your shirt, loosen your collar. You'd like to remove your stockings and heels and just be barefoot, but you suppose it's not a good idea under the circumstances. The car waits for you in the driveway. There is a gust of wind and a splattering of rain and then something strange happens—the sun beams through the clouds, so bright that for several seconds you are blinded by it—and then just as abruptly it vanishes, leaving you cold. Another gust of wind sweeps the For Sale sign off the windshield and into the air. You watch the piece of paper sail through the air to the ground, rest a moment, then resume its flight down the grassy incline, into the road where it is swiftly trampled by a passing car.

The car is not locked. You climb into it, laughing a little, feeling like a movie star. For a moment you just sit there, smelling the old leather, the faintest scent of roses. Inside the glove compartment—what a strange old term it is—*glove compartment*—you find a pair of gloves. They are white calf and luxurious. You try them on, but they are too small. You do not have thin, elegant hands like the magician's dead wife. Your hands are square, simply manicured, the nails cut short. You examine the paperwork. The old man's wife was named Inez. In the photo he'd shown you she was wearing heavy beads and a white blouse and long dangling earrings with stones. You say her name aloud, *Inez.* You put the key into the ignition and the engine fires up. You laugh out loud like a child. As Flora suggested, you drive around the neighborhood, passing large elegant homes with empty yards. You never see people outside. It's the strangest thing about L.A.—beautiful lawns with no one on them. It makes you feel as though you are the last woman on earth after some apocalypse. It is one of the reasons you took the house in your neighborhood; you like the street, the crooked sidewalks, the eclectic collection of neighbors. It reminds you of where you grew up, in the "poor" section of Short Hills, near Millburn Village. At night, from your bedroom window overlooking the backyard, you'd watch the trains fly past full of sleepy commuters on their way home from the city. The modified ranch had a separate section where your parents saw their patients, totally removed from the rest of the house. On your days off from school, you'd see them—the patients—pulling up in their cars, trying not to look conspicuous, walking up the short driveway and slipping through the side entrance, a door with a small rectangular window of shaded glass. As a kid, your parents' profession embarrassed you. You rarely had friends over after school; if you did, you'd spy on the patients and make fun of them, but you never really thought it was funny. In high school, a brilliant student, you retreated into your studies. The other kids despised you. You had one or two friends, both nerds. Sometimes you'd go to their houses, large, immaculate homes full of breakable things. It would occur to you much later, after you'd finished at the conservatory and entered the work force in Hollywood, that the gatekeepers of the film industry were, for the most part, a collection of neurotics and social incompetents just like you. Unlike the high school cheerleaders and handsome football stars who populated their films, they had been gloomy, brainy misfits—now they were the arbiters of the cultural landscape, constructing dreamy fake-realities that had precious little to do with any of them.

On impulse, you drive down the boulevard and cross over into your neighborhood and turn onto Lomita Avenue and pull up in front of your house. It is a typical Spanish bungalow with a clay roof. If you owned it, you would completely redo it—but it is only temporary, and as soon as the renovation of your villa is finished you will be moving out. Your life will change. Still, you have liked living here. You will miss it.

It begins to rain again and now the sky is getting dark. You pull out and start back to the old man's house. By the time you get there, you have decided to buy the car.

5

The car makes you happy. Everybody notices it. Even the guards at the studio gate make a fuss about it. It is a marvelous car and handles the road like a dream. You look for excuses to drive it. You make visits to your villa out in Malibu, an arduous journey in traffic, but you don't mind it. Instead, you admire the sunshine, the glittering ocean, the beach. The villa is a wreck; you got a deal on it. Other, more particular buyers didn't like the fact that it had been home to an iconoclastic woman with seventeen dogs. She was the reclusive daughter of a Swiss actress who'd been killed in a terrible accident. The daughter's dogs had been in several movies, beginning with Laddy, the famous yellow Labrador, in the early seventies—the show had been syndicated and you could still see it sometimes on Nickelodeon—once you'd even seen it in Tokyo, dubbed in Japanese. Unfortunately, the old villa still has a slightly doggish odor, and several of the once magnificent bamboo floors have been destroyed, but the view is spectacular. The windows are tall, the rooms full of light. There are narrow walkways down to the beach, overgrown with roses. Whenever you walk the property you can't help wondering where all the dogs are now, and whatever happened to the daughter. You had met her once, at the closing—she was a white-haired woman in her sixties in a mangy old fur coat who smoked Tiparillo cigarettes and asked the lawyer if he might provide her with a glass of chocolate milk.

In truth, when you'd bought the place, you felt a little embarrassed. It was something you had to focus on with your therapist. And yet, compared to some of the homes you've been to parties at, unbelievable homes overlooking the beach, yours is modest. Even Harold's house in Beverly Hills looks like a wedding cake and has a swimming pool fit for a community center. You feel a surge of pride—you'd earned your money—you have nothing to apologize for! And yet this guilt persists. "Is it so wrong to live nicely?" you'd asked your therapist, a spiky-haired woman with a pierced nose, and she'd just looked at you, blankly, and said nothing. It dawned on you that, like your modest psychiatrist parents, your therapist made far less of an income than most of her patients, including you, so it wasn't really a fair question. It wasn't one she could answer. You have to decide for yourself. Sometimes when you drive through certain undesirable sections of the city, you regret your success. Sometimes you think: *It's not my fault I have so much.*

Of course you didn't always have it. You started out with nothing like everybody else. After the conservatory, you'd had a string of fragmented industry jobs that kept you going for years: production assistant, wardrobe assistant, script supervisor, secretary, reader, assistant story editor, story editor, development executive, assistant producer, producer. When you'd finally made it to Gladiator you were still something of an innocent, a starry-eyed optimist with big dreams that were gradually disintegrating. Until then, you'd been working for Maura Holt at Fox, developing the Kingpin series based on the graphic novels, having foolishly assumed that working for a woman would be better for your career, that a woman would be more understanding and sensitive about the movies she made—not true—she was like a Titan goddess, wielding her powers like a javelin. Your life took on the characteristics of the films themselves, a kind of strange, grainy, apocalyptic reality. You rarely slept and were continually plugged into indispensable gadgets. Of course you had a million excuses for not living like an actual human being; you were addicted to the possibility that you would get something for all your trouble—for taking so much abuse; for existing in some hybrid plastic sycophantic whirlwind that promised you a future. You had heard Cory Rogers had died—Harold Unger was looking—but in truth you weren't that interested. Gladiator Films had a reputation for being sexist, not only because of the movies they made, hard-core thrillers and gangster movies that raked it in at the box office, but because none of their top people were female. When Unger called you, explaining that his good friend Leo Zaklos had suggested you to him, you decided that the job was an opportunity. You sensed that you and Harold would work well together, that he'd understand you and, at the very least, appreciate your history—you shared aspects of being marginally accepted in certain circles—nothing you could say to his face—but you sensed that he had experienced things in life that had shaped his perspective in a way other men, straight men, could not absorb.

During your first month with the company, sequestered in your second-floor office, your bird's nest as you liked to think of it, with leafy, pendulous avocado branches pressing up against the windows, you spent whole days cleaning out Cory Rogers' junk (there was a poster of Tracy Lords over his private toilet—it was *signed*), reading over the scripts he had bought and developed, most of them awful, one of which was slated to go into production the following year. It was a thriller called *The Adjuster,* written by somebody you'd never heard of, a client of Miles Beck's, an agent you generally avoided. It was the most disturbing script you'd ever read. The protagonist, an insurance adjuster, abducts a coworker who has refused his advances. He drugs her, puts her in the trunk of his car and parks it at the airport, leaves the keys in the ignition. The car gets stolen by a group of thugs who go for a joyride. From inside the trunk, the woman hears the thugs getting high; the pulsing music; a girl getting raped—she waits in terror, praying they won't open the trunk—of course they do. After reading a few more scenes, you felt physically ill. You went into Harold's office and threatened to quit. "Maybe you should find somebody else," you told him. "I can't make films like this."

Harold smiled knowingly and flipped through the script. "I admire the fact that you have a conscience," he said. "That's a rare commodity. It's why I hired you."

Then he took out his lighter and set fire to it. You stood there watching it burn. He dumped the burning pages into the trash can.

"Happy now?"

You nodded, somewhat embarrassed, and walked out.

You had no delusions that you were a creative genius; there were few of those in your business. But you were something of a snob. It was your pedigree, being a member of the Ivy League. And yet months later, after the release of your first movie, *The Hold Up*, which was a box-office hit, you had little trouble rationalizing the fact that you were not making Great Works of Art.

The work was demanding, consuming. At the end of the day, you'd find Harold in his office, his feet up on the desk, his shirt unbuttoned, smoking a cigar, gazing thoughtfully out the picture window. He'd invite you in for what he called "a confidential," and you'd sit on his Chippendale sofa drinking martinis, confiding too much about your pathetic social life. For a man in his sixties, he had progressive ideas about sex. "People should be having more of it," he was fond of saying. Rumor had it that when he'd first come out to Hollywood he'd been married—it wasn't until he'd met Mitchell that he'd come out. You saw in him a man who had come to terms with himself. The struggle had been difficult, but it had informed his professional life. He knew people; he knew how to talk to people. He was like a psychic or a priest. He could look at you and know what you were thinking. As a result, the good people admired and trusted him, and the bad people avoided him. For a stocky, hairy-chested schlepadik from Brooklyn he packaged a hell of a product, and he had the numbers to prove it. But he had a dark side. When he broke out his temper, you didn't want to be around. When he got his teeth into something he did not let go, not for anything. "It's the way I was raised," he told you. "You don't give up."

"You are how you live," he told you once, and you had silently scoffed, but now, after months of seeing Harold in action, you have come to believe it to be true. What it says about *you* is another story. Unlike your harried, generic office that reveals as little as possible about you, Harold's office is comfortable and inviting—the furniture an odd mix of Windsor and Eames chairs, his desk an eighteenth-century gateleg table; the floors covered with kilims. A Joan Mitchell painting hangs on the wall like a dream of summer leaves.

Once, after a half dozen mint juleps at Vern Rudnick's famous Kentucky Derby party, he admitted to you that he'd been married. "I did it for my mother," he told you. "It was a mistake. You can't do favors like that for people." He told you he had a daughter named Ruby who wouldn't speak to him. "You kind of look like her," he said.

One Friday afternoon in October, Harold invited you into his office for a glass of wine. "You're a Jew, right?"

"Theoretically," you said, a little put off.

"Here," he tossed you some matches. "You're a woman. Light the candles."

It was something you hadn't done in years. Striking the match, you realized you were nervous, but you remembered the blessing perfectly. For some reason it made you proud and he smiled, pleased at your happiness. "Don't get excited. I'm not very religious," you clarified.

"It's not really about religion. It's about ritual. Celebration." He raised his glass. *"La'chaim. Shabbat shalom."*

"La'chaim."

"Rituals are important," he said. "They're like the adjectives in a sentence, they keep people engaged."

"They're also dangerous. Look at Iraq; Afghanistan. Look at Israel. Cultures where rituals cause violence, and then violence becomes ritual."

"Yes, this is true. Some are healthier than others. But I don't think people could survive without them."

Your only ritual was your nightly glass of vodka. And you couldn't remember the last time you celebrated anything.

"I actually minored in biblical studies," Harold said. "I was considering becoming a rabbi."

"Really?"

He nodded deliberately, one of his endearing characteristics. "But then I realized that it was the stories I liked so much, not the religion—they'd even written special effects into the text." He laughed. "Good stories. That's why we're here, isn't it? That's why we're doing this."

"Easier said than done."

"Money has become too much of a factor. Money and art." He shook his head. "Not a good combination. You have to decide which side you're on. Me, I've made my peace with it. It took me a while, but I've finally accepted the fact that entertainment takes precedence over art. You saw *Sullivan's Travels*."

"Yes, of course, one of my favorites."

"I'm making films for the common folk, just like Shakespeare."

You smile, even though it is not enough and you both know it.

"Anyway, it always comes back to Story. Sometimes you have to look back to move forward. You have to go back to when stories were told out loud— great legends," he says dramatically. "You have to reread people like Homer and Dante and Shakespeare—of course everybody steals from Shakespeare. But I don't think a pure story exists anymore, do you?"

"Not in this town."

"Everything's derivative on some level. Ask me how many times I've seen *King Lear*?" Harold reached behind him and held up a rumpled paperback edition of *The Odyssey*. "Have you read it?"

"In high school."

"They make you read all this great stuff in high school when you don't appreciate it." He tossed you the book. "It's a great story. A masterpiece."

"Now that's what I call good poster copy."

You put the book in your bag, but you had no intention of reading it. Instead, you would be reading screenplays that were like airbrushed versions of great paintings. They were like the velvet reproductions they sold out near the airport, furry versions of Van Gogh's *Starry Night* displayed on a chain-link fence. Apparently people bought them. They took them home and hung them up in their living rooms. You wondered if they'd ever even seen the original painting or, for that matter, even knew of its existence.

Harold's cell phone beeped with an incoming text message. He glanced at it then looked at you again. "We've become a culture of sound bites. It's tragic, really. Have you ever noticed how many sounds there are? These beeps everywhere. It's maddening." He looked at you wearily. "It occurs to me that I'm starting to sound like an old man."

"The question is, with all our portals of communication, are we actually communicating? I'm the first to admit I'd be lost without my BlackBerry. It's alarming, actually, how much time I spend typing out these incredibly cryptic messages. The truth is: I don't want to talk to anyone. I really don't."

As if on cue, his cell phone rang. "I need to take this."

"Go."

You drank your wine, something knocking around in your brain. Over Harold's desk was a lithograph bearing the company logo with the word GLADIATOR in large black letters at the bottom. The Gladiator, great muscled warrior, the hero in the arena, unprotected, willing to risk everything to win. To *survive*. The gory *spectacle* of it, the carnage. You thought Odysseus. You thought army; marines. You thought suicide bombers, Blackwater mercenaries.

Harold had gotten up and was standing at the window, nodding his head as he listened to the person on the other end of the conversation. You drank your wine and considered the books on his shelves. There was fiction, poetry, philosophy, books about art and film. Harold had gone to City College. It was unusual to see bookshelves that actually had books on them, as opposed to DVD boxes. Books, *epic masterpieces,* that's what had gotten you into this business in the first place—the fat, glorious books you'd read as a kid, great love stories like *Anna Karenina* and *Gone with the Wind*. Filmmakers like D. W. Griffith, Billy Wilder, Hitchcock. You couldn't help wondering what they would have thought of *The Hold Up*. Was it even possible to turn out movies like theirs anymore? The world was different now. Maybe the people were different, too.

You could tell from Harold's placating, mildly ingratiating tone that he was talking to Bobby Darling about the new Braden Quinn film that Gladiator was going to make. A disruption at the window caught your eye. Bobolinks flashed behind the leaves of the avocado tree. The sky was pink.

"The wine is nice," you said when he hung up.

"A good way to end the week." He finished his glass and stood up, pulling on his blazer. "You got plans tonight?"

"A little light reading. I have a stack of scripts in my office."

"Maybe you need to get out more." He smiled at you. "Come, take a ride with me."

In his hundred-thousand-dollar Mercedes with the top down you submitted to Harold's itinerary. "I always go to services on Friday night. I'm very superstitious, I never miss."

"I haven't stepped foot in a synagogue in years."

"If nothing else you might meet someone. Take it from me; there are some very cute guys in here. And what could be better, they're all Jewish."

"Ha, ha. You sound like my mother."

"Anyway, it's *Sukot*. It's a good time. Festive. You'll enjoy it."

The synagogue had a ceiling with a gold dome. Harold put on his *tallis* and *kippah*, then took your arm and like an old married couple you walked down the aisle looking for a place to sit. A man got up and stepped aside to let you into the pew. The rabbi was young, passionate, a recent graduate of rabbinical school. You found yourself admiring him. Aside from the fact that it was a little strange being there with your boss, being there *period*, you tried to relax. You tried to be open to it. You were not a person who could easily submit; perhaps you were a cynic. Any kind of group where there was a focused belief system made you nervous. It was cultlike, creepy. You were not willing to give in to God, to be His servant. You were not necessarily willing to worship Him. What had He done, really, for peace? The world was evil; chaos. The idea of some higher power was too abstract for your literal mind. It wasn't for you. Instead, even at an early age, you learned to intellectualize, packing your delicate beliefs into a little box to store up in your closet along with your little Torah, your little white bible upon which your name had been inscribed in gold letters. Spirituality made you queasy. And yet, sitting there, hearing the prayers of *Sukot*, you felt an almost uncanny sense of joy. Even the smell of the air reminded you of autumn back home. You thought about your conversation earlier with Harold, what he'd said about rituals, and you found yourself thinking it was true. Rituals were like landmarks, reliable symbols that gave people a reason to get up every morning.

You were like a foreigner from a strange land. You had no home, really. Your life felt temporary, ungrounded. It was hard being in L.A. Underneath your capable exterior, you were impossibly fragile—always the first in line to stand in your own way, to defer to someone else. Your sensitivity was both a gift and your nemesis.

After the service you explored the *sukkah*, a wood structure designed to commemorate the harvest. There were tables laden with vegetables and fruits, pumpkins and squash. Children ran in and out, laughing. You held a lemon in your hands like a baby bird.

Later, back at the studio parking lot, Harold kissed you on the forehead and thanked you for joining him.

"It's a beautiful synagogue," you said.

"You're welcome any time."

You nodded, but you had no plans to return. You were not a person of faith. You didn't believe in religion; you didn't believe in anything.

Then he did something strange. He reached out and gently touched your cheek with his open palm. "It's good for the soul," he said. "In a town like this, you can forget you have one."

6

In November the weather turns cold. Everybody is wearing sweaters and coats. They complain, but you can tell they really like it. They like walking around in beautiful sweaters, long woven scarves. The first several minutes of every meeting is dedicated to a discussion of the weather. It's all right with you; you don't really mind. The days are bleak. The wind unusually strong. That morning your lawn was covered with sycamore leaves.

There are meetings and more meetings. Meetings go late, meetings are canceled and rescheduled. You are charming. You are funny and edgy and dangerous and benevolent; you have croissants and raspberry jam; you have sashimi and drink too much sake and promise too many things; you have grilled trout with almonds; you are not in love, it's not your cup of tea; you are looking for something darker; you are intrigued; you haven't laughed so hard in years.

You feel as if something has been lost. You cannot explain it. You are on your hands and knees like a blind person, and yet you have forgotten what it is that you are trying to grasp.

Perhaps it is the beginning of winter, the grim prospect of hibernation that you remember from your youth. And yet, this is Los Angeles, there is no true winter here. Your days are complicated with the hopes and dreams of strangers. Writers come to tell you stories, to peddle their ideas. They are all the same. Most are dull little packages. You are eager to hear something new. Something *fresh*. You don't know what it is, but you will know it when you hear it.

And then, during a screening of a rough cut of *The Promise,* a film you executive produced, something unexpected happens. At twenty-four frames per second, in the span of eight minutes, you witness three murders, two explosions, and an admittedly thrilling car chase through the narrow streets of São Paulo. Two minutes into the second act, you begin to feel a creepy sense of isolation. Watching a love scene, you discover, surprisingly, that you are offended—and you are not the type who is easily offended. You glance around in the darkness at the others in the small screening room: Harold; Armand, your assistant; Buddy Meyers, the film's director; Jim Gage, his assistant director; and Vic Peters, his editor. Their faces are calm, almost placid. They absorb the images without dissent. The only other women in the room are Bethany, an "intern" (Harold's cousin's daughter), whose IQ is even less than her body weight, and the women from the commissary, soundlessly delivering coffee and pastries. You sit back and watch. Of course you had read the scene in the script, and yet Buddy's interpretation of it gives you pause. The fact that he is dating the female lead, Claudia Wells, who is twenty years his junior, probably hasn't helped the situation, and the camera, as it grazes her body, seems to proclaim *feast your eyes.* Antonio Ramirez plays a misunderstood gangster; Wells plays the wife of his boss, a ruthless mobster. She has left her husband, who has threatened to kill her. They are on a desolate Brazilian beach and it has begun to rain—the sky is black—the wind gusts at the ocean, the sea grass undulates—they run up the beach to a cement shelter—a public restroom—as the rain comes down. It is a grimy, disgusting place with cement floors and gray stalls. Closeup of Ramirez's hand twisting the lock as Wells dries her face on a paper towel. She turns, sees the way he's looking at her, and knows what is to come. She waits, cautious—he advances on her with a predator's certainty, violently sweeping her into his arms—the camera backs up and we realize that there is somebody else in the room—a dubious shadow in one of the stalls—watching. Cut to the lovers, the tops of her thighs, his hand as it rips off the lacy g-string then curves around to lift her up—a swift shot of her buttocks as they come in contact with the cement block wall, someone's graffiti under her flesh—anonymous initials inside a heart—and he pulls her onto his hips and opens his pants, the punitive sound of his buckle as it drops and dangles—and he's in her, pushing her up against the cement—bashing her into it—as their passion insinuates itself onto the sound track—the sound her back makes as it hits the wall— the grunt that escapes her mouth each time she hits—which the audience will misinterpret as pleasure, excitement, ecstasy—and the camera watches their hips as we register the velocity of their fucking—his fingers clutching her naked skin, the muscles in his arms, her torso, her flushed breasts, her face, her grinding pleasure as her lover pursues his climax and, finally, her face as they "come together," panting with euphoria.

You stand up, shapes of light flashing across your body, and for a split second you are part of the scene. Your voice cuts through the sound. "Can we stop a moment?"

The projectionist stops the film. Dim lights come up.

"What? What's the matter?" Harold says.

"What's with this scene?"

"What do you mean?"

"I'm getting really tired of this bullshit."

"What?" Buddy Meyers looks confused. "What are you talking about?"

"What's the scene about?"

"What's it about? It's pretty simple, Hedda. It's about sex," Bud says.

"I don't understand." Harold glances around uncertainly like someone who's been accused of shoplifting. "What's the matter?"

"The scene offends me," you proclaim.

"What?" Harold jerks like he's been pinched. "The scene offends you?"

"Yes, it offends me."

Buddy and his AD chuckle.

"The scene offends you," Harold inquires again, as if he can't believe it. As if it's impossible to offend a woman like you. "Why?" He smiles a little, humoring you. "Why does it *offend* you?"

"I think it's very sexy," Armand interjects, and you shoot him a withering look that tells him to shut his mouth if he plans on keeping his job.

You realize what you're up against here. *Only the history of modern cinema.* You think of *Klute*, the legendary scene when Jane Fonda, a prostitute, checks her watch while her trick's fucking her. To your memory, it is the only scene in the history of movies that actually indicates how remotely satisfying sex can be for women.

"Who has sex like that?"

The men look at each other, their solidarity building.

"Evidently you don't," Meyers mutters.

You ignore the comment. "It's not like she's going to come in that position."

"Speaking from experience," Jim Gage snickers.

"Yeah, speaking from experience. She's hitting her head on a cement wall—you're telling me that feels good? He gets to come, and she gets to have stitches."

"It's just a sex scene, Hedda," Harold says. "You're taking it too seriously."

"Really?"

He opens his hands as if it's obvious.

"Why is *this* what people want?" You present the question, sounding more like a high school principal than a producer.

"Because it's sexy, it's hot," Buddy Meyers answers.

"Hot for who?"

Harold frowns, uncomfortable, and looks embarrassed.

"Hot for who?" you repeat, but of course no one answers.

"What is this all about?" Harold asks as if it's obvious that you are having some sort of mental breakdown.

"It's about a lot of things. It's about all those seventeen-year-old girls out there who are going to think that this is what it is—that getting pounded against a cement wall is a turn-on. It's about all those confused women who wonder why they're not having orgasms when their husbands and boyfriends do this to them—I hate to break it to you guys, but contrary to popular opin-ion, it's not necessarily *about* the penis."

Buddy Meyers sighs audibly. "I feel like I'm being lectured. You're starting to sound like my ex-wife."

"Look," Harold says. "Look, Hedda—"

"No, let her talk," Buddy concedes. "I want to hear her perspective."

You persevere: "The scene—it gives men license to be violent. It tells women they should want to be taken, that being submissive is sexy. 'Fuck me harder. Do whatever you want to me, I'm a bad girl, I deserve it.' I know it's not intentional . . . but I think you underestimate the effect it has."

"It sure as hell has an effect on me," Gage says.

"We're saying: This is what love is. This is the best sex you can have. We put it up there on the big screen and people believe it. They think it's real."

"But it is real, Hedda," Meyers argues. "Maybe not for you."

The men in the room are looking at you in a way that makes you feel naked. Somehow, you feel as though you are on trial. They are watching you closely, judging you. Their eyes accuse you of being frigid, that, perhaps, this is your own personal issue and has nothing to do with the film. That perhaps this isn't a concern for most women. Most women, their eyes suggest, have no issue with orgasms like you do. Their wives and girlfriends, for example, are completely satisfied. Their wives and girlfriends and mothers even come up a storm every night. But you—a woman like you, with your pale skin and ratty blond hair and hawkish nose and insignificant breasts, are lucky just to get laid, let alone fetch a determined lover. They are actually feeling sorry for you.

Nobody says anything for several minutes. The air closes in, your cheeks flush. An awkward tension fills the room. And then Meyers asks, "So what would you change? How would you shoot it?" He chuckles as if over his own private joke then trains his eyes on you, lightly, as if you are somehow touched in the head. "How would you shoot it—let's say from a feminist perspective?"

Just the way he says the word burns you up. You can feel your face turning colors. You scramble for ideas, but you are flummoxed, empty. You are beginning to feel embarrassed. Jim Gage whispers something into Meyers' ear and they both snort with mockery.

"It's not even about feminism," you say quietly. "It's about behavior. We just keep going over the same ground. The women are always at a disadvantage. I think it's confusing, that's all."

"I think you're overreacting," Harold says, which feels like such a betrayal.

"Maybe." It's suddenly clear to you that they don't really care. If anything, the discussion is purely academic. "Maybe I am."

"You haven't answered my question," Meyers says accusingly, his ego stinking up the room like a nasty fart.

"How would I shoot it?" You look at him. "I don't have a clue."

Meyers grunts as if he's made his point. "Look, I can't change the way people behave, that's not my job. I'm in the entertainment business. That's what I do. I entertain. And judging from my numbers, I'm pretty fucking good at it. As far as I'm concerned, that film's in the can."

Surprising everyone, he gets up and walks out. You stand there, feeling oddly ashamed. Harold is glaring at you. Without wasting another minute, you gather your things and walk out.

It isn't until you're in your car that you begin to cry and you hate your tears, you resent the ease with which you've come undone. It is so definitively female—and yet it may be the essence of your strength, you just don't feel it now. Your colleagues always seem to bring the attention back to you, suggesting that your criticism is a consequence of some personal problem. They interpret the things you say as though you are speaking a different dialect of the same language—the subtle differences of inflection seem to weaken your position and they can easily rationalize and discount your opinions. It is, you admit, a sophisticated form of passive aggression.

Back in the screening room, you couldn't possibly explain all of the reasons and ramifications of why that scene bothered you, because to do that you'd have to review the entire Western canon—you'd have to break out your old Henry Miller books, your Norman Mailer, in order to illustrate for them the myriad ways in which we have condemned women to living lives of subservience—even now, yes, even now! Centuries of cultural propaganda dispensed by a male regime!

You drive onto the freeway, trying to calm down. Maybe you should see your therapist. You try to breathe. How *would* you shoot it? Meyers' question comes back to you—the way he'd said the word *feminist*, like it was some sort of disease. You review the scene in your head. First, the location sort of bothers you. Realistically, it is not the most conducive to sex—and yet, perhaps you can work with it—yes, perhaps the location is sexy, the implicit contrast, the seedy texture, the beauty of love in a brutal, impossible place. You're not sure about the strange voyeur in the scene—what does it represent? The fact that we are all voyeurs in some way—that there is always some stranger in our midst, watching us—that we are never alone? Maybe, in some way, it's a Jesus reference—it's not impossible—but then you remember that the screenwriter is a Scientologist. You suppose, if you shot the scene, you wouldn't have them actually fuck. You'd have them kiss. You're thinking *From Here to Eternity*—the legendary kiss in the surf—you're thinking *Witness*. Yes, you decide, that's all they would do, they would kiss. You don't really need the sex, it's gratuitous. Not that you're a prude—no. You remember having sex like that, standing up. First of all, it was awkward—you couldn't get past the idea that your boyfriend was struggling to hold you up while attempting to fuck you—you were maybe twenty pounds heavier at the time, too—but then again, he wasn't built like Antonio Ramirez. You felt like one of those acrobats in the circus, doing some elaborate trick, and you remember changing your minds and finding a bed, instead. Perhaps the lovers in the scene could lie down on the floor—but that appeals to you even less. Once, you had sex on a dirty floor—it wasn't necessarily the most pleasant thing—you did in fact contract a strange viral rash—you'd had to go to the dermatologist for treatment. So, yes, you decide that if you were to reshoot the scene, you'd have them simply kiss, and it would be a wildly passionate, beautiful kiss—it would be enough.

On impulse, you get off the freeway and drive into Santa Monica, toward the beach. You turn down Colorado Avenue and head toward the pier. The sun is bright, the air warm—maybe you'll take a walk. Thinking back on it now, you realize that much of your information about sex came from movies. Growing up in the seventies, you were empowered by films like *An Unmarried Woman* or *Kramer vs. Kramer*—even *Manhattan* seemed to encourage you to be sexual for the sake of your own pleasure—if Mariel Hemingway could have sex with a forty-year-old man, why couldn't you? And yet, still, it seemed like the sex was for *him*. You remember not fully believing that she was as ravenous a lover as Woody said she was and, in retrospect, it reeks of wet dream. You were further confused by *Swept Away,* which had been directed by a woman, Lina Wertmuller—the first woman director you'd ever heard of. You remember feeling somewhat betrayed by her treatment of the female character, a wretched aristocrat, who, on a yacht in the Mediterranean, verbally abuses the impossibly sexy Giancarlo Giannini, a member of the crew, who later, when they are castaways on a deserted island, retaliates by depriving her of food and sodomizing her (another cinema first for you— you had not yet seen *Last Tango in Paris,* which had come out a year or two earlier). When you'd watched the Wertmuller film at Yale, the discussion by your mostly male classmates had revolved around the political implications of the film, the fact that the male character was a communist, and that the rape was a political act, not a sexual one—it's a familiar argument, one you've heard since. But, to this day, you can't get past the flagrant misogyny of *Swept Away*.

Now that you have succeeded in getting yourself into a state, you turn down a side street near the beach, looking for a place to park. You rarely come here—and you are slightly worried about being alone—but you are desperately thirsty and need to pee. Miraculously, you find a parking space and retreat into a dark little bar called Sullivan's. Feeling a little lost, you use the bathroom, wash your hands, then go to the bar and order a drink. Vodka neat with half a lemon, just the way you like it. Just having the drink, having a reason to sit here in one place, alone, without anyone saying anything to you, without having to speak, is a relief. The bartender has the eyes of an undertaker. They haven't turned on any lights and the place is dark and quiet. The windows glint with late sunlight. You notice the tail of a cat slipping under one of the tables. Somewhere outside you hear chimes. There are only a few people in the place, regulars. You like it here, nobody knows you, and you stick it out at the bar for a couple of drinks. At last you begin to relax. You think of going home, but for some reason you don't want to be alone. Just as you are about to leave, someone taps you on the shoulder. "This may be awkward," you hear him say. "But we were lovers for a while, back in film school."

You turn to see Tom Foster. "Tom?"

"Shove over, sailor, and let a man buy you a drink."

You move to a table in the back, near the games and machines. It is dark now and the place is crowded. Your conversation is punctuated by the smacking collision of balls on the pool table, and the cheesy, jubilant gush of the pinball machine. Although it has been nearly twenty years, Tom Foster looks almost the same. He is a big man, well over six feet, and yet he is thin, almost gaunt. His arms are long, his hands swift, powerful. The same dark, intelligent eyes. For so large a man, he moves with unusual agility, even grace. You remember his tendency to be slightly vain and yet, in fairness, it is part of what makes him interesting. And so you are not surprised by the beat-up leather coat and motorcycle boots, the twine bracelets around his wrist that resemble the delicate twigs of a bird's nest. He tells you about a documentary he has just shot, about a homeless shelter in Hollywood, and you remember the expression on his face, the passion he has for his work, the particular shine in his eyes. In your twenties, you had been students together at the Conservatory. Somehow you'd fallen in step with each other and become fast friends. Your lovemaking was almost an afterthought—in truth you were better at being friends than lovers, mostly because you had a tendency to get jealous and resented the attention he paid to other women. He was like a peacock flaunting his feathers. He lived in an efficiency apartment on Franklin Avenue that had a Murphy bed. Making love, you'd hear the cats yowling in the Dumpster outside the bedroom window. He'd write his screenplays at the kitchen table on an electric typewriter. You both smoked Camel straights and drank too much bourbon. Once, he even made you dinner, pork chops and canned soup—you didn't have the heart to tell him that, even though you were only a Reform Jew, you still didn't eat pork. You were in your Lauren Bacall phase. You wore dark red lipstick and parted your long blond hair on the side and were fond of saying: *You wanna know how to whistle? Just put your lips together and blow.* You had a tiny apartment in Beachwood Canyon, on a strange little street called Glen Alder Terrace. The apartment was in a compound of crooked Spanish cottages, set into a canyon, with red rooftops and rusty windows without screens. A long paint-chipped stairway led up to a plateau where the little cottages stood under the avocado trees. Sprawling thickets spit their purple berries onto the steps; you would carry them inside on the soles of your shoes, dappling the floors with purple, star-shaped stains. It was a strange place with lots of spiders. Sometimes at night you'd hear coyotes. Once you caught one going through your trash. It was after midnight and there was nobody around and you were frightened, standing there alone with a wild animal. The coyote looked at you with the sheepish eyes of a drug addict, a jumble of tin foil in its mouth, and ran away. You had trouble sleeping in those days. Being alone made you anxious. Sometimes you'd wake in the night, sweating, feeling a weight upon you—the weight of a horny ghost. You'd watch TV late into the night; reruns of the old shows you'd grown up on, and drink until you were too drunk to think about all of the terrible things lurking out in the dark. Your neighbors were movie people: a script girl, a set decorator, a sales rep for Fuji Film; they ignored you. In one of the cottages lived Leo Zaklos, a bumbling iconoclastic lunatic who was now considered a screenwriting genius. Once, you'd knocked on his door to borrow some bug spray. He leaned there in the doorway, leering at you with his plump slippery lips, his stubby tobacco stained fingertips, and convinced you to come inside. You could scarcely walk, the floor was covered with filthy clothes, garbage, but he lured you out to his terrace in the back, a splendid enchanting place dripping with hanging orchids, where he convinced you that he was one of the smartest people you had ever met. You introduced him to Tom, and the three of you became an unlikely trio, watching movies every night together and ripping them to shreds.

Despite your efforts, you could never make Tom fall in love with you. He made it clear that he was not available for possession, leaving you continually frustrated. In those days, Tom was obsessed with the beat poets and the writer, James Agee, who'd come from the same place, Knoxville, Tennessee. Tom liked the fact that Agee had lots of women, a ruthless connoisseur, and yet, beneath the mythology Agee was unkempt and unhygienic—allegedly, he rarely brushed his teeth. Like Agee, Tom took pride in being enigmatic, aloof. Days would pass and you wouldn't hear from him and he'd show up looking scrappy and hung over and stinking of cigarettes and perfume fresh out of the Conservatory, he'd sold his first screenplay, an action thriller, for over a million dollars—you've never quite forgiven him for it. After a while, you lost touch. You'd run into him from time to time at parties, always with some Victoria's Secret model on his arm. You didn't really care; he was an asshole. You'd heard he'd gotten married to some Italian woman, a poet, and had started making documentaries. You never thought of yourself as being the jealous type, but whenever you'd get a scrap of news about him—the wedding announcement in *The Times*, for example—you had to choke down your rage.

"I'm looking for a producer," he says to you now. "Trouble is I can't find anyone with any balls. You wouldn't happen to know anyone, would you?"

"I might."

He orders more drinks and reaches out for your hand and holds it for a minute. His hand is huge and rough, a farmer's hand. As much as you think it's strange, you don't pull away. "I remember these hands," he says, then looks at you. "How've you been, Hed?"

"All right, I guess. Working hard."

"You're good at that."

"Too good."

"Married?"

"Please. You?"

"Sort of."

"What does that mean?"

"We're sort of separated."

"No such thing."

"She lives over in Rome."

"Italy?"

"Another one of my impulsive mistakes."

The drinks come and you hope he'll change the subject. He doesn't. "She's very beautiful. I guess you could say I fell in love with her accent."

A little stab of jealousy. "I'm a sucker for accents, too," you say because you are drunk, because you like his, which is warmly southern and conjures in your mind the lazy summer afternoons of his childhood.

"Look, Hedda," he says. "I know it's weird running into you like this."

"It is weird."

"But maybe there's a reason for it. Something corny like destiny."

"I doubt it. I don't believe in destiny."

"All right. I respect that. You always were brass tacks."

"That's right, that's me. I'm all about the bottom line."

"Look," he says, impatient. "I got a story for you. You interested?"

You really should go home—you are not in the habit of hearing pitches in seedy bars—but you say, "I guess I could hear it."

He finishes his drink and holds up his glass and the pretty waitress with the tits comes over. "Thank you, darlin'," he says to her, handing her his glass, gazing briefly at her cleavage. You give him the benefit of the doubt. It's like Pavlov, you decide, they can't help themselves. He is a victim of the culture. Perhaps it's not his fault, and perhaps it's not the waitress's fault either for smiling at him with encouragement, all too happy to forgive him for not knowing any better.

But she does not smile at you. "Another round?"

"Why the hell not," you say.

"That's my girl." He grins.

You sit back, pretending to be interested. "Okay, hit me."

"I've been teaching up at Santa Cruz," he tells you. "I'm a lecturer in the film studies program."

"La-di-dah."

He explains that after one of his talks a student came up to him, a Muslim girl, Fatima. "She's wearing the *hijab* and *abaya*, you know, she's covered. I can only see her eyes. And she hands me this story she wrote. It's on loose-leaf paper, ripped out of a notebook, the most perfect handwriting I've ever seen."

Through a series of miracles, the girl had been chosen as an exchange student to attend UC Santa Cruz as part of a diplomatic effort called the Iraqi Student Project. Fatima had been living with an aunt in Syria, having been sent by her father after her mother's death in a car bombing in Baghdad. The story was based on the real-life tragedy of a Baghdad woman, the mother's best friend, who'd been accused of adultery and put to death. The girl did not think that the car bombing that killed her own mother was an accident.

"My script is based on her story," he tells you. "It's a love story between an American soldier and an Iraqi woman."

"Is that even possible?"

"The soldier and the woman were trapped inside a building for several days after a bombing. People thought they were dead. At first, they don't speak; they're enemies. Then, as time goes on, they become very close. They don't want to return to their lives. They'd rather be trapped, together, than go back to their lives in the world."

"Then what?"

"They get saved. It's immediately assumed that they've been lovers. The fact that the woman was with this man for all that time—it's assumed that the soldier's taken advantage of her, that she's succumbed to his advances."

"Has she?"

"You'll have to read it to find out." He grins. He goes on to explain that the woman's husband accuses her of adultery; the woman is found guilty and sentenced to death. One of the characters, an Iranian feminist lawyer, has committed her life to banning the stoning practices of the Muslim clerics. "She's my Erin Brockovich character," he says.

"How does it end?"

"Just the way it happened. She was stoned to death."

"You might have to tone down the ending," you say, thinking of what Harold is going to say to you when you pitch this to him. Foster grins at you with his beautiful mouth. You ask, "How soon are you going to be done?"

"Soon."

But several weeks pass without another word from Tom Foster. Through the grapevine you hear that he's shooting a documentary in Hollywood. People have seen him with his crew. You begin to wonder if perhaps you imagined your meeting with him. And you resent the fact that it has brought up issues that you don't particularly want to think about—not about *him*—no—we've already established that he has a form of attachment disorder, unable to fully embrace love, commitment; any expectations of intimacy will somehow be betrayed, or, at the very least, manipulated, and yet, still, your imagination has already begun spinning a sticky web of fantasy. No, we are not talking about Tom Foster here, we are talking about you—the pages from your repertoire of angst that you haven't necessarily dealt with yet, the fact that you haven't had the decency to marry some reasonable, perfectly acceptable man and given your parents grandchildren. Or the fact that your womb is like a tomb, swiftly closing its doors, sprouting toxic mushrooms and jagged barnacles. Or the fact that, on some occasions, you feel desolate, rubble-strewn, like a field after the apocalypse. Food has lost its flavor. You can't seem to consume enough alcohol to take away the twinge of desperation—the fear that all of the people you have made promises to, all of the people you have taken money from will come back with their hands out, wanting their payoff. You don't sleep—not really. You lie awake, anxious. You have fears you do not discuss, not even with your therapist. Whole scenes play out in your head each night. Intruders, rapists, killers.

You are a very private person. In truth, you are shy, you are unassuming. You keep your real persona to yourself.

People don't know you. They think you are somebody else.

In the privacy of your head, you review your conversation, reimagining the table where you sat, his large expressive hands, the faintest smell of leather from his old coat. One drunken night, you dig out your old photographs from the Conservatory, ogling him like a schoolgirl, and you feel as though you are under a spell that can only be broken by seeing him again. But it is not likely. Although he is considered to be smart and talented, he is on the periphery of your social circle. The likelihood of his Baghdad movie ever getting made is slim to none, at least not in your realm. Perhaps a smaller independent company might take a chance on it, although you highly doubt it. Finding the money isn't going to be easy. Not so long as there are wars going on.

Still, you have to admit, the story got to you—and the fact that it is true makes it all the more appealing. *Based on a true story.* You can't get out of your head the look in his eyes as he told it to you, intimate as a love poem, across the table of the noisy bar. On Google you find pictures of his wife, a beautiful woman with slightly bucked teeth, sphinxlike eyes, round breasts like pomegranates. You remember sensing his disappointment with your flat chest, your boyish hips. Still, that didn't stop him from wanting you.

For the first time in months, *years*, you feel a keen excitement—and a terror that you won't ever hear from him again.

And then, without prior notice, the script is delivered to your office by messenger on a rainy Wednesday morning in December. You tell Armand to cancel your meetings and hold your calls. With some degree of anticipation that is unavoidably personal, you curl up on the couch and begin to read. Tom always was a good writer, but this script is unusually powerful—it gives you a stomachache. You begin to sweat and your throat goes dry as if you are there in the Iraqi desert. You can almost feel the hot wind against your skin and you acknowledge the tension in your body, the result of being completely at his mercy. Three quarters of the way through the script you realize the hours have faded; it is nearly three o'clock. You feel as if you're about to explode. Bedraggled, overwhelmed, you emerge from your office. "That good, huh," Armand asks.

You cannot bring yourself to speak. You bum a cigarette from him and walk out into the open corridor. The air is warm; the clouds seem to be brewing another storm. "What about lunch?" he asks. "Shouldn't you eat something?"

You tell him to order you lunch from the commissary; you'll eat in your office. "I need to take a walk," you say. "I need to think."

You walk across the lot, from one end of it to another. Your pace is quick, ferocious. You are like a disgruntled teenager, smoking defiantly, hot tears streaming down your cheeks.

Your mind is jammed with disturbing realizations, not only about the war, the despicable mistreatment of women—but about your own pathetic complacency. Unlike Foster, you have forgotten what it feels like to be on the edge. Perhaps you traded in your ideals, your dreams, when you took this job. You have forgotten those early impulses that got you into this business in the first place—your desire to stir people from sleep! Yes, you know it's dramatic—but you are in the drama business. It is entirely the point. When you consider the work you've done, the handful of films you've produced, you acknowledge their success at the box office—you are proud of their success—and yet, in truth, they are banal and unimportant. Standing there on the now-vacant set of a gangster picture, you reckon with the truth. You have gone off course. You have sold out.

"These are the kinds of stories we should be telling," you implore Harold in a breakfast meeting the next morning. "Not this . . . this crap." You point to a stack of scripts on your desk about which Armand had written promising remarks. "These aren't the reason I took this job," you tell him. You hold up Foster's script. "This is an important story. This is why you hired me."

Harold shakes his head; he is not convinced. "This is a loaded gun, Hedda."

"Fire it," you say, and walk out.

After a week of silent deliberation, Harold knocks on your door. "Okay," he says. "We'll do it. Get Foster over here."

You leap from your chair; you take the old man into your arms. You kiss his cheeks, tears in your eyes. "I love you for this doing this. I won't let you down. I promise."

You celebrate with Tom in your empty villa. He picks you up in his old Ford Bronco and drives you out to Malibu. You let the windows down in the truck and the wind blows too loud to talk. The sun is low, the ocean dark. You stop to get champagne—ice-cold Veuve Clicquot—and sit outside on the broken stone terrace and drink it. The evening casts a golden light. The wind is swift, your hair sweeps about your face. All the trees are moving at once. The orchids and chimes that hang from their branches sing their love songs. Even from here you can smell the sea.

"You gonna give me a tour of this place, or what?"

Like a tour guide, you lead him around your house, a complicated excursion amidst the contractor's tools, the stacks of flooring and drywall. "It's on the map of the stars, you know. A very famous dog lived here once."

"What are you going to do with all this space?"

The question jabs at your heart. It reminds you that you are alone, as if it's something to regret. "I haven't quite figured that out yet."

"I'm sure you'll think of something." He stands at the French doors, looking out, his arms stretched across the open space. "That's quite a view. The sky is orange."

"It's a beautiful night."

He turns, comes toward you. "You've done well for yourself, Hedda."

The comment makes you unspeakably proud. "Harold wanted me to buy a house. He thought it would be good for me to put down some roots."

"So you bought a mansion."

You shrug. "I got a good deal on it."

"*Mazel tov.*" Since he's not a Jew, you're not sure how to take it. On the one hand, the words mean *good luck;* on the other, they mean something else. They mean: *spoiled rich Jew, showoff.*

"It was a wreck when I bought it."

"It's still a wreck."

"But it's got good vibes."

"You're the one with the good vibes," he says. "You'll make it beautiful."

You can't help blushing; you look away, out the windows, down the sprawling hill to the ocean. "The ocean is rough tonight."

"Maybe it will rain."

"It's windy. I love the wind, don't you?"

"Do you have any music? We could dance? It would be very Gatsbyesque."

"No, I don't have any music."

"We have the wind," he says. "The chimes."

The chimes clatter and sing. He comes closer, takes you in his arms. You dance slowly across the open space, the darkness spreading across the floor, silent as mist. "I've thought about you," he says. "I've thought about you a lot."

"I've thought about you, too."

"You're different. You're different from most of the women in this town."

"Like your wife?"

"Yeah, like my wife."

"Are you in love with her?"

"No."

You don't say anything. You put your head on his chest. You dance like that for a long time, pushing around the shadows.

"Are you afraid?" he asks.

You are too afraid to answer. You let him kiss you and while he's kissing you you are already thinking about the countless ways that you will mess it up—that it will cause problems for the film—that after this night—after you let him have you, which you know you will, he will be gone from your life—he will disappear.

Silently, you climb the grand, winding staircase. You make love on the floor of what will become your bedroom, strewn with dust, smelling of fresh paint. It reminds you of the scene in *The Promise* and it makes you smile. But this is different, you decide. This is your house, your beautiful house, clinging with wild roses, the black ocean in the distance. And he is someone you know. Someone you met long ago, during a time of life when you were purer, less corrupted. It is something he is searching to find inside of you; something you need back from him too.

He stretches out alongside you, rolls on top of you, kisses your neck, your face, your tiny breasts, your belly, the tops of your thighs. You pull him up. You love his body, his weight, his beautiful shoulders, his chest—the way he smells. His long legs, his enormous feet. The look on his face. How you have survived without this for so long eludes you. And as you tumble together, your body upon his, his body upon yours, your hard kisses, your spit, your sweat, you feel your longing renewed. You give yourself to him; you feed him pieces of your soul that you will never get back.

With the project in development, you work together on the script. You spend late hours in your office at the studio. Sometimes he comes to your house. Usually it is late at night, after he's been to the editing room, cutting his documentary. You drink together, talking, your bare feet curled up on the sofa. Sometimes you will eat a little something, an omelet maybe, or some hard salami, sharp cheese, olives. It is like old times, you think. Only not really. You are different now, and so is he, and the truth is you miss your old self, that courage you had, the ease with which you survived without comfort. Without safety. Shooting edgy sixteen-millimeter films with no money; living off baked ziti and peanut butter sandwiches. Barely having the cash to process your film, let alone rent the Steenbeck. The risks you were willing to take for your art—because that's what it was—that's where you began, making something called art. But money will do that, you realize, suck away at your courage. And anyway, you're not making art anymore—not really. *You are making money*.

Watching Tom Foster makes you happy. The way he sits there, his long, lanky body, his big feet, his enormous shoes. Sometimes you will walk around the house in his shoes, just to see what it's like. He wears clogs, old boots with broken laces. His shirts are deep caves, the pockets of his trousers filled with pencils, lint, useless matches upon which he has scrawled intermittent lines of poems. He talks about his film, the famed documentary, his eyes lit with passion. There is a girl in the film, sixteen and homeless. She has been living at the shelter. She has a talent of playing the harmonica. He has her playing in the film, sitting on some playground swings. The girl has freckles, her hair is long and blond. "Wholesome American stock of the Midwestern variety," he tells you. "She was living in her mother's car for about three years till the mother got a boyfriend. Left soon after that. Says he broke her arm. She doesn't talk about it much."

"Did you try to contact the mother?"

"Sure, I tried. Couldn't find her. She's totally off the grid."

"Now what?"

"I'm not sure. I'm looking into it. She doesn't want to be part of the system. She doesn't want to live with strangers. Maybe it's all right."

"What if it isn't?"

He shakes his head. "I don't know. I have to think about it."

It comes to you that his life is larger than yours. The way he puts himself out there for strangers. On the one hand, it humbles you—you admire his passion—on the other, you think it's a marvelous distraction from all the other stuff in his life he'd rather not deal with, like his unconventional marriage to the Italian shrew. Countless people seem to depend on him and he never complains. He seems to welcome the confusion. "I'm happy to help," he is fond of saying. Even his wife is something of a stray cat. Still, you haven't quite forgiven him for staying married, especially now that you are fucking him on a daily basis. On the rare occasion that he tells you about her, Lucia—just her name is enough to make you ill—you imagine that he is talking about a character in one of his scripts; it is the only way you can tolerate the folklore. A few times you've been up to his house in Laurel Canyon, a striking modern cube that juts over the cliff. The walls inside are covered with extraordinary photographs, most of them black and white and exceptionally valuable—Harry

Callahan—Dorothea Lange—Edward Weston—Ansel Adams—a serious photography collection for which he is renowned. The furniture is spare, Scan-
dinavian. Only once you slept beside him through the night. It was there,
in his bedroom, with the white moon shining through the skylight that you
first told him that you loved him—you admit now that it was a mistake. *Too
much information.* His wife was in Italy somewhere, at her family's vineyard.
Of course her dilemmas were always fascinating and exotic. While he slept,
you snooped around the house, opening her drawers, fingering pieces of her
stationery, a box full of feathers, a book crammed with poems—much to
your dismay, they were all in Italian. Evidence of his life with her everywhere
you looked, the espresso machine, wine from the family vineyard, *please,* the
hand-painted plates from Sicily. You find yourself wondering if her absence
is in some way more meaningful to him than the flesh and blood time he
spends with you. It makes you weak; you don't like thinking about it. It is as
if there was a tiny crack in your heart that leaks your pain, there is no drug for
it, but you are stoic, you can put up with a little pain. And you don't believe in
jealousy—as your therapist would say it undermines your self-respect—and
yet there's this weight in your chest, this rage. You lie awake at night, stewing
over it. It's your own fault for falling under his spell. *Your own fault!* And yet
you refuse to compete. You are a fascinating, accomplished woman, terrifically
exciting—everybody says so. And you have worked your fingers to the bone
to get where you are! You are smart—smarter than *her*—smarter than him
too while you're at it—but she is the phantom wife, persistently unattainable
and, like some devious icon, forever in his thoughts.

One morning, you fly to San Francisco together then drive down the coast
to Santa Cruz. In person, Fatima Kassim is graceful and lovely. Her head is
covered, but she is wearing a Western skirt, a long-sleeved blouse. You drink
tea together in the student union and she tells you about her mother and the
woman who was murdered, her mother's best friend. "They were like sisters,"
she says in nearly perfect English. "They were good women. They were good
Muslims. It's not right, what happens to women in my country. Before the

invasion was different, but now it is very bad. It is much worse now. Before we went to school, to the cafes. We could wear what we wanted. We had *life*." She shakes her head, her eyes filling with tears. "Not now. Now we don't go out. The suspicion—that's all they need to condemn you. If you are a woman, you have nothing. We cannot drive, we cannot wear trousers, I could not be wearing this," she tugs on her skirt. A look of shame crosses her face, but you are not certain for which she is more ashamed, her country's treatment of women, or the newly acquired clothing. "If you are seen in the street wearing makeup someone will throw acid in your face. Just before I came here, a woman who was not wearing her head scarf was murdered. One of the girls in our village was raped on her way home from school, she was just twelve years old. And do you know what she did? Because of the shame? She set herself on fire. They said it was some kind of kitchen accident, but we knew. All of us knew the truth." Fatima looks across the table at you. "People should know. They should know these things happen." She nods, as if she is resigned to something. "You make your film. You tell the truth."

In silence, you and Tom drive back to San Francisco. On the way, driving up the coast, he wants to stop to go kite surfing. There's a place he knows, friends of his who have equipment right on the beach. They are toned, handsome men in wetsuits. They make a fuss over you, the only woman. They give you coffee in a thermos and warm bread. For a few hours, you sit on the beach watching them surf, attached to kites that are like enormous wings. You can't help thinking of Icarus, the dream of flying. The power of being up in the air like a magnificent bird. Of using your body, your strength. The détente that forms between the body and the elements: the ferocious sea, the relentless wind. You envy it. That feeling he must have; that rush. The freedom. It is something to see, watching him, being part of this scene—the wild ocean, the cold sand beneath you, the smell of the water, the wind shouting in your ears. You fall in love with him all over again. Maybe you are not strong like him. Willing to stake your life, willing to take such risks. And yet, you are making his film. You are putting yourself on the line for him.

Driving into the city you tell him how you feel, that the movie about

Fatima's mother and her friend terrifies you. There could be serious consequences for her. If word gets out about her involvement, and eventually it
will, she could be in danger. You express this to Tom.

"She's already in danger," he says, "simply because she's female. Anyway,
she's here. For now, she's safe."

"They can always send her back."

"She's willing to risk that."

Still, you don't feel any better. You fear you have no business making a
movie like this now, with so much trouble in Iraq. With American soldiers
fighting over there. What do you really know about Islam? Who are you to
question their laws? You're an American, you can't relate to their way of life,
their rituals. Maybe it's none of your business.

"As long as we're over there, it's our business," Tom argues.

"Convince me that's it's all right to risk Fatima's life. Because that's what
we're doing." He doesn't say anything. "Why are we making this film?"

"If you have to ask, you shouldn't be involved." He pulls over to the side
of the road and looks at you in a way that makes you feel sorry you started
the conversation. The Bronco shakes with the wake of passing cars. "We're
making it, because she has to go back there one day. Because it's not just
about Iraq. It's just as much about us as it is about them."

"It could be dangerous. That's all I'm saying. It could piss some people
off."

He looks at you. "That's the whole point, isn't it?" He reaches across the
seat and takes your hand. "We're into it now, Hedda. For better or worse.
No turning back."

You spend the afternoon in San Francisco, walking the streets. He pulls
you into the contemporary art museum and you wander together through
the open bright spaces. A museum is a good place to be with your lover, you
think. Something about the white walls, the art, allows so much possibility.
It is a place where you are free to be anonymous. The work, the art, lures
you out of yourself, into another realm, an abstract arena of pictures and
sounds, dreamlike and abeyant. Much of the work is informed by war, images

of genocide and apocalypse. Landscapes of broken cities, destitute villages. Dead people; ghosts. Languages of nonsense conveyed by passionate graffiti we cannot understand. The consequences of wars devised in strange, foreign lands. For some reason you think of Harold, his obsession with *The Iliad* and *The Odyssey,* the visceral evocation of bloodshed, the legends of wars between men, the enduring characteristics of heroes.

It's late, and you're both hungry. The restaurant is noisy and close, with tight leather booths and white tablecloths. You drink two bottles of wine and decide to check into a hotel. You make love all night over the noisy street below, the unruly behavior of strangers. Your bodies sweat. Deep sounds erupt from your mouths. It is reckless, bitter sex, each of you fully aware of your own inability to save the world from ruin.

7

On the plane to Abu Dhabi, the magician's wife, Inez, comes to you in a dream. She is wearing her long white driving gloves, the same ones you had found in the glove compartment that first day you drove the car. You are a passenger in the car and she is driving and the sun is very bright, you can hardly see. You are in the desert. The light is fierce, and yet Inez is laughing. She hands you her necklace, a string of heavy white stones. When you look at her now, you see that she is wearing the *abaya*, her head covered. The veil is like a shroud, and when she turns to you once more you see that she has no eyes, only empty black holes. You put the necklace around your neck, but the string breaks and the stones fall into your lap.

You wake, muddled, smelling roses.

The sound of the plane reminds you that you are in flight, that the crew is all around you, and that your lover, Tom Foster, the film's screenwriter, is in the seat beside you. You have agreed to keep your affair a secret. It isn't something that Harold needs to find out about right now, with so much money on the table. As progressive as he is, he would not approve of it and you know he would think less of you. Everyone is asleep. The journey is long, and you are not fond of planes or of flying through mysterious channels of airspace. The idea that your life hangs in abeyance, that progress of any kind is suspended, fills you with anxiety. How strange to think that you are up in the sky, moving from point A to point B and yet you haven't even the slightest understanding of the physics behind it. Glancing out the window at the pink clouds you can't help hoping that there's a God out there, even

111

though you have proclaimed yourself a nonbeliever. Thousands of feet below are the ancient cities where life began—this is a reality. You remember your summer in Israel, living on a kibbutz, visiting Jerusalem. It had amazed you at the time, just being there, in the Holy Land, amid so much history. Although you were hesitant, you indeed felt a kinship with the Israelis, you were proud to be a Jew. At the Wailing Wall, you can remember feeling moved, tucking your prayer for peace into a deep crevice between stones. And yet the culture was so different, even the simple negotiations of daily life were rife with dissent. It was the Middle East. It was not America. You suppose that living in the desert changes you somehow. Perhaps the heat, the dry air, the need to protect what you feel is rightly yours. And yet, the boundaries of territory are philosophical, subject to debate. Living so close to God—the idea that the Holy City is God's homeland—the place where history began—that changes people. It permits the possibility of something larger, something beyond one's ordinary scope. Of course it is far more complicated than that, and you are smart enough to know that power, in any form, is often an illusion.

These thoughts make you nervous. You don't like being at the mercy of others. You don't like the fact that your country is at war and you don't fully understand the war. Even now, making a film about it, you are still full of doubt, uncertainty. In truth, you feel completely powerless. You feel very small, as though you are an insignificant speck of sand in the eye of an infantryman who, within a matter of hours, might be dead.

With only ten days in the United Arab Emirates, your crew will have to work quickly and efficiently, transforming the neutral landscape around Abu Dhabi into the war-ravaged desert of Iraq, a sweeping white landscape that gives nothing back, nothing at all, only heat and rage. And you will be shooting in Iraqi-style homes on city streets that resemble Baghdad's. One soldier Tom interviewed had described the first invasion as an unlikely parade of tanks and Humvees rolling out of Kuwait City down a strip of vacant highway in the middle of nowhere, no human presence around for miles save for the distant clusters of Bedouin tents. That same summer in Israel, you bought a Bedouin bracelet in Jaffa—it was once the ankle bracelet of a young bride, a silver tubeful of sand. It makes noise whenever you move, the rattle of tiny stones. You are wearing it now, for good luck. You shake it, wondering how old the sand inside of it actually is. Centuries, perhaps. The fact that there are still people living out there in the desert in tents amazes you. You can't imagine living like that, with nothing, and you reject the idea fiercely; you have no patience for such nonsense.

The pilot announces your arrival and something inside of you flips over and your mouth goes dry. Tom squeezes your hand and gives you a look. "This is it," he says. This is the last leg of your shoot; you are eager to get it wrapped. Most of the interior scenes have already been shot back home on a sound stage. Everybody is excited about being here, in the real Arabian desert. Based on what other filmmakers have told you about Abu Dhabi, the accommodations should be first class. It is a country of superlatives, you've been told—they have the best, the biggest, the tallest, the most amazing. Still, you are not entirely comfortable being so close to the Saudi Arabian border and you feel determined to be on guard, to look out for your crew whom you have begun to think of as a kind of family.

When the plane touches the ground you are not without gratitude. The terminal is surprisingly modern. It is not what you had expected. Customs is an agonizing process that takes over two hours. The officers are extremely cautious, and yet the fact that you are from Hollywood intrigues them, makes them blush. Even though you have the necessary paperwork, your permits, they detain you with questions. When you finally step outside into the afternoon light, your first thought is about the heat. You had been warned about the heat, but this is altogether different, a Dante's *Inferno* sort of heat, the sort of heat you feel *inside* your body, in your throat, all the way down your esophagus, in your head, behind your eyes, inside your ears and nostrils. You can only hope you will get used to it. Already your shirt is soaked through. Like a Girl Scout leader, you evaluate your exhausted crew. They perk up when they see the fleet of Rolls Royces sent by the hotel for the ride from the airport. You find yourself smiling as you enter the luxurious car. Gazing out the window on the way to the city you notice the bands of wavering heat.

The sky so blue it is almost translucent. You are struck with the beauty of the landscape, a dry, brown, mysterious beauty, so vividly in contrast to anything you have seen before. Like the intriguing beauty of a stranger, it beckons you near and promises nothing.

The city is an architectural spectacle, sky scrapers of glass and metal shooting into the heavens, refracting the sunlight. The men on the sidewalks, in their white *kandouras* belted with narrow black rope, their heads covered with the white cloth, *ghutrah,* remind you that you are somewhere in the middle of the desert, and that, for now, you must suspend your sense of logic, for it is of no use here. The approach to the hotel is dramatic, a spectacular edifice surrounded by gardens. The Emirates Palace is enormous—the sort of excessive grandeur rarely seen in your own country. Entering the lobby is like stepping into another world. The hotel is newly built. Marble floors, a dome ceiling, crystal chandeliers laced with real gold. Distantly, you think of Iraq—its once magnificent buildings gone to rubble, how strange it seems knowing the destruction continues *right over there* and yet here, here it is beautiful, perfect. Here there is peace.

Maybe you are just tired after the long flight, but you feel conspicuous, profoundly aware of your middle-class American roots, drawing attention to yourself as only an American can, in your schlumpy sweat suit, your clunky bag of indispensables (vitamins, pills and medications for any possible problem, dental floss, makeup, Tampax, Nikes, your favorite Patagonia cap), and the way you move, with carbonated overflow in comparison to the serene aerodynamics of the locals. As a female, you are sensitive to the feverish curiosity of strangers. Their eyes coat your body like paint.

Your contact from the Dubai production company is waiting for you, a slim Arab man in an expensive suit, Italian shoes. *"Salaam aleikum,"* he says, bowing slightly, wishing you peace.

"Aleikum assalaam."

His name is Al Hassim and he is very friendly, very organized, and speaks impeccable English. "How was your flight? Are you feeling well?"

"Yes, thank you," you say, and return the solicitation. More than any other location you've shot in you feel the need to be polite, conscious of the possibility that he is judging you, adding you to the larger pool of nasty Americans who have tainted your reputation as a citizen of the world.

"I am well, yes, thank you for asking." Again, he bows slightly, out of courtesy. Briefly, he reviews the schedule for tomorrow. "Your facilitator and translator will be here at five a.m. Of course the weather will be splendid. It's a two-hour drive to our location in the Rub' al-Khali desert."

It is late. Most of the crew retires to their rooms to sleep. You and Tom and Bruno find the café—some of the actors join you. You are served sweet tea and dates, cognac. Tom is his usual charming self, flirting with Rosa, your gorgeous star, but instead of feeling jealous you are glad for it, hoping it will put her at ease before the difficult scenes ahead. "I'm going to turn in," you say, finishing your tea, using the fact that you need to call Harold as a worthy excuse to be antisocial. In truth you are feeling fat and disgusting after the long flight, already dreading the early call. You want to brush your teeth, take a shower. Your room is lovely. It is like your own private Kasbah, surrounded floor to ceiling with gold fabric. French doors lead to a private terrace, inviting the warm black wind of the desert, the sounds of distant bells, horns, music from the cafe. You step outside briefly, looking down at the dark beach, the velvety water of the sea. Out there is a world you cannot begin to understand. As sophisticated as the city is, you cannot get past the cultural differences; the few women you noticed outside the hotel were clothed in *abayas*. And yet inside the hotel is a different world. It is as if you have traveled to a made-up land on the opposite end of the universe and as safe and peaceful as it seems you can't ignore the fact that there are wars close by—wars that have endured for centuries and yet, in the shadow of the modern world, seem obscure and unfounded, colored by the nuances of political subterfuge. Their logic is buried somewhere, under thousands of years of sand.

The telephone line crackles with static and you disconnect the call. You will try tomorrow, after a good night's rest. Your body feels jittery, enervated, unpleasantly bloated, and you find your way to the shower, anxious to feel clean. Standing under the water it occurs to you that you are not as strong as you'd like to believe. Underneath your sultry arrogance you are still only a woman, physically inferior, vulnerable to the whims of men. No matter how hard you fight, no matter how deft your analysis, you are still the weaker sex. It is something you would never admit to in public, and yet you know it is the truth. Under certain circumstances—a war in your own country, for example—the prowess of your intellect would lose value. The men, with their brawny appetite for power, could easily take control.

But then, maybe you are underestimating yourself.

Still, it is something you think about from time to time, something you don't discuss. And it is precisely the reason you are making this film.

You step out of the shower and dry off, the plush terrycloth like a white stole, then pull on your boxers and T-shirt and climb into bed. Such elegance, you think. This place, this city in the middle of the desert, drenched in the kind of luxury few Americans will ever know. This is oil money, you realize. Everything it touches glitters and shines.

Only a short distance from here, people are getting killed. On this borrowed desert, your crew will re-create the theater of war, machinating scenes of terror that may or may not be wholly accurate. And yet, the world will believe them to be. The world will assume that you have done your homework, that you have gotten the facts. It is the business of art, you argue, to create an authentic sense of reality otherwise known as a suspension of disbelief.

PART THREE

POINT OF VIEW

8

One of his uncle's friends worked at the airport and had arranged the job for Denny at the gatehouse. Denny guessed that his uncle was getting tired of him lying around the house all day complaining about his leg. They had told him it could take up to a year for his benefits to come through, and there wasn't even any guarantee he'd get any. A bullet had hit his thigh and taken out a chunk of flesh the size of a baby's fist, but he'd been lucky, he hadn't lost his leg like some of the others, and he was still alive. There would be surgery in his future, but not without benefits. He had to wait and see and it was hard to wait and he was sick of watching TV. The world he saw on the screen was too loud, too much. He felt bad about his situation and sometimes, in a weird way, he almost missed the war, even though not a day went by that he didn't hate it with every cell of his body. Still, you could get used to hating something. He missed his M16. His weapon was like an old girlfriend who'd walked out on him and there was just this empty space now. Being without it gave him an ache in his belly. Sometimes he couldn't eat. Sometimes he would wake up with a start with his heart going about a million miles a minute and all he could do was cry. He was not the sort of person who cried easily, but now he cried all the time. When he'd first come home, he spent most of his time on the couch when his aunt and uncle were out at work. He would watch the shadows of the sycamores roam around on the ceiling. Sometimes he dozed off and there he was, back in Baghdad, clattering pictures, faces jeering, sounds booming. He had made up his mind that he was going to get a gun. Even back here in America, in his home state, he did not feel safe without it and he knew that, first chance he got, he'd buy himself a pistol. His aunt Marie didn't want him there either—she had been glad to get rid of him when he'd enlisted—it was the first thing he'd ever done that she'd been proud of. She had a theory that he took after his father who had disappeared when he was a kid and got himself killed in a motorcycle accident. His mother had died a couple of years later, when he was only seven, and he'd been living with them ever since, feeling like he was taking up too much space. He knew about loss. Now he could hear his aunt wrestling with the vacuum hose, slamming it into the furniture and muttering about her no-good nephew who might have done them all a favor in getting himself killed and giving the family some honor for once instead of more heartache. She knew heartache, oh how she knew heartache! He had almost gotten killed, but almost didn't count, almost wasn't good enough for her. In a fit of anger, he had taken the framed picture of his commander in chief and shattered it on her kitchen floor and stepped all over it with his one good foot, grinding up the glass with his desert boots, and now she wasn't speaking to him. Nobody could believe he would do something like that because it was that very photograph that had kept her going all these months when she was worrying about him night and day, clutching her rosary. "I'm not your mother, but I might as well be," she scolded him.

What Marie didn't seem to get was that he'd enlisted for her. To give her some clout in the neighborhood. And people started looking at him different. Maybe he wasn't the fuckup they thought, maybe he could make something of himself and come home and marry one of their daughters. But now, since he'd been home, people ignored him around the neighborhood. It was like they didn't know what to say to him, almost like they felt guilty or they felt sorry for him. They put on fake smiles like either he was touched in the head or dangerous or both. It was all the same bullshit he'd been dealing with since grade school because nobody gave a fuck about him and maybe people thought he was stupid for going over there in the first place. He thought it had something to do with fear, because they knew you'd killed people and that changed the way they saw you. Nobody ever said it, but he could tell. Even his aunt Marie looked at him funny and always kind of got out of the way when he came into the kitchen for something. Uncle Hector kept scrounging around for work to keep him out of trouble but now when time passed and he had nothing to do, trouble found him. "It's in your blood," his uncle would say. "It ain't your fault."

The job was boring, but it was something to do. He didn't mind it. He had to catch a bus at quarter to seven out to the airport, an hour or so drive from East L.A. That part wasn't so bad. He didn't mind the bus and he usually would try to sleep. At the airport, he bought an egg and cheese sandwich off the breakfast truck and walked three quarters of a mile over to his post in the gatehouse in long-term parking. That was his favorite time of the day, walking through the windy open space out to the lot, hearing the whining engines of the planes. Long-term parking had four gates—his post was the gatehouse all the way on the end. It was a tight space, but had a window and you could see the planes taking off. He had a computer register and the credit card machine. Close quarters was all right with him, like being inside the tank. It always brought him straight back to the first few months of his tour. Flying over to Kuwait City, his first time on a plane, his first trip overseas. He could remember the excitement, like it was some kind of vacation he was going on—not the worst fucking decision he had ever made in his life. But that was behind him now. He was out; home. And he was alive.

There were things he noticed on his shift. People came and went. They carried bags and packages. They would park, walk to the terminal tram. Some had kids. Some went alone, in business clothes. There was once a group of nuns who'd poured out of a van. They reminded him of pigeons in their gray veils. Passengers came and went. They would stand there waiting for the tram. Some had more patience than others. Some smoked. Once he saw somebody take gum out of their mouth and stick it on the side of the shelter, right on the face of some actress in an ad like a big pimple. They didn't know they were being watched, but he could tell a whole lot about somebody when they had to wait. You could catch people doing embarrassing things, picking their noses or butts, smacking their kids. Anyway, that was neither here nor there. It was just a job and he was just trying to keep things interesting. In the army, you learned to size someone up pretty fast. Some people would lose their tickets and make up some cockamamie story. Others didn't have enough cash or their credit cards didn't work. You had to come clean for him to raise the gate and he let them know it.

Soon as he made enough money he was going to get his own place somewhere. He was going to buy himself a car so he didn't have to ride the bus with all the cleaning ladies and gardeners. They reminded him of Hajis, and sometimes when there was one that was a little dark, with the oily greenish skin, or some kind of cloth on their head like the towel heads in Iraq, he had to stare at the floor and count, that's what they told him to do at the crisis center, just breathe and count—anyway, they had given him some pills and sometimes they worked and sometimes he wouldn't take them because he thought, if he did, something might happen to him, something terrible. He knew what they were trying to do. Shut him up. It was a government conspiracy. They didn't want people knowing what it was really like over there, what it had done to his head. On the other hand, he had acquired certain skills that were useful to him now. For one thing he was a marksman. His body was toned, he was stronger than before. Problems would arise and his body would react without even thinking about it, like one of those slick intelligence operatives in the movies, nothing could really stop him—he was a fucking machine. He could read people. He could look at someone's eyes and know things, intimate things. He could guess whether they were honorable, or whether they paid their bills or cheated on their taxes or on their wives. Like one of those police dogs, he had a nose for deception. In the long run he figured it would be useful somehow.

His doctor at the VA told him about a priest who had a support group in a nearby church. They'd been meeting on Sunday afternoons, for two hours. Everybody had been to war, either Iraq or Afghanistan. You went around in a circle and you could say whatever you wanted and sometimes the father asked you questions. Denny didn't mind going, but he never really said anything much. He liked being inside the church. For a period of time in high school he had considered becoming a priest, but then he'd had his first girlfriend and changed his mind. They sat on the hard metal chairs near the windows with the blue curtains. The curtains rippled and snapped sometimes, if there was a breeze. Watching them was like a kind of mystery, like the wind had a story to tell. The church was very old, no air-conditioning, and on hot days you could work up a sweat sitting there. Something about the heat and the smell, the damp linoleum floors, the dust, reminded him of the desert. Hot during the day, hot and dry, and cold at night. You were constantly in a fever state, sweating in your body armor, your Kevlar, and then, at night, shivering under your sweat, the kind of shiver you get when you're sick. When it was his turn he said, "At night there were so many stars. I'd look up." He shook his head, his eyes watery. "I've never seen a sky like that." He didn't tell them that it always made him cry. He didn't tell them that the stars in Iraq were like the teeth of the dead.

Nobody could really help you. You had to sort things out on your own. Denny tried. He carried his stories around in his pockets, in his fists, like stones. After an hour they took a break. They stood awkwardly like kids at a school dance, drinking lemonade and eating cupcakes made by some of the church ladies, with pink icing. During those interludes it came to him that he was better off than most. There was this one woman, her name was Chloe. She didn't say much in the group. When it was her turn, she'd freeze up and stutter and then she'd start to cry. One time she took off her prosthesis and showed everybody her stump. It was weird; nobody said anything.

They all had something in common, something you couldn't put into words. When you're over there, everything you've been taught in church goes right out the window. The more he killed the better he felt. That was the truth. You got praised for killing. You were part of a team, an exclusive brotherhood. Knowing you can die at any second changes the way you see, the way you think. He never would have believed he had the capacity to kill with his bare hands, but he'd done that too. Once. It was either succumb and die, or kill. His body went cold and rubbery, unbreakable. The killing was an intimate, terrifying dance. He was the fucking terminator. And the victory—he didn't want to call it sexual but it was pretty close. It was primitive.

———

He had this one friend from work, Javier. Javier was chunky and suave. He had a girlfriend and liked to read poetry. He carried around this huge volume of e. e. cummings and used to sing out poems when nobody was around. Javier was not a soldier, but he had gone to prison once for something stupid. They had an understanding. They shared something that didn't need to be discussed. So that Thursday night Javier asked Denny would he mind taking the night shift and Denny said no problem. Denny didn't mind doing favors for Javier because he knew they would be returned. It was something he missed about the army. He missed his buddies; they were the brothers he'd never had. That was the only thing about being over there that felt right and he would have done anything for them; he had killed for them and they had killed for him. You couldn't mess with that bond. You didn't find it anywhere else.

The night shift was slower and cooler than the day shift. His aunt had sent him with tortillas and limeade and he'd just finished eating. For some reason it wasn't very busy. Somewhere around nine o'clock, maybe a little later, a car pulled into the lot and parked under the lights. Denny happened to notice it because it was vintage, a BMW. He had always liked foreign cars, especially old ones, and it brought back good memories of the only teacher he had ever liked, Mr. Ruggeri, who taught the vo-tech classes at his high school and didn't make him feel like shit every chance he got, like his other teachers. From where he sat in the gatehouse, he watched as the driver got out of the car, pulled on his jacket, took a small suitcase out of the backseat, and walked toward the tram. It could have been the lighting, but he looked a little bit like a Haji. But that was of no consequence anymore. He had to keep reminding himself of that. There were perfectly nice Muslims living in this country who deserved to be left alone.

On his piss break he walked over to check out the car. It was a sweet little car with leather seats, a wood steering wheel. He ran his hands along the sides of it. Something caught his eye, a metallic reflection, and he saw that the man had forgotten his keys. There they were in the ignition, attached to a rabbit's foot. He had also broken the cardinal rule of airport parking—he'd left his ticket in the car. The ticket was up on the dashboard where anybody could see it. Denny caught his own reflection in the dark glass and it suddenly occurred to him that it might be a setup. There were probably cameras all over this place. He glanced around to see if anybody was watching him. Maybe it was a test they did on new employees, he thought, and peered over at a coworker, May Lynn, who was on her cell phone behind the filthy glass. There were no cars in the line—it was quiet. He felt all alone, the slight wind grazing his skin, this weird balmy quiet. You'd get that kind of quiet in the desert and it was sometimes nice, but it didn't last.

It's not your car, so keep walking. And that's what he did. He walked around the parking lot like a person getting exercise on his piss break, but he couldn't get those keys out of his head and, with the way things were going in his life, it took a great deal of effort and concentration on his part not to run over there and take it and drive the fuck out of there and never come back.

Routine made a difference to Denny. It got him through. They don't tell you how different it is over there. Things you don't expect, emotions. You're flying over there and you're a little excited, you think it's this great adventure, you think you're a fucking badass now that you made it through basic training, your initiation into hell. But it's not all that simple, and you don't really know what you've gotten yourself into. Then you land; you arrive. The heat is the first thing you notice. Then the light, the smells, the people, everything with an edge, an extreme—kind of like waking up with a severe hangover—and then the realization creeping up the back of your neck that you're stuck there. There is no way out. Basically, you learn pretty quick that you're totally royally fucked. And it's like abstract. Everything about it is abstract starting with the light, the heat, the open space. For the first couple of weeks in Kuwait City it was like Christmas every day, unpacking crates of supplies, and he was like, yeah, I can deal with this. He had felt like it was under control, it was going to be all right, and maybe it was true that everybody back in Washington was looking out for him. Then it came time. They woke everybody up in the middle of the night—St. Patrick's Day, 2003—and said they were moving out. Drowsy with sleep, disoriented, his unit did what they were supposed to. They set out to make war.

A lot of stuff happened to him in Iraq. Not just with the Iraqis, but in his battalion. He had gone over as one person, and come back as somebody else. He learned pretty quick that if you let them see your weak side they would hurt you for it, they would make you suffer. You could not be weak. It was not allowed. It was like some kind of perverse club—you had to be totally in or you were fucked; you were dead. You had to want to kill. You had to want to kill so bad you couldn't wait for it, you couldn't wait to go out there. You went to bed thinking about killing and you woke up thinking about it. That was the only way you survived. And there was no church in hell that was going to forgive you for that.

Once you get over your first kill, something twists up inside you and you suddenly have a purpose, a reason for being there. You experience a kind of reckoning. Kind of like when you shake up a can before you open it and it sprays all over the place, that's how fucking crazy it was—something that could be a big joke, something maybe you dreamed up as a gag, but then you're wet and everybody else is all wet and nobody's happy. And instead of Mountain Dew you're covered in blood.

Halfway through his tour he started crying a lot. He would bawl like a baby. It would come on suddenly, gush out of him. Sometimes they locked him up, they said, "Get the fuck with the program, dickhead." They made him feel stupid and he'd suffered a whole lot of that abuse already in his life and he didn't need it over there. He had seen things. He had seen children getting blown to pieces. He had seen an old woman lose her eye. His best friend, Ross, had gone down right next to him and Denny had tried to save him and had held him in his arms and cried over his body, but nobody could do anything. He had watched Ross's soul go up to heaven, a kind of yellow mist. It's a weird thing when you hold a dead person. There were soldiers down everywhere he looked, limbs splayed out. Pieces of bodies. They all worked together to keep people alive. He had learned to tie a tourniquet; he had learned CPR. Sometimes it worked. Everybody was pretty upset. He didn't like to make excuses, but it may have been the reason for what they did to the girl.

There were four of them and she had come out of nowhere, maybe she was thirteen, fourteen, he didn't know. At first they were all just joking around, not funny, but kind of in a sick way, not letting her pass, and then all of a sudden Hull was doing her and Denny realized what was going to happen next, and if you didn't go along you were fucked, they'd never let you forget it, and even though Denny went last and couldn't get hard and was just pretending, he was still guilty, and she had bit him so hard he still had a scar. Hull wanted to kill her afterward, but Denny convinced him to let her go—said she wasn't worth it, that maybe they'd get away with it the way things were—and she had gimped off on her hands and feet like a beat-up kangaroo, spit dripping out of her mouth and this awful little sound coming out. They all just laughed. And when Denny puked in the shadows they laughed some more. They never let him forget it. Later that night Hull jumped on him, pinned him down, said he'd kill him if he told. "I'll fucking kill you and make it look like a Haji."

A few nights later Denny woke out of a deep sleep and saw Jesus standing over him in these purple scrubs, the kind you see on doctors, and he had a long white beard just like they say. He told Denny he was going to be all right, that he should be patient. Soon he would be out. He went and told the shrink he had seen Jesus and the shrink snickered and told him to stop being such a pussy.

Now he dreamed about the girl almost every night. In the dream she put her veil over his nose and mouth and he would wake gasping for air, feeling suffocated. He had brought the war home with him. There were things he couldn't get over. They had told him to put it behind him, but he couldn't. There were things he had done, they had all done them, and you hoped they went away, but they didn't. They really didn't. Because you didn't forget shit like that.

One thing he had learned over there was to sense when bad things were going to happen. It was a feeling you got sometimes. He had it now. Even in his aunt and uncle's house he didn't feel safe. If something dropped on the floor, he just about jumped out of his skin. His hearing was keen, like a dog's, he could hear *everything*. His stomach always in knots, his jaw clenched. It was like some essential piece of himself had been left behind in that desert, something he would never get back. It was stuffed into an old suitcase, lost in some airport terminal with all the other lost bags. Anybody could walk along and take it. Unprotected, he was out in the open, in full view of a sniper, just waiting to get the shit blown out of him. Let it happen, he thought. *Let it happen now.*

Two weeks before the end of his tour he got shot. They tell you it's going to hurt, but this was medieval pain, this was the pain of the rack, stretching your flesh into something else. It was like nothing he'd ever experienced. You couldn't compare it to anything. Maybe like a train running into you. Something to that effect. And he could remember lying there thinking, please God, just take me. Take me out. He was in a hospital for a while, and then they sent him home, an honorable discharge, but he couldn't get his mind around the honorable part. That was almost a year ago, and now all he had to do was wait for his benefits to come through. He just had to put it all behind him. He had to move on. He had to.

That same Thursday night, after his shift, he met up with Javier and his girlfriend at a bar in Hollywood, a pool hall. It was the night that changed his life. There was this girl there, Daisy. She was the most beautiful thing he had ever seen, she even looked like a Daisy with her slender white petals. Denny didn't know how to talk to girls. For most of the night he just watched her floating around the room. She kept going outside with different people. He could see her standing on the curb, smoking, watching the cars. When she came back in, Javier made him go up and talk to her. She shook her blond hair off her shoulder and asked him about his limp and he told her he'd just come home. "What was it like over there?" she asked, and he used his stock answer, "Hot."

"You're a hero, I guess."

"Yes, ma'am."

"Well, you deserve a medal." She smiled.

"I don't know. I don't think I deserve anything."

"I can tell just by looking at you."

"Tell what?"

But the music came on too loud to hear her answer. She led him onto the dance floor and they danced—basically *she* danced and he sort of stood there trying to move a little bit. She didn't care. She took his hand and moved it back and forth and he watched her hips, her little badminton tits going back and forth inside her shirt.

They shot a rack together and she wasn't any good at pool. She let him buy her a drink. The four of them took Javier's car and drove to Venice and walked along the beach. They went into a bar and he took her hand under the table and held it tight. The girl asked him about Iraq and he made himself sound like a hero. She put her hand on his arm, and then he took her hand and held it under the table. It was sweaty, they were both nervous. Later they walked on the beach, putting their feet in the water, and he tried to kiss her. "Where'd you come from?" he asked her.

"You dreamed me up."

He didn't know what to say to that. It scared the shit out of him. They made out on the beach and her mouth tasted like cherry cough syrup. Her breasts were small and pointy. She told him she was sixteen. He was twenty-one, not much older, but still, he could get in trouble. "You look older."

"I know. People tell me that all the time."

"Can I see you again?"

She took his hand and wrote her cell phone number on it and gave him a big, juicy smile. "Bye, bye, sailor boy."

If you kill for Allah you get virgins in the afterlife—it's a big selling point to a common Islamist terrorist. They make it sound so great. He found himself thinking about it that night on the bus, wondering if the girl, Daisy, was a virgin. Maybe she was, he thought. His first girlfriend had been a virgin, but he didn't remember anything all that great about it. Her name had been Christina, a red-haired girl from his high school who smoked menthol cigarettes and had pimples—he'd had acne too. Even though he'd practiced, the condom was tricky to put on and it broke, finally. The girl had been upset and called him a pathetic excuse for a man. Now that he thought about it, screwing a virgin was overrated. If he had his pick, he'd rather have someone experienced in the afterlife. Somebody really hot like a porn star who knew what she was doing. Come to think of it, he'd never really had anyone who was great in bed. No, he decided, when it came to sex he'd only had amateurs. Well, that was all right; he wasn't complaining. He took whatever he could get.

When he finally got back to his aunt and uncle's house, he took off his clothes and got into the shower. It was still like a gift to stand, unhurried, in the shower. He realized he was crying. It was maybe two a.m. and he felt scared. The windows were black, he pulled the shades. Anyone could be watching the house, he thought. Wrapped in his towel, he stood in the hall for a minute, listening, but the only thing he heard was his uncle snoring. It was an endearing sound, and again his eyes welled with fresh tears. Before the war, he had taken all that shit for granted. Not now. Now he cried over stuff like that, because he realized how much it mattered to him. They had always fought, him and his uncle, and his uncle was always right. For a long time, Denny couldn't get his shit together. He didn't know; he felt bad about everything. He had just wanted them to be proud of him, to do something that made them feel like raising somebody else's kid had been worth it.

In his room, he sat on the edge of the bed, shaking. He felt the presence of someone there, a spirit. Maybe it was his mother. He could still remember his aunt leading him down the hospital corridor on the day he'd said goodbye to her for the last time. How she'd held him and apologized for being so sick. For leaving him behind.

It came to him now that he'd never forgiven her.

He had not been born destined for nice things. Everything was secondhand, even his girlfriends. It wasn't his looks, because he *had* looks, he was good-looking—his mother had been white—his father, Marie's brother, had looked just like his aunt, strong Mexican faces, dark eyes. He had those eyes too, and feathery lashes that made all the girls jealous, but he had his mother's fine skin, her good teeth and wide lips. But not everybody could put up with his jumpy manner, Attention Deficit poster boy—he'd spent a lot of time watching recess from the classroom windows, which was pretty stupid when you thought about it, just about the last thing he'd needed. So yeah, now he was bitter. Maybe that's why he'd enlisted in the first place: to get the fuck out. He wanted to make use of himself. He wanted to prove that he could be something.

He went to sleep and in his dream the girl was there, the one. She came this close to his face. She was about to bite him when he woke up.

He cried and hated himself some more. What kind of fucking faggot cries like this? They had been right; he was a fucking pussy.

Next morning, his day off, he slept in. Somewhere around noon he woke up to the sound of the doorbell. Nobody ever rang the doorbell in their neighborhood. Weddings and funerals, maybe, but not regular social calls. He glanced out the window and saw a police cruiser. The house smelled of coffee and his aunt's tamales. He could hear her heels clacking on the tiles as she walked to the door. This was it, he realized, they were here for him.

Denny shuffled into his clothes, old tennis sneakers, a jacket, and was out the back door. He was a skilled athlete—a magnificent warrior—and the stretched out yards behind the neighboring houses became the broken hovels of Baghdad—in his head, through his eyes, he was *right there*—the sounds and smells, the vivid white light. His heart was beating in his chest and he felt light, agile, as he slalomed through swing sets and fallen bicycles, the holy Jesus statues, climbed the chain-link fence, hit the pavement and kept running.

There were the usuals at the bus shelter. They looked at him sideways, turned away. Maybe on account of the sweat; he wiped his brow. The bus pulled up and he got on, dropped his money in, took a seat in the back. He had a *don't fuck with me* look on his face. At any second, he might take the whole bus out. That's what he would do if anyone messed with him. The bus went along, stopping every couple of blocks to pick people up. He got off at the airport and walked up to the lot. It was almost three. Luckily, Javier wasn't working yet, only May Lee and he avoided her, and two other people he hadn't met, but knew by sight. The sky turned pearly, the clouds pushing down. Maybe it would rain. The lot was pretty full. The car was still there. It was waiting for him. He got into it like it was his and started it up. The engine responded with a lusty roar and he shifted, hit the gas. He wound around toward the exit and stopped at the gate furthest from his. The girl took his ticket; she didn't recognize him. "Fourteen dollars."

He paid her and smiled and she raised the gate and he drove through it.

It was a swell car. He thought he could smell roses. He hadn't bothered to check the registration or to look in the trunk. There was something inside of it, he thought, rolling around. Later, he would check. Now he had two things on his mind. Buying a gun and finding Daisy.

9

On Saturday morning Hugh woke in the motel room. The sounds of the boulevard filled his room, somebody whistling, a woman's shrill laughter, the beeping of a horn, a siren, a crying baby. It began to rain. Hugh sat there for a few minutes with his hands pressed together in his lap as if in prayer. Suddenly, the whole sky was full of rain. He sat there watching it.

He had made his peace with himself about the incident with Hedda Chase. It was over and done with and out of his hands.

On the whole, it was a confusing time for him. On the one hand, he wanted to leave his wife. On the other, he was afraid to cut the ties to his old life. He called himself a writer, but what did he have to show for it? Here he was in this stinking motel room. He'd gotten this far, he realized, he could not go home now. Empowered, he called his wife's cell phone. When she finally picked up, he could hear a lawn mower in the background. "They're mowing their lawn again," she explained. The neighbors were neurotic about their grass—there wasn't a single dandelion on it. As much as Hugh complained and made fun of them, Marion seemed to admire them. "I'm making a garden for us," she said.

"What?"

"I'm outside. I'm making a garden. We're going to have beautiful tomatoes this summer."

He could tell she was back on her antidepressants. "Marion," he said. "I'm not coming home."

"What? The mower—I can't hear you, Hughie. *What?*"

He shouted into the phone. "I'm not coming home."

"What? I can't—*what did you say?*"

He hung up. What was the point? He sat there for a moment. He opened his briefcase and riffled through his papers and pulled out a copy of his screenplay, *The Adjuster.* He thought it might be salvageable in some way. Perhaps if he just told his own story. Perhaps if he simply told the truth. Would people be interested in a story about a man like him—misplaced—working in the wrong job, married to the wrong woman, living in the wrong house? Everything wrong. Once you bought into that life, how did you escape it? Of course you could not. You were stuck. Vulnerable to the judgment of strangers, people you didn't care about and yet you cared what they thought. And, once you admitted to failure, like savage crows they feasted on your remains.

When he called Ida, her voice sounded groggy. "I need a favor," she said, and asked if he'd be willing to come over and read her script, she was having trouble with the ending and wanted another opinion. She had a deadline. "I've been up all night."

"I happen to be good at endings," he told her.

Ida lived in Westwood, on Roebling Avenue. The neighborhood catered to people from the university. She lived in a white stucco duplex with black shutters. He found a parking space down the street and ran through the rain all the way to her door. Ida's neighbor, an opera singer with the Los Angeles Philharmonic, was singing in her apartment—whatever it was sounded familiar to him—it was Italian, he knew that.

"*La Bohème,*" Ida told him, letting him in. The place smelled of coffee. "I always cry when I hear it."

"Has she broken any glasses yet?"

"No, silly." She gave him a hug.

"You're not going to cry, are you?"

"I'll try not to." She smiled up at him. "It's good to see you."

"You too."

She made him breakfast, a cheese omelet, and they drank coffee by the big picture window, watching the rain. Then they went into her den to read her script. They drank a pot of coffee as they turned the pages. They sat on adjacent couches, the same sort of setup as his therapist had, but in this case it was conducive to reading the script out loud and he liked the way her face looked when she read, like a third grader giving a school presentation, a mixture of pride and a little fear. The script was about a boxer struggling with Lou Gehrig's disease. In the beginning, the man is an asshole and a drunk; in the end, just before he dies, he's practically a saint. The story was based on her father's life. It was the sort of script Hedda Chase would have loved, he thought. "You've underestimated yourself," he told her. "It's very powerful."

Ida smiled as if she were relieved. "That means a lot to me, coming from you."

"You don't know me very well, Ida," he said grimly. "I'm not who you think I am."

"No?" She tilted her head, thoughtfully appraising him. "Who are you?"

He shrugged. "I guess I'm trying to figure that out."

She looked dissatisfied with his answer.

"With you? I feel like I'm myself," he tried to explain. "But before, back in New York, back with my wife, it was like being somebody else. Someone I didn't like. Does that make any sense?"

"We're all imposters to some degree."

"I don't know."

"It's true."

"Who are you pretending to be?"

"Me?" She hesitated and frowned. "I'm not pretending."

"I don't believe you." His smile leaked out.

She laughed nervously.

"You're a big fucking faker and I know it," he said. "Come over here."

She came over to him and sat down on the couch and let him kiss her. "We've barely opened my suitcase," she admitted.

"The truth is difficult."

"Yes, but it's all we have."

They stumbled into her bedroom, a tiny room with a single window and a torn yellow shade. He watched her as she pulled off her shirt then took off her pants, all the while hearing nothing but the rain. Stripped to her underwear, she stood there waiting for him. She was small and square and round hipped and busty. She was a woman on the verge of something, he thought. Defeat, maybe. Like the boxer in her script, she had one more good fight.

"I want to know you," she said. "Is that okay?"

"I can't promise anything."

She nodded like a person at a funeral. Her eyes were glossy and black. Her skin mottled with the tiny shadows of raindrops. She kissed him and her mouth was soft and lovely and very warm. The rain fell harder. They stood there kissing with the rain running down the windows, washing everything clean.

———

Foster's film was called *Transients Welcome*. The screening was at the Film Forum in Hollywood, in one of the old theaters. Entering the crowded lobby with Ida at his side made him wistful, bitter over the years he had wasted being somebody else. He held her close, protectively. They had rolled around in her bed for hours just kissing, her skin flushed, hot to the touch. He had turned her onto her stomach and had run his hands down her naked back.

They shuffled into the middle of a crowded row and took their seats. Ida was wearing her smart little half boots and a short skirt. It was an outfit Marion wouldn't be caught dead in, but then Ida was younger than Marion by a good ten years. Hugh liked the fact that she was younger, it made him feel superior. Perhaps he could guide her in some way; he could have a positive influence on her life. The theater filled rapidly. The people seemed excited. Ida put her knees against the back of the seat in front of her as if this sort of thing were old hat. She was like a gangly kid, her knees greenish and knobby. She'd been out here for years, trying to make it. She had deals in the works. Even though none of her scripts had been produced, she'd made good money; she was a good writer and they called her when they needed her.

The room hummed with excitement. People talking, removing their jackets, settling down. He could see Tom Foster in the first row, sitting next to a dark-haired woman in a red dress. Tom had on a black blazer and a white scarf. The lights dimmed and a man came onto the stage, a man people seemed to know. They laughed at his jokes. He spoke about Tom Foster, his work, his courage, his past films, his awards. "Enjoy this spectacular film," he said as the room went black and the large screen filled with light.

The film was dark, raw. It was like a poem, Hugh thought, a somber, beautiful love song. The sound track evoked his compassion with a single piano. The film was shot in color, its hues spare, unvaried; serene. Foster had found beauty in ordinary places. A child's shoe left in the road; a dented beer can tumbling in the gutter; a junkyard at twilight; a sulking mutt pacing by the fence; the metallic carcasses of dead cars. Sunrise like the smeared rouge on a whore.

The first story was about a bearded man in a pink raincoat. At one time, he'd been a noted mathematician. He'd worked at a think tank in Santa Monica. At the think tank he'd come up with new ideas, change. People knew his work, his brilliance. Then one day, quite suddenly, he stopped. His wife left him. He stood there in an empty house. He walked out and never returned. Watching the man's face in closeup, Hugh felt tears burn his eyes. There were so many people living the wrong lives. Hugh understood; he knew what it was. It was a heartbreaking dilemma. Now the man was living in the shelter on Argyle Avenue; he was a better man now, he told the camera. His life was honest.

When the next story began, Hugh saw a familiar face. It was the girl from his motel room, Daisy. Hugh could hardly believe his eyes. He found himself clutching the armrests of his seat. His hands had begun to sweat. The waif-like creature who had slept in his motel room now wandered the streets of Hollywood with her little pet rat. She had on a long black coat and saddle shoes and there were ribbons in her hair. In voice over, she told the story of her life, growing up in rural South Dakota, how she had left home, an eighth grader with a broken arm—she could not bring herself to talk about the incident, only shook her head and wept. Since the arm hadn't been set properly, it would never heal right and you could tell it was slightly crooked, something like a broken wing. She had no money; she had nothing. For a while she'd been a prostitute. There were scenes of her putting on makeup like a child playing dress-up. Then she's in a motel room, kneeling in front of some creep—you saw nothing of the creep or of what she was doing to him, only his hand entwined in her golden hair, and you could hear the guy breathing, the sounds he was making. Watching it made Hugh squirm in his seat. For a while she slept in a playhouse in someone's backyard. The playhouse had been purchased at Toys R Us. It had yellow shutters that you could close and a little red door. If she curled up real tight she could fit and nobody saw her. During the day, after they went to work, she crept into the people's home, a bungalow somewhere in L.A. She'd seen the maid using the key, stored in a drainpipe alongside the house. She marveled at the toddler's room, the expensive toys, the clouds on the ceiling. The stocked refrigerator. The spotless bathroom. She helped herself to whatever she wanted, the freshly baked cookies, the change that had collected in a dish on the windowsill, always careful to keep things precisely as they were. She looked at the pictures of the family on the refrigerator, a life she'd never known. She knew their schedule; she'd watched carefully. She found things out about the couple; the husband was having an affair. He'd bring the girl home on his lunch hour. It had made Daisy so sad that she'd written the wife a letter and put it in the mail. A week later the wife and her little girl moved out and Daisy went to the shelter. There were shots of Daisy doing a hula hoop, there were shots of her playing a harmonica. She could play Bob Dylan. She was pretty good.

After the film, Hugh scanned the audience to see if she was there. He didn't see her at first, and then he spotted her splintered blond hair as she walked up the aisle on the other side of the theater. She had on makeup and looked older. Her boyfriend was young, maybe in his twenties, with longish black hair and the gritty shadow of a beard. He walked with a limp and wore a loose-fitting camouflage jacket in the colors of the desert—for some reason he looked familiar to Hugh. She suddenly looked across the sea of red seats and caught Hugh's eye and for a moment held his gaze. Hugh couldn't tell whether she recognized him or not. He hadn't mentioned Daisy to Ida. He felt awkward about the fact that he'd had the girl to his motel—he doubted Ida could understand that part of it. Out of the context of the street, she was like an actress or a celebrity, not some poor, homeless girl. She flashed an apologetic smile and raised her hand to wave, but was swiftly obscured by the crowd. The moment made Hugh uneasy and he turned toward Ida and they walked down the sloped aisle toward the stage. Foster was standing down front, next to the woman in the red dress who tossed back her dark hair like a restless horse. When Tom saw him, he smiled apologetically. "Hey, thanks for coming, man. I'm sorry I left you stranded the other night."

"The film was terrific."

The woman looked Italian, and had a compelling gap between her two front teeth. "This is my wife," Tom said. "Lucia."

"It's very nice to meet you, Lucia." Her hand was slim and cold, slightly limp. "This is Ida Kent."

"We're having a small party if you want to come," Foster's wife said in an Italian accent.

Hugh started to decline the invitation, but Ida spoke up. "Of course we'll come."

Foster owned a mid-century glass cube in Laurel Canyon. The house had been built in the fifties by a famous architect but had been ignored by a succession of indifferent tenants, mostly rock stars and actors. On the outside, the place had a seedy, forlorn appearance, overgrown with desert grass that looked silver in the moonlight. Everybody was around the pool on the crumbled cement decking, their faces lit from below by the small patio lights, creating a theatrical effect like footlights on a stage. The pool was oval, painted black, a bottomless pit—an abyss. Hugh thought of jumping into it. In his mind, he pictured himself at the bottom in complete darkness, with nothing to cling to, nothing to pull him out.

He wondered if the girl would show up; he hoped she wouldn't.

After a while the wind picked up, gusting at their elbows, their necks and hips, rolling across their backs. Hugh looked over the side of the cliff and saw that it was steep, complicated with dark clusters of brush. Ida wanted to go inside to see the house. She knew about Tom's photography collection. They went in and helped themselves to a tour. They went down a narrow corridor and found Tom's bedroom, lit only by the skylights. The floor was scattered with books; Ida stepped on them as she crossed the room like stones across a stream. Tom's diploma hung over a desk in a small alcove—he'd gone to Bowdoin. There were some photographs too, of his parents and brothers, a swell-looking family around a table at their country club, and another photograph of his lacrosse team at Deerfield. "Quite the pedigree," Ida said.

"We should get out of here."

They drifted back out to the crowded living room. Hugh smelled weed, but couldn't locate the joint. People were crammed into the kitchen, trying to get up to the counters for more booze. Tom and his wife were sitting with some people around a glass table, the base of which looked like the stump of a sequoia. They were drinking and eating peanuts, cracking them out of their shells. As if partaking in some impromptu ritual, they scooped a handful, opened the shells, popped the nuts into their mouths, and tossed the shells into a pile that had formed in the center of the table like a castle of sand. Hugh watched Tom's wife, Lucia, with interest. She took out a package of Gauloises cigarettes and lit one and sat like a man with her legs spread out and her elbows on the table. She had changed out of her red dress and was wearing a pair of baggy trousers and a white blouse that she'd buttoned improperly, accidentally revealing the satiny strap of her bra.

Ida nudged him fiercely and whispered into his ear, "That's Leo Zaklos."

"Who?" The man was sitting at the table next to Foster's wife.

"You know, the screenwriting guru," she hissed. "He teaches at the Conservatory. Let's go in there."

They went into the kitchen. People appraised them casually, but made no effort to welcome them. Apparently, it was the VIP table and they didn't rate. They stood there, leaning against the wall, trying to look casual as they drank their drinks. Apart from his reputation, Zaklos, a stocky Romanian, might have been cast as a grubby, commonplace thug. Hugh figured his outfit, a black leather motorcycle jacket and blue jeans held up by suspenders over a Mickey Mouse T-shirt, was not accidental, and neither was the straggly white ponytail or the gypsy rings on his fingers. In any case, Ida seemed terribly infatuated. Stacked on the table before him were a couple of rumpled poetry books, Theodore Roethke on top. At his feet lay a black Labrador named Lily who, unfazed by all the attention, rolled onto her back and snored. The whole place smelled like dog.

"You're Leo Zaklos," Hugh said, shaking the man's hand. "I've always wanted to meet you."

Zaklos looked up at him and smiled half-heartedly and shook his hand warily, as if he might catch something. "Do I know you?"

"Hugh Waters," Hugh said sheepishly. "I'm from New York."

"Waters. Why does that sound familiar?"

"He's a friend of Hedda's," Foster said.

Hugh could feel Ida looking at him. He said, "We knew each other back in the eighties."

"Ah, Hedda," Zaklos said. "Love of my life."

Lucia snorted with distaste. He decided that Tom's wife had the social grace of a porcupine.

"Here, sit down," Tom said abruptly, as though it had just occurred to him how rude he was being not offering them a chair, as though he felt sorry for Hugh and his drippy, insignificant girlfriend, as if letting them sit at the VIP table was an act of mercy. He reached for two folding chairs and set them up like a magician preparing to do a trick. Everyone watched, expressionless. Hugh and Ida sat down, insinuating themselves into the circle.

Lucia snorted again and waited for Tom's full attention. "Why do you have to bring *her* up?"

"Shouldn't she be here?" Zaklos asked.

"She wasn't invited," Lucia said. "I don't socialize with my husband's girlfriends."

"Apparently she's away this weekend," Tom muttered to Leo, covertly suggesting to Zaklos that there'd been a breach in their love affair.

"Getting a little spa action for the Cannes trip, perhaps," Leo suggested. "Are you going?"

"Of course we're going," Lucia said, then started talking to Zaklos in Italian and although nobody else at the table spoke Italian, including Tom, they were hanging on her every word. Tom met Hugh's eyes across the table. Hugh nodded with sympathy. There was a bond between them, only it was a secret. It had been established that night at the strip club, Hugh thought. They were like brothers, and words were not necessary. They only had to look at each other to know what the other was thinking. In truth, Hugh had never had a relationship like it, not with anyone, let alone another man. For a period of time he had thought he might be gay. Once, in high school, some of the boys in his gym class had accused him of getting a hard-on in the showers—it wasn't true, but the rumor had had an effect on his status with girls at the time—they'd veer away from him in the halls—and it had been something he could not talk about, he'd had to deal with it silently, like some kind of disfiguring virus. From time to time he let himself dream about being with a man, but the idea never seemed to stick.

"I have your tapes," Ida said to Zaklos. "They're marvelous."

"Thank you, my dear."

"Every script must have a premise!"

"I can see you're a good student."

Hugh thought his tone was patronizing, but Ida didn't seem to notice. "What do you mean exactly?"

"One thing leads to another," Zaklos explained.

"Lust leads to betrayal, for example," Ida said. "That's always a good one."

"Betrayal leads to destruction," Lucia said darkly.

"We are all bound to be destroyed," Tom said dramatically.

"No doubt." Zaklos nodded. "Destruction can be sexy."

"Only in movies," Lucia said. "Not in real life."

"You want to show how people change," Zaklos clarified. "A character starts here and ends up over there. Protagonist, antagonist, conflict, resolution. It's pretty simple, actually."

"Change is good," Tom said.

"Not always it's not so good," his wife said.

"Change is necessary. Once you figure out the premise you basically have your movie." Zaklos asked them to go around the table saying premises that pertained to their own lives. "I do this with my students."

"What fun," Ida said, "I'll go first. Education leads to success." Somewhat bashfully, she explained how she'd gone to a community college before transferring to UCLA. "Not that I'm this big success or anything. But I'm the first one in my family to go to college."

"Good for you," Zaklos said.

"My father's brother screwed him in the family business," Tom said. "It brought us down. We lost almost everything. I guess I'll go with deception leads to destruction."

"Hamlet 101."

"Betrayal leads to divorce!" Lucia backed out her chair and got up. "I don't like this game." She shuffled off in her clunky shoes, making a lot of noise, and joined a group in the living room, laughing too loud, shrugging her hair off her shoulders like she didn't care about anything, especially Tom. She was the sort of woman who wanted to be watched and admired from afar. Obviously, Lucia wanted Tom's attention. Everything she did was for his benefit, but Tom couldn't see it; he was dumb to her games.

"What about you, Waters," Zaklos said. "What havoc have you wreaked?"

Hugh laughed nervously. He couldn't help feeling that Zaklos didn't like him; he liked Ida better. Maybe it was because Ida was kissing his ass every chance she got.

"What's *your* premise?" Ida asked in a way that made him think she'd turn on him if it benefited her career.

"I suppose it would have to be betrayal," he said flatly. "Betrayal leads to destruction."

"Let's have the gory details."

"I was betrayed by an important person, an influential person. A promise that was taken away," he snapped his finger, "like this." He had broken a sweat, he was trembling as if with a fever, and yet perhaps they didn't notice. "Nobody has that right." He spit out the words.

"It's pretty standard in this town," Zaklos commented ironically.

Ida put her hand on his back. She looked worried and a little embarrassed.

"Sounds to me like something's already been destroyed," Zaklos said. "You might want to go with destruction leads to revenge."

"Yeah," Hugh said. "That sounds about right."

"Good luck with that." Zaklos looked him in the eye. "That sounds like my kind of movie."

Hugh held up his empty glass and stood up. He left the table and poured himself another drink and took it outside. He wasn't used to people like this. Sitting at the table, he'd felt his mind scrambling to come up with clever things to say. Now he had a headache. The cool air felt good; he felt a little better. Somebody was having a fire somewhere and he could smell it on the wind. He bummed a cigarette from someone and smoked, looking out at the city below. The city was a vast place with thousands of lights. Where was she now? he wondered. This was the third night. If she wasn't out of the trunk by now she could die. He felt his stomach jolt, his shoulders tense.

He turned to look at the house, the yellow lights against the darkness. He saw Ida sitting at the table, laughing with Zaklos. What could possibly be so funny? he wondered. She had already forgotten him.

He decided to have another drink. He meandered through the crowd back into the kitchen and poured whiskey into his glass. "Look who's here," he heard Tom say, and when he turned he saw Daisy and her boyfriend standing around the table. It was weird seeing her here, among people he knew. He hoped she wouldn't bring up that night in the motel. He didn't want these people, Ida especially, knowing that he was staying in that seedy dump. Daisy had on a light blue dress that was too short and said OUCH across the chest. Hugh wondered what she'd done with her pet rat. She'd brought the boyfriend with her and was telling everyone how he'd just gotten back from Iraq. *He's my hero,* is how she put it.

For a soldier, he was a scruffy-looking character in need of a haircut and shave and he walked with a noticeable limp. There was something about his face, an expression that lingered, like a boy who'd been scalded. His face was on red alert. The dog got up and started barking at him for no reason. "She does that sometimes," Zaklos apologized, stroking the animal. "She has nightmares just like us. Come on, you can pet her."

The War Hero reached out timidly to stroke the dog and Hugh could tell he didn't really want to pet it, he was just trying to be nice. Lily's tail whipped against his leg. "Nice dog," he said. "Nice dog."

The dog sniffed at his legs curiously then settled down onto the floor at her master's feet as though she'd had enough of his phony sweet talk.

Somebody handed the soldier a beer and a chair and he sat down and pulled the girl onto his lap. Daisy grinned at Hugh hazily. *Here it comes,* he thought. "Hey, I know you. What are you doing here?"

Hugh said, "You didn't tell me you were a movie star."

She blushed and everybody, including Ida, assaulted him with suspicion.

Foster said, "You two know each other?"

"He let me stay in his room one night," she said like a starry-eyed teenager. "You didn't tell me you were in the business."

"I'm just a writer," he said sheepishly.

"Still," she said.

"We met in a coffee shop," Hugh told the others. "This is a total coincidence. It was raining. I just wanted to help her out."

"What a saint," Ida said wryly.

"According to William Burroughs there are no coincidences," Zaklos said, savoring the implications.

"I watched you getting dressed," Daisy muttered. "You looked so sad."

Ida pulled her hand away and folded them on the table, her mouth sucked into a frown.

"Nothing happened," Hugh protested. "It's not what you think."

A sound came out of Zaklos' mouth, a snort that felt like mockery. "It's all right, man, calm down."

"I don't want anyone thinking—"

"What, that you're somebody else?" Zaklos smiled meaningfully.

"Yeah," Hugh tried to laugh. "Something like that."

"I didn't know you were a writer."

"We're working on something together," Ida lied. He had to admit, she was good at keeping her name in play.

"What's it about?" Daisy asked, leaning sleepily on the heel of her hand.

Hugh and Ida exchanged glances and Hugh said, "It's about a man who works in an insurance company in the city and he's had it with his life; his job is the wrong job, his wife is the wrong woman, he hates where he lives. Every day he goes into work, submits to the routine. Then, this one day he meets this woman in a Hoboken bar. She's a woman of color, her name's Jolene. They begin an affair and his life begins to change. At first, there's this Kafkaesque menace. Everything dull and dreary, routine. Then, because of this woman, his world brightens. He starts to see things in a new way." Hugh smiled as the premise occurred to him. "Love leads to resolution."

Zaklos coughed, cleared his throat. He had a strange expression on his face. "You're kidding, right?"

Hugh laughed abruptly, trying to hide his disappointment. "Of course I'm kidding." In truth, he'd been turning the idea around in his mind; he thought if he'd told his own story, it would be more real, more authentic, somehow. Going along with Zaklos, everybody started laughing, even Ida. They laughed and laughed like it was the funniest thing in the world.

"I think it's great," Daisy whispered into his ear.

"You do?"

"These people are assholes. Don't listen to them."

"What happened to your leg?" Ida asked the soldier.

"Caught a bullet. It really screwed me up. Imagine my surprise when I get back here and nobody want to pay for it." He grinned at everyone like he was talking about something else, something nice. People around the table gravely shook their heads. "And since I've had a few beers I'm gonna tell you all a dirty little secret."

Everybody sat there looking at him, waiting. They were like people waiting in a doctor's office to have some procedure. This look on their faces of anticipation and something else: guilt.

"This was friendly fire," he pointed to his leg. "It wasn't some Haji done this. This was us."

After an awkward moment, Ida said, her face jammed with concern, "It's a terrible, terrible war. I don't understand it. I just don't see what we're doing over there. I mean, aside from the obvious reasons."

"Yes, ma'am," the soldier said. "A lot of people say that."

"Did you know?"

"Ma'am?"

"Did you understand what your role was?"

"I was trying to do some good." He looked around the table. "That's all. It's pretty simple."

"I'm sure you were," she patronized. "But did you know—did you understand your purpose? Did they make it clear to you?"

"I didn't come here to talk politics, ma'am."

"No, that's right, you didn't," Tom said, handing him another beer. "Drink up, my friend."

Ida shook off the insult and smiled at the soldier. "Well, we all really appreciate what you did over there, that's for sure."

"Thank you, ma'am. I appreciate that."

Ida nodded at him almost tearfully, then excused herself and walked off in search of the bathroom. Sitting there, Hugh felt a little embarrassed.

The soldier whispered something to Daisy and she said, "We have to go."

"You just got here," Tom said.

"We're in love," she offered as an explanation. "We're going to Las Vegas."

"Come on, darlin'." He stood up and put out his hand and she took it like somebody under a spell.

Everybody said good night and watched them leave.

Hugh got up and pushed through the crowded room to the French doors and went out after them. The music was loud. In the strong wind, his shirt billowed out like a sail. "Daisy!" They were walking across the terrace near the pool. The wind was so strong that his words came right back to him. "Hey!" he called again. "Wait up!"

Finally she turned around, her hands on her hips like she didn't want to hear it. "It's past my bedtime," she said in the coquettish voice of an older woman. "Good night, Mister Daddy."

The boyfriend gazed at Hugh with sinister dispassion. There was something in his eyes that made Hugh think he'd seen things he could not explain. He gripped the girl around the waist, protective or possessive, Hugh couldn't decide which, both probably. "Good night," the boyfriend said, and they walked off.

For some reason, Hugh felt dejected. It was something he couldn't really understand. He knew he had no right to judge her, but he did.

Without turning around, she raised her hand in a little wave of arrogance. The soldier grabbed her hand in the same way one might attempt to contain an annoying insect, with one swift movement, and she giggled. Hugh knew it was none of his business, but he followed them anyway. He wanted to help. "Look," he called. "You were great in the film. Maybe you'll be a famous actress one day."

She turned, impatient, affecting some atrocious bravado. "I wasn't acting," she said. "It was real, remember? And anyway, I'm already famous."

"Maybe you should go home. Maybe you should see your mother."

Daisy looked down at the ground. She was weaving a little bit and Hugh wondered if she took drugs.

"Your mother's probably worried about you. Maybe you should give her another chance."

"You don't know my mother," she said. "You don't know anything about her,"

Hugh reached out and touched her shoulder and within seconds the boyfriend had him on his back, leering over him with an expression on his face that Hugh had never witnessed on a human being before, an expression that told him he was about to die. The back of his head began to pound and he could feel the blood trickling out.

"Mind your own business, freak," the soldier said, and spit at him, leaving a gob of yellow phlegm the size of a used condom on the pavement beside his head.

Several minutes later, Hugh woke up on the ground. The first thing he saw was the brightest star. For a dreamy moment, he was somewhere removed, a very pleasant place very far away from everything he knew. He wanted to stay there and rest.

Then faces. Peering down at him with confusion, as if he was some kind of an alien that had dropped out of the sky. Somebody was about to call an ambulance, but he sat up and said, "I'm fine. I'm fine." His head was killing him. He touched his hair and felt a glob of blood like a jellyfish. Ida helped him up. "I'll take him to the hospital."

She drove the Mercedes. In the emergency department, they had to wait several hours for someone to look at his head. Finally, a resident sewed him up and gave him some pain pills and they left. The sky was just beginning to get light. It was the color of a teabag that had been used too many times. Crossing the parking lot Ida took his hand. "I'm sorry you got hurt," she said. "That guy was a monster."

"I'm okay." He didn't really feel like holding hands and was glad to get into the car. The sun was starting to rise in his rearview mirror.

"Take me to your motel."

"I don't think that's a good idea."

"Why not, Hugh?"

"You're not going to like it."

"I want to know you," she said. "I want to see where you live."

"All right. If that's what you want."

The motel lobby was dark and empty when they got there. It was light enough to see the sort of place it was. She didn't say anything, but he could tell she was a little shocked by it. Maybe she had made something up in her mind. Maybe she thought he had money, class. Back home he did. Back home, he was a respectable citizen. But this motel was seedy, he knew it, and his heart had turned seedy, too. For now, this was who he was. He opened the door and they walked in.

"You said you wanted to know me."

"Yes." She looked around uncertainly, a little frightened.

"What if I'm not the man you think I am?"

"Show me," she said. "Show me who you are."

"I'll show you," he said. "Take off your clothes."

He watched her in the glare of the open window. Naked, she stood there waiting for him. He looked at her. Then he went to the windows and yanked the curtains closed. The room went dark. He sat down on the bed and had her stand between his legs and he caressed her and she went damp and milky like a baby calf. Her body was warm, soft, and she was trembling just a little. He was still angry at her for laughing at him with the others. It wasn't nice of her. He wasn't sure he could forgive her.

"Why don't you lie down?"

His head hurt. It felt dense and heavy. She climbed onto the bed and he stretched out beside her in his street clothes. "Turn over," he said.

"What?" She sounded frightened.

She lay on her stomach expectantly. "Keep quiet," he said, opening his pants. "Don't say a word."

They woke a few hours later. There was a little blood on the sheet. She had cried. She lay on her side, turned away from him, remote. That was all right with him, he didn't want to look at her now anyway. He could hear people in the adjacent rooms getting up, starting the day. A man with a deep, guttural laugh. Toilets flushing, water running through the pipes. The shades were drawn and the room was dark, nearly black, save for the stripe of bright light that was the slit in the curtains. Outside beyond the awful room there was a whole world.

Ida sat up, pulling the sheet around her. Her hair was mussed and her eye makeup had run. In a kind of personal fury, she started getting dressed, pulling on her shirt, her little skirt, her boots.

"You were right," she said. "You're not who I thought you were." She shook her head and looked at him fiercely. "I thought you were somebody else."

Then she walked to the door and went out.

For some reason he called Marion. The phone rang and rang. His wife wasn't picking up. He tried to imagine what she might be doing. They'd been married for nine years. It seemed to him that he should be able to figure out where she was, but his mind came up empty. It came to him that he was completely alone. You think you know someone, and then you realize that you've just supplied your own convincing version of them—eventually reality takes over and you realize that the person you've made your life with is a complete stranger.

10

After he'd taken the car he'd driven around in the rain for a while, looking for a place to buy a gun. The rain was a comforting distraction and he was glad for it. The pawn shop was behind a Chinese restaurant on a side street off the Sunset Strip. It was a tiny place, a little larger than a phone booth or a coffin, depending on your mood, and the man behind the counter was an ex-marine. He showed Denny one or two pistols he wasn't interested in, and then when Denny told him he'd just come back from Iraq he took out the Glock 17, a 9-millimeter semiautomatic handgun. It was the same gun the Iraqi police officers used, a sweet little weapon—the man would not say where he'd gotten it. It was light, ready to fire once you loaded the clip. He counted out his money. After he bought the gun he ate in the Chinese place, watching the chorus of sweaty cooks, the wild hiss of the woks, the shimmer of passing cars.

Having the gun made all the difference.

After that he'd called Daisy on that number she'd given him, but she didn't answer. Something in his gut told him he needed her; he didn't think he could go on without her. To pass some time, he drove down to the public library and went in to wait out the rain. In an empty corner, he fell asleep for a while, until one of the old librarians shook him awake and said it was time to go. It was nighttime when he stepped outside, and it was still raining.

Finally, she picked up her phone. "Can I see you?"

"Something happened," she said. "Something sad."

She wouldn't tell him anything over the phone. She was staying in a room over the bowling alley on Pico. He parked the car in the bowling alley lot, near the fence. She had a part-time job washing the lanes, waxing the floors, and they let her sleep upstairs. Nobody answered for a while. He just stood there in the doorway feeling stupid with the rain blasting down. A cat watched him from under some orange crates somebody had piled up. Every so often it shook the rain off its whiskers then licked its paws. Finally, she came to the door. In her hands was the dead rat, her pet. "What happened to it?"

"It got into something."

"Maybe there was some poison around."

"Help me bury it."

They went outside in the rain. There was a patch of dirt, a failed garden. They dug a hole and put the rat into it and covered it back up. She crouched down with the rain on her back and he put his hand there.

"Things won't be the same," she said.

"That's true. They won't."

"Are you scared of it?" She looked up at him. "Dying, I mean."

He thought of lying, but then admitted, "Everyone is."

"Not me."

"No?"

But she reconsidered. "Maybe a little. Do you think there's a heaven?"

"Yes," he said, "yes, I do."

That seemed to cheer her up a little. She took his hand and they went back inside and dried off. She had a mattress with just a light blanket and they lay there together without doing anything, just curled up like that, and the next thing he knew it was morning. You could hear the sound of the bowling alley downstairs, the sound of the pins falling down. It was a good sound. Chairs moving. Bottles clattering. She had to work for a couple of hours. He told her he had to get out of L.A. for a while. "Come with me," he said, and she looked out the window with the light in her eyes mulling it over and then looked back at him. "I guess I could go with you."

Then she told him about some film she was in, a screening that night. "I want you to see it first," she said.

Thinking back on it now, seeing her up on that screen had been weird. That wasn't the Daisy he knew. She wasn't the person he'd put together in his head, based on what she'd told him or the way he felt when he looked into those crazy blue eyes. During the screening, he'd shifted around in his seat. He guessed he wasn't the type to share his problems—and he had *plenty* to complain about. Then again, maybe a film like that could enlighten people. Maybe seeing that stuff would convince people how fucked up things really were, deep-down, under all the other bullshit where it counts. There was just so much here to take for granted, and maybe that was all right. Maybe that was the American way. But when he thought about it, you couldn't compare some of the things he'd witnessed in Iraq—random acts of terror he called them—in a single day there were too many to count. He could appreciate what these movie people were trying to do, but when you came right down to it, things weren't all that bad here. People didn't know how good they had it.

Now she was sleeping. They'd been driving for three hours and the moon was high. Flat, open land stretched for miles. They were about halfway to Nevada. She'd been mad at him for hitting her friend, but Denny didn't feel too bad about it. He'd taken one look at that son of a bitch and had his number.

He had a little money left. He was old enough to gamble. With a little bit of money he could make a fresh start.

Daisy stirred on the seat. "I'm thirsty."

"We'll stop. We'll get some breakfast in a little while, soon as the sun comes up." He glanced over at her uneasy face. "You just leave everything to me, honey," he said. "I'm going to take good care of you. You know that, don't you?"

She nodded at him. Nobody had ever taken care of her before. She'd pretty much been on her own. One day he would track her mother down and tell her what he thought of her—he would do it, too.

All he had to do was gaze into her smile and his whole world went bright.

He wanted to do things for her. Work—he wasn't lazy—he could make her happy. He had a strong body. He could do anything. Make a life for them. Maybe even have kids one day. All he had to do was get to Vegas. A plan had taken shape in his mind, a way to get out. An army buddy of his had told him about a guy down in Vegas who sold fake passports. They were probably expensive; he'd figure that out later.

She moved over and curled up under his arm. That night on the beach, they had talked a little about their dreams. She had confided in him, said she'd done things she regretted. Made mistakes. She was just a girl who'd had a little bad luck. Same with him. But she hadn't been corrupted, yet, like some of the girls in his neighborhood. The way he saw it, she was meant for him, handpicked by the higher powers above. Soon as they got settled some place he'd take her to church. It would be nice to be in a church with her. He could just about picture it. They would confess, they would pray for absolution. Light some candles together. They could let go of the past. They could start over.

"There's something in the trunk," she said.

"What?"

"Something's rolling around in there." She turned around, looking out the back windshield. "That, don't you hear it?"

"It's just some junk of my uncle's," he lied. He hadn't told her he'd stolen the car, it would spoil everything. Daisy thought he was a big success. Big, handsome hero back from the war. Stupidly, he had forgotten to look in the trunk. He would sell it, that's what he would do. Find some shifty dealer who didn't need any papers and he'd get rid of it. Buy something else. One of these days the owner would come back from his trip, looking for it. Somebody could put two and two together, the fact that Denny had never come back to work, the fact that the car was missing—it would appear suspicious. Hopefully, that guy had gone on a long trip someplace.

"I'm sorry about before," she said. "When I cried."

"I understand."

She put her hand on his leg. "You make me feel safe."

It was the highest compliment. "I'm glad, Daisy. I feel safe with you, too."

Sometimes in Baghdad he would see kids, he would talk to them. A couple of times they'd played soccer with the boys in the neighborhood around their encampment. They'd all had a good time and for that hour and a half it was like there wasn't even a war going on at all. Sometimes they gave the kids their MREs. He'd never seen anyone eat so fast. They were hungry, skinny kids, curious what the big American soldiers ate every day. Kids were the same everywhere. They just wanted people to be nice to them. They just wanted to feel safe. It wasn't all horror and killing. They'd done a lot of good things over there. But that wasn't the kind of stuff people heard about or read in the papers. They had made a lot of people feel safe. There had been important moments, graceful exchanges. And there had been times when he'd actually felt like a warrior, a true hero. It was the best feeling in the world. One thing people back here didn't get: Heroic acts happened on a minute-to-minute basis. The military was full of heroes and that's what he tried to focus on. People like him and Ross, who'd done some good, who'd made a difference.

After a while they came to a truck stop and got out to stretch their legs. It was still dark and the air had cooled and there was a little wind. Truckers had turned in here for the night, their trailers like huge sleeping animals lined up in rows. Daisy went in to use the restroom. He walked around to take a look in the trunk. Right away he noticed some dents in the top. The trunk was locked. He tried the key, but the lock was stripped. He would need a crowbar.

Then he heard something strange. Something that lowered his body temperature about a hundred degrees. It sure as hell sounded like somebody was in there. Somebody moving around like they were in pain.

Maybe he was hallucinating. He hadn't slept for a while and had drunk too much beer. No; he wasn't hallucinating. He'd put money on it. There was somebody in there.

"What's in there?" Daisy said, smelling like toothpaste and truck stop soap, drinking from a bottle of water.

"Just some junk. Come on, let's go.

The road was empty and dark. The moon shone down on the distant canyons. He turned on the radio, hoping she wouldn't hear anything coming from the trunk. "Find something you like," he said.

She tuned in a Beatles song and sat back, looking sleepy.

"Why don't you go back to sleep?"

"You don't mind?"

"No, honey, I want you to rest."

"All right."

He looked over at her pale face. "You feeling okay now?"

"Uh-huh." She bunched up her jacket to make a pillow and leaned on the door and he reached over and pushed down the lock so she'd be safe. While she slept, he drove and tried to think. He was in enough trouble; he didn't need any more of it. It came to him that he was cursed. Bad luck followed him around like a starved puppy. Maybe he was just stupid. Stupid people got into trouble, that's what his uncle always said. How was he supposed to know there was somebody in the trunk? Seemed like he was always taking the rap for other people's crimes. That girl in Baghdad—couldn't have been more than thirteen—and what they'd done to her. He should have taken Hull out, that's what he should've done. He regretted it now. Should've done it before they'd hurt her. But he'd been too freaked out. They'd all just jumped right in before he could stop them. He guessed the girl had told her parents and he guessed the parents had told the police. He wondered whatever happened to Hull and the others. Far as he knew, they were still in Iraq. He was the only one who'd gotten out. That meant he'd be tried here at home, in a regular court—if they caught him, that is—and he didn't plan on getting caught. It didn't seem right that he'd have to go to jail—he hadn't done anything to the girl. He was innocent, but there was no way to prove it. Only the girl could say. And he knew she wouldn't. All around it was a bad situation. War brought out the animal in you; it had brought a monster out of Jason Hull. Every time

Denny thought about it he felt sick. When he reimagined the incident in his head, he took Jason out and saved the girl, but in reality that girl had suffered horribly and he couldn't erase those memories, flashes of anguish that were stuck there, like splinters, in the softest tissue of his brain.

Another thump came from the trunk. If there was somebody in there they were alive. If there was somebody in there it meant that the man who'd parked the car at the airport was not coming back. Leaving the keys and the ticket had been deliberate. The car had been waiting for a sucker like him.

PART FOUR

HOPES AND·DREAMS

11

Making the film is harder than you thought. The desert, the heat. Some members of the crew are afflicted with heatstroke. Your director, Bruno Morelli, is a taskmaster—a great believer in method acting. Every morning at daybreak he insists that the actors run three miles through the desert to warm up. And although you are proud of your work on this film, your exceptional organization, your fastidious attention to detail, the dailies disappoint you— the final scenes in particular. You feel, what—compromised?

In real life, the woman had been stoned to death—a sentence declared not by a court of law, but by her family members to protect their honor—to display their shiny new fundamentalism inspired by extremists who had cropped up through the rubble like vigorous weeds. And so the accused adulteress was captured, buried up to her waist, and pummeled with stones over the course of several hours. In truth, it is not easy to kill a person with stones. It takes time. In real life, as in Tom's original script, the woman had died. But Harold and his backers in Australia have insisted the ending be changed. "You're going to have people running out of the theater if you don't."

And so it was changed. Now, determined to survive, the character frees herself and runs away into the desert—a highly unlikely scenario. The ritual disallows anyone from going after her—her survival is considered a miracle—but in truth her prospects are limited and, under the circumstances, her doomed fate is inevitable. Bruno contends that it will make people think. As they are leaving the theater, they will understand that freedom is a fickle, arbitrary condition, more vulnerable than people realize.

At this point, after being here, you are not entirely comfortable with the film's subject matter. You are a stranger in this city and, although you enjoy its luxuries, you cannot abide its traditions or the fact that women are infrequently seen in the street without male escorts and are generally in traditional dress, the black *abaya*, their heads covered with the *hijab*.

Your facilitator reminds you that the women are wearing beautiful clothes underneath. In the nearby malls there are shops representing all the top designers. "It is like Rodeo Drive," he tells you. And it's true, you have seen the shops with exquisite clothes, lingerie—he tells you that the women here buy such garments, but they are reserved only for their husbands. This information doesn't satisfy you. In fact, it's almost worse—as if the women are in collusion with their own oppression.

But who are you to say they are oppressed?

Still, this is shorts and tank top weather. Those black robes are *hot*. You realize it is their tradition, a sign of devotion to Islam. But the men get to wear white. Of course the men need to be out more, on the streets. The men are working. They are going to prayer. They are actively supporting their families. Whereas the women are inside; they don't need to wear white. They are inside, where they belong.

You wonder what it would be like, staying inside your house all day, doing chores. Cleaning and cooking—in your Versace underwear. You are not the sort of person who likes chores, or cares particularly about keeping house. Even Harold begged you to get a cleaning person. You never liked the idea of someone poking around your things, some stranger changing your sheets, doing your laundry. It's not for you. You can't imagine being forced to wear those long black robes, especially in the heat. What would it be like? The veil, swathed in black cloth, the strangeness of it—as though you don't really exist. As though only your husband defines you. You don't get it. It makes you furious. That summer, when you'd lived in Israel, you'd taken the bus across the desert into Egypt. You remember the endless chain-link fence that split the countries in two, the same sand on either side. Nobody had told you to wear long sleeves. It was hot, nearly a hundred degrees. You had on a sleeveless shirt. Everywhere you went Egyptian men touched your arms, as if it was their right. The train station; the marketplace. They forgave you for walking around like a whore because you were American. You didn't know any better.

Maybe you are a stupid, ignorant American woman with no moral conscience—you have no understanding of Islam. Maybe you can't argue with thousands of years of tradition. After all, tradition—religious faith and devotion—is important. It is a very good excuse to keep things exactly as they are.

And why should you care? You don't live here. This is not your country. *Go home, American woman! Slut! We don't need your opinions. Your views are not useful here.*

Two days into the second week of filming, your actors are besieged with a strange stomach virus. You too spend an afternoon bent over the toilet and you can't help thinking that there is some devious reason behind it, that, perhaps, you have overstayed your welcome and it is time to go home. You begin to question making the film in general—you begin to sense that you have crossed some imaginary line, and that, somehow, there will be serious repercussions. Not only here, but back in America, the land of dizzying delusion. Your fever is high, a doctor is summoned. You don't like the doctor, his greedy eyes. Tom feeds you tea with mint off a spoon. He holds you in his arms. At one point, with his mouth whispering at your neck, you think you hear him crying. Sick and weak, you lay in bed, listening to the strange world outside, a place where your life has little importance. You think: It is possible to die here.

In your final days in the Emirates you begin to experience a shift, a transition. You have been bewitched by the colors of the desert. A sky that blooms every morning and every evening like a lotus flower with its black and blue and red petals. The heat, perhaps, has altered your internal rhythm. Your dreams are flagrant with images. The people that you meet, the children, the sense of space without boundaries. Sand. Heat. A landscape that takes everything, that demands your devotion and yet gives nothing back.

The next afternoon you are well enough to return to the set. It is the final day in the desert; tomorrow you will all be flying home. After lunch, the weather changes, the sky turns a feverish pink. There is talk of a sandstorm, and your facilitator urges everyone onto the bus. The equipment is carefully packed and returned to the trucks. For several hours, you wait, marooned, while the storm engulfs you with its thick putty-colored cloud. It is a strange, slow-moving manifestation, like a grotesque otherworldly invasion in some 1950s horror flick.

That night the crew celebrates with an elaborate party in a private dining room. It is a country where alcohol is forbidden and yet you are Hollywood People, they encourage your indulgence, knowing that you will not be happy without it. The waiters look on with hungry amusement. Near dawn, Tom comes to your room. He undresses you slowly and, as a joke, wraps the sheet around your head, across your nose. Only your eyes are showing. "My beautiful Arabian princess," he says. "So mysterious."

But you pull off the sheet, freeing yourself. You can't help thinking there is something stagey about his lovemaking, a kind of ceremonious finality. He is unusually rigorous, demanding, and afterward you are drained, spent.

"You are my country," he whispers, holding you. "You are the language I speak."

On the way to the airport you look out the window in a dreamy state, the sky streaked with violet and pink like a watery painting. A vivid white light beams through the clouds. You can't help feeling superstitious. Maybe there is a God. Maybe there is a reason for everything, some grand scheme.

Going through customs, you are on guard, anxious to hurry through. The officers examine the equipment with agonizing patience, and you have good reason to be nervous, because the images that you have captured on film are far more dangerous than any form of contraband, and the noble ideals behind them that demand a safer world, a real and permanent peace, have somehow become the most dubious of all.

Back in L.A. you work harder than necessary. Every hour is consumed with postproduction details, meetings, telephone calls. You find that you have acquired a new patience from your weeks in the desert. As an experiment, you leave your BlackBerry in the car when you go to the gym, taking a whole hour to yourself, without disruption. When you finally get home at night you are surprised that there are no messages from Tom. It is as though he has completely forgotten you. At first you are hurt, you feel dejected. Armand has told you that his wife is in town. People have seen them together, at restaurants and parties, *looking very married.*

Then one night, he comes to your house to break the news. "She wants to stay this time."

"Lucky you."

"Hedda," he says. He tries to touch you.

"Don't." You get up and fix a drink. You swallow the vodka like water.

"You know I love you," he says, trying to gather you up in his arms.

"If you love me so much, you'll leave her."

"It's not that simple."

"Yes, it is. Now go, get out."

It's a good thing, you tell yourself; you're too busy for love. You focus on work, the film. A preview is scheduled. You find yourself in a kind of postpartum malaise where there is too much to get done and too little time. You rarely sleep. You spend more and more time with Bruno and Lucy Price, your editor, in the editing room, watching the film take shape.

Harold invites you for seder. You cannot refuse. Although you are considerably on edge and probably shouldn't be around anyone at all, you put on a suit, heels, and drive to his home in Beverly Hills. He has invited Important People. Harold's partner, Mitchell, greets you at the door, kisses you on both cheeks. He takes one look at you and asks, "Okay, what's wrong?"

"You don't want to know."

"Come into the kitchen. We can throw the matzo balls over the roof, see what happens. I always wanted to redo the garage."

But then he looks at you and sees your tears. He takes your hand and leads you up the back staircase, down the hall, away from everyone. "I'm sorry, this is so stupid."

"You're tired, you've been through a lot." For a moment he lets you cry. "Harold says the film is brilliant. You shouldn't worry. It's going to blow people's minds."

"I don't know," you say. "I'm not sure. Anyway, it's not about the film."

"Okay." He nods knowingly. Even with all your discretion, everybody seems to know about you and Tom. Mitchell takes your hand. "Look, honey, it's his loss. That wife of his—*please*—that's not a real marriage. Real married people live together. They slowly drive each other crazy in one house, in the same state, in the same *country*. Yeah, I know; an insanely ridiculous concept. It's called commitment—the son of a bitch!"

You cry; you let it out, knowing all too well that it will destroy your face, your perfectly constructed sense of calm for which you have earned your reputation. "I'm such an idiot," you say in the wobbly voice of a teenager. "I don't know why I allowed myself," but he cuts you off.

"Hey, I know you're a big control freak, sweetheart, but we're talking about love, here. Love is this . . . this amorphous creature. It's a fucking monster. It eats you alive."

"I hope nothing illicit is going on," Harold jokes when you come downstairs together holding hands. "Although you do make a very nice couple."

Mitchell kisses him and you smile at them, bittersweet. You've never had what they have, you realize. Not even close.

"We're all ready to begin," Harold says, gently guiding you to the table. He doesn't seem to notice your glassy eyes, your slightly mottled skin. Gratefully, you approach the table, kissing people as you make your way to your chair at the other end, and the seder begins.

The table is set with a fine white cloth, beautiful dishes. An unusual centerpiece with poppies and irises. Harold and Mitchell sit at opposite ends of the long table. You feel a tender admiration for both of them and you try to relax. It is an interesting mix of people. The famous costume designer, Sonia Moss, wearing a magnificent vintage shawl she bought in Prague. Tony Roth, whose string of espionage movies made him one of the richest men in town, and his wife, Lara. And Harold's old friend, the director Dick Brower, in his late eighties, who has brought along his young lover/attendant, a cheerful Adonis named Gus. Some of the old guard—in a business managed by people who are barely out of diapers, proponents of the coloring book approach to filmmaking, you included. Here's a character, color him black; here's another one, color her yellow. But the older guests at the table grew up in a different time, and their saturated Technicolor aesthetic promised a wiser, more civilized world—the images you clung to as a child that structured your days, nurtured your hopes and dreams.

Everybody gets a turn reading from the Haggadah. When it's your turn, you read a paragraph about the epic journey across the desert, the heat, the fact that the Israelites had no flour to make bread. You can't help thinking about your trip to Abu Dhabi. The desert is the same desert. The heat the same heat, the sun the same sun. The best thing about the trip was the food, the warm bread and meat, the sliced cucumbers and ripe tomatoes, the sweet dates.

"From something terrible came something good," Harold says.

"What, matzo?" Ben Appelman scowls. He is the youngest person at the table, a wunderkind screenwriter fresh out of USC whom Harold has decided to nurture. "What's so good about matzo? It sits in your stomach like a lead weight and makes you constipated for weeks?"

"Let's do the prayer over the matzo," Harold says, holding up a piece, launching into the Hebrew prayer.

Mitchell reads some more and they do the prayer for the wine. More wine is poured.

"Somebody open the door for Elijah," Mitchell says.

A table setting awaits the ghost of the prophet Elijah. Since you are at the end of the table, across from the phantom's place, you get up to open the door, to let him in. Standing there you take a moment to enjoy the gentle evening breeze, the first stars on the darkening sky. Across the street, a man and woman are having an argument, screaming at one another across the expansive lawn. The woman takes off her shoes and throws them at the man. You close the door.

"Welcome Elijah," Mitchell says to the imaginary prophet as he pulls out his chair and pours a glass of wine for the thirsty spirit. He pantomimes patting the prophet's shoulder. "Enjoy yourself."

The dinner is served. Of course there's no surprise that it's amazing, Mitchell has his own cooking show on the Food Network. Matzo ball soup, homemade gefilte fish, brisket—it makes you nostalgic and you remember your mother's seders with all the Conservative relatives who took forever to get through the Haggadah, but paid generously if you found the *afikoman*. Tonight, back in New Jersey, your parents are having seder at the temple and you are glad that they are at least with people, instead of being home, just the two of them at the kitchen table. It occurs to you that you could have flown back for the holiday, it would have been a nice thing to do, but in reality you don't have the time. Holidays are not something you work into your schedule.

You eat and drink and your face is flushed with happiness and, during a brief philosophical interlude, you conclude that Harold was right about rituals, that this is what matters most, *this*, right here, having a meal with friends. The rituals in life that define who we are. When you come right down to it what else is there?

And yet, even such earnest introspection cannot erase the other thoughts inside your head. Louder, ferocious thoughts: *you need to go, you've spent enough time here, you need to check your BlackBerry, you need to make some calls.* Sitting here like this is a terrific waste of your time with so many other pressing things to be done. It is because you are a predator—ravenous for power—that every aspect of your life is a tacit negotiation—even here at this holiday table you are wondering if something might be gained from the evening, maybe the boy wonder will agree to write something for Gladiator at a reasonable price—or perhaps Harold has other ideas for him. It is entirely possible that your power has deceived you into believing that you are not expendable. This is something you will think about later, when you are lying alone in bed. It will drive you to new heights of savagery. And what a convenient distraction from everything else, what a terrific excuse to remain distant, unknowable.

As a result, your terrible loneliness is nobody's fault but your own.

Toward the end of the meal, as the wine bottle makes its way around the table, you happen to notice Elijah's glass. It's empty. The fact that you are slightly drunk makes you wonder if you've imagined it. You reach across the table and tap Ben's arm and he looks at you with his baby face and warm brown eyes. He is the definition of a "nice Jewish boy," the sort of boy people used to try to fix you up with back in college—except for the fact that he's gay. "This may sound weird," you say conspiratorially, "but did you drink his wine?"

Ben sees Elijah's empty glass and shakes his head, wide-eyed. "I don't drink." He gestures to his own glass, which is full.

How is it possible, you think? Before you can stop yourself you tap on your glass with your knife to get everyone's attention. "Something amazing has happened," you announce to the table. "Elijah has finished his wine." You hold up the empty glass. Everyone stares at it, astonished.

"Seriously?" Mitchell asks.

"Look, it's empty. I didn't drink it and neither did Ben."

"It's a sign," Mitchell says somberly, then shakes his hands at the sky in an affectation of some Hollywood Moses, and speaks in a heavy Yiddish accent, "It's a miracle! It's a miracle!"

"That is pretty wild," Ben says.

"It is a miracle," Harold affirms seriously, and raises his glass. "Here's to you, Elijah," he says, addressing the empty chair. "You've reminded us that what we don't see is often so much more revealing than what's right in front of our eyes."

12

The preview of *Oath of Allegiance* takes place in a movie theater in Glendale. Of course Tom doesn't show. You're starting to think that he set you up—running into you by accident at that bar in Santa Monica—what you thought had been a coincidence—perhaps he'd followed you from the studio that night. It was possible. In times like these, where it's next to impossible to get a movie made—especially a movie like this—you almost wouldn't put it past him. You suppose the sex, your affair, was just a fringe benefit of the deal. And then you think: not for him, but for *you*. He threw it in; no extra charge.

Now that the film is done, he doesn't need you anymore.

You sit with Bruno in the back. The theater goes dark and the film begins and that's when you see them, Tom and Fatima, slipping into one of the rows. At first you don't recognize her because she looks like any other American woman, dressed like a college student in jeans and a Santa Cruz sweatshirt, no sign of the veil. Your heart beats a little faster as you watch them take their seats.

At last you lose yourself in the film, watching the heads move, trying to decipher what people might be thinking. Just before the credits roll, Tom ushers Fatima out. You feel a little spurned, excluded. The film fades to black and, for a brief moment, silence descends upon the room as if from the heavens above, and you are certain that your life, your career as you know it, is over. But then there's applause as the credits roll. It resounds through the theater, loud as a helicopter. People stand and clap at the screen. When the lights come up, they exit respectfully, like mourners leaving a funeral. Later that night, reading over the comments in Harold's office, you discover that many in the audience had been moved. Some admit to crying during the film, swept up in the woman's plight. Some, the ones with children in Iraq and Afghanistan, identified with the soldier. They wrote of their frustration, the fear that their sons and daughters have been manipulated into fighting an unwinnable war, a war with no authentic purpose, being faced with problems beyond their emotional realms. You leave the studio feeling victorious. Perhaps it is true that you have accomplished something important. That this film—this bold and artful rendering—will have a significant effect.

The calls begin that night, when you return home to your rented bungalow after midnight. As you always do before you answer, you check your caller ID: Unavailable. "Hello?" You can tell someone is there, you can hear them breathing, the sounds of the street in the background, and yet they say nothing. The line disconnects.

Your number is unlisted. Very few people have the privilege of knowing it. And yet it is no accident. Someone has managed to get your number. Or perhaps it is someone you already know.

It rings again. "Hello . . . hello?" At first you repeat your greeting, as though there is some disruption in the line, as if the caller, whoever it is, can't hear you. "Who is this?" you demand, only to hear the finite click as the caller disconnects. In the days that follow there are more calls, and you begin to worry that your line has been tapped. Feelings of paranoia consume you. Anyone you happen to see becomes an extra in your own private thriller. The gardeners across the street; the letter carrier; even your neighbor. You are certain that you are being watched. You notice a strange car on the street when you come home one evening—a Ford Taurus sedan—just the sort of innocuous car for a terrorist. Then Bobby Darling calls your cell phone. "We may have a problem," he says. "I got a call from Cannes this morning. They have concerns about showing the film."

"What concerns?"

"They're afraid of having a riot."

"What do you want to do?"

"Show it, of course. You can't buy this kind of publicity."

And then, a few days later, you are driving in your car listening to NPR when a report comes on: a strange fire has occurred in one of the dormitories at UC Santa Cruz. *The fire ignited in the room of a foreign student on exchange from Iraq, Fatima Kassim, who was found, hours later, burned to death, dressed in her* abaya. After their investigation, the fire department determines that the fire was the result of arson. The following morning you receive a telegram at your office from her father: *Underneath it all, she was a good Muslim girl; in our country, betrayal is never denied. It comes with a price. She paid dearly.*

Distressed, you leave work early that afternoon. To think that you might have somehow been responsible for her death fills you with grief. Driving home, the sun is bright, a blaze of fire. You try to call Tom. He is the only person you really want to talk to, but he doesn't pick up and you do something you have sworn you would never do, you call his home. Lucia answers the phone. For a moment, you are tongue-tied, and then, meekly, you ask for him—she says something in Italian and then translates: "Why do you call here? What do you want?"

Trembling, you hang up. You drive, trying to focus on the road. You pass the house where you bought the car. The house looks dark, sprawling with ivy, the window shades pulled. You wonder how the old magician is doing. When you finally pull into your driveway, it occurs to you that you should make some changes; you've been cavalier about your safety. There should be a light over the garage, for example, with a motion sensor. And there should be lights on timers inside the house. You make a mental note to call an electrician in the morning. Maybe you're being paranoid, it's a good neighborhood with very little crime, and yet you feel strangely exposed as you cross the driveway, past the shed, to your porch. The sun is setting sharply, reflecting in the windows of the shed, and for a second you are momentarily blinded. Something catches your eye, but you don't stop to acknowledge it. Instead, you continue onto your porch, unlock the door and go inside, relocking it behind you. Your heart is beating fast. You need a drink.

In your kitchen, you fix a drink and watch the news. Another report about Fatima Kassim. There are shots back in Iraq, of her father mourning with other family members, the women all in black abayas. Thankfully, they do not mention the film or your connection to the girl. Moments later, your mother calls to express her concern. She has seen the report on the news. "Come home for a few weeks," she implores you. It's not safe, she tells you, who knows what may happen? "I can't do that, Mother, I won't," you say, your voice sharper than necessary. You don't mean to be like that, but the fact that she is worried troubles you even more. You stand in your kitchen, drinking. You try to eat a few crackers. Since your illness in Abu Dhabi, your normal appetite has not returned. An unquenchable thirst preoccupies you. The vodka is good, the vodka is necessary.

The doorbell rings. Through the window, you see Tom's car parked at the curb. He walks into your kitchen with his camera bags, the final cut of his documentary.

"Thank God you're here," you cry, hugging him, hiding your face in his chest. Tears rush to your eyes, there doesn't seem to be any point in hiding them. He takes out a handkerchief and gives it to you and you cry some more. "I thought I saw someone in my shed."

Tom walks to the back of the house, into your bedroom, and peers through the Venetian blinds. "I don't see anything," he says. "You're probably imagining it. The film's not even out yet."

"I saw you at the screening. Why didn't you tell me you were bringing her?"

"She didn't want anyone to know. She took a bus; I picked her up downtown. We stopped and got some food. She was so happy. You saw her—she had taken off the veil. She was wearing flip-flops, for Christ's sake." He shook his head, his eyes filling with tears. "She looked like any American girl."

"What happened?"

"I put her on the bus. That's the last I saw of her."

"Some people are saying she did it herself. How does a person set herself on fire?"

He shakes his head. "No, I don't believe that."

"It's something that happens sometimes in the more religious neighborhoods. Women do it to avoid shaming their families. Either that or their family burns them and makes it look like an accident."

"That sounds more like it."

"I feel responsible."

"She came to us, Hedda. She wanted people to know."

"Still." You shake your head. Tears roll down your cheeks.

"She was happy here. She was beautiful. Somebody got to her. She was obviously being watched."

You cry; you let it out—everything you've been holding in for months. Not just about Fatima, but about the film, the uncertainty of your life—Tom.

"Look, you have to remember that it's in their culture, it's not something you can necessarily change."

"I guess I can't accept it."

"You can't accept it because you're American. Because you live here. Because here you have a voice; you have rights." He puts his hands on your shoulders, slides them down your arms. "It's why we made the film, isn't it?"

"I know." You look at him, nodding, and perhaps for the first time you accept what you've done. "I'm glad we made it."

On the day you'd met Fatima Kassim you remember thinking how beautiful she looked in her veil. She loved her country; she loved being a Muslim. It was in her heart, she'd told you, it was *inside* of her. She was devoted to Islam. She had told you that the invasion had changed her beloved country. How before, even though there were many problems, at least things had been better for women. At least a woman could go out without fear. There had been life, joy, in the streets of Baghdad. Not now.

"We just marched in there like some splashy Hollywood production thinking we could dazzle people with special effects."

"Yeah, well, we're way over budget at this point."

"Yeah, and we're losing our audience. If it were me in charge, I'd shut down the whole production and come home."

"Why don't you run for president? I'll vote for you."

"Only if you'll be my running mate."

You end up in bed.

"This was a mistake," you say. "You should go."

"I'm taking you to Bruno's party. He's expecting us. Get dressed." He tosses you your clothes.

But you stay where you are. You watch him as he buttons his shirt, pulls on his trousers. You have become so fond of watching him in these moments.

"I have to ask you something," you say. "For the record."

He turns and looks at you.

"Did you set me up?"

"What?" Stalling.

"The film. Running into me that time?"

He hesitates, buckling his belt. "So what if I did? It was a good cause. You're all going to benefit. You'll see." He turns and looks at you. "They're talking Oscars."

"Fatima didn't."

"No, she didn't." He sits down on the edge of the bed, strokes the hair from your face. "Look, Hedda. I wish things were different."

You shake off his hand. "Don't insult me."

"You're no different than the others."

"What?"

"You think you're so fierce, don't you? So independent. You don't need anybody, right?"

You get up, pull on your clothes. Your heart is pounding. You refuse to cry. "That's right, Tom. I don't need anyone. Not a fucking soul."

The party is crowded. Everyone from the crew is there. And lots of writers. Bruno likes to hang out with writers because he likes to talk, he likes to sit around drinking and smoking and bullshitting until the wee hours—and who else would put up with that? An Antonioni disciple, Bruno is a visual genius. He was your first choice for *Oath of Allegiance* and you are convinced that, because of him, the film is a magnificent creation. Born in Sicily, Bruno is earthy and dark, like peasant bread. He has a way of getting people to fess up to their better qualities, even the ones who are hard pressed to find any. His face lights up when you and Tom step through the door. He is glad and perhaps a little relieved that you've shown up. In a tight three-way hug, you commiserate about Fatima's death. "A terrible tragedy," he says. "Absolutely terrible." He shakes his head as if he, too, is trying to reckon with his guilt. "We only wanted to tell her story," he confesses. "It is just another terrible story. We are not in short supply of those, I'm afraid. Come, have a drink. Try to enjoy yourselves."

You drink too much, talking to all the wrong people, encouraging people you have no interest in working with to call your office for a meeting. They nod and smile like people who have swallowed some mysterious pleasure drug and are just beginning to feel the effects. Tom lingers on the periphery, talking to his wife on his phone. Apparently another emotional crisis. Briefly, you reflect on your lovemaking that afternoon, the pleasure experienced then and the regret you're experiencing now. *Go ahead, speak to your wife.* Bruno comes around and puts his arm around you and the two of you disappear together, down to his office to smoke a joint. Smoking pot is not something you do, you don't believe in doing drugs, but tonight you just might indulge. You feel like you are standing at the edge of a very tall cliff, preparing to jump. You picture your body falling through the air, your arms out, your legs spread.

"I told you you were wasting your time with him," Bruno says, sucking a hit. "Really, Hedda, you're too smart to be in this mess."

You take a hit. The smoke burns your chest, you cough.

"He can't commit to anyone," Bruno criticizes—not that he's any better—he's notorious for sleeping with the actors in his films, the script girls, the makeup people. "I don't think it's in his DNA."

"That's a lousy excuse," you say. "Can't you come up with something more original?"

Bruno shrugs. "He's never going to commit to you. Married men never leave their wives. I know you know this." He shrugs again like the Italian that he is, as if you're an impossible adolescent. "You're a woman," he says. "You should know better. Where are your pretty fangs?" He reaches out and touches your cheek, gently, like a brother.

The door opens, a sudden intrusion. A man you don't know stands there, his eyes prickling with insinuation. You can't help thinking he has the look of someone who is marginally deranged. He is taller and slimmer than Bruno, with the shadow of a beard, a not unattractive man, you think, and yet there is something disarming about his presence. He has an angry face, you decide, as he surveys the two of you with what looks like contempt—or maybe he just needs a bathroom. "Down the hall on the left," Bruno instructs, and you assume that they are friends, that he is a guest you have never met.

Sufficiently stoned, Tom takes you home. He parks out front and walks you to the door, but does not come in. "I better go," he says. "I have to get home." Just that word *home* makes you cringe.

"I don't get it," you say. "This sudden devotion to her. You're suddenly so . . . so *married*. You didn't seem so devoted to her at five o'clock this afternoon."

"I didn't want to tell you, but I don't see that I have much of a choice at this point."

"Tell me what?"

"She's pregnant. We're having a baby."

He watches you closely as if you are a subject in one of his documentaries, savoring your reaction. But you learned long ago to keep your feelings to yourself. It is an essential skill in a town like this and you have mastered it.

You save your tantrum for when you are inside, alone. The first thing you do is pour yourself a very large glass of vodka. It's childish, you realize, to behave this way, but you can't seem to help yourself. And you *know* he loves you! Why is it that you're always the one who ends up with nothing? You're supposed to be so smart, such a success, but your life is joyless and isolated. Your existence is almost arbitrary. When it comes right down to it you have little to show for all your hard work. Nobody cares! Not really they don't. They're all so involved in their own little cubicle lives. Somehow, you can't help feeling used. If you dropped out of the world tomorrow, nobody would even care! Well—your parents would care, of course. And Harold—he and Mitchell might be a little sad. But nobody else! And certainly *not* Tom!

Son of a bitch!

Staggering into the kitchen you try to find something to eat. It would be nice to have some food here, but you haven't been to the market in weeks. You rarely eat at home; you rarely enjoy a meal, period. It's true, you are enviably thin—but so what? *You are so fucking hungry.* You could eat an elephant right now. No wonder you can't think straight! And the irony is that your entire existence revolves around meals—not that you actually eat much. Breakfast meetings, ridiculously expensive lunches and dinners—with your photographic memory you have memorized all the menus, and how pathetic that you don't even taste the food. Because of course it's not even about the food. It's about getting what you want, what you need, by the time dessert comes around.

Hoping you won't throw up, you stumble into your room. Clearly, it is time to go to bed. You are too tired, too flustered, to wash your face and you fall into bed and sleep. You wake an hour or so later with the light glaring down in your face like some sort of vile interrogation. You turn it off and fall into dreams. Again, you dream of Inez, the exquisite dead wife of the magician who once owned your car. She is waiting for you, now, her gloved hand outstretched. She is your guide, to the desert inside your soul, where nothing grows.

13

In the morning, your alarm fails—you had forgotten to set it. You wake at eleven. Jumping around the house in an attempt to get dressed, your cell phone continues to ring and the sound is like an electric drill to your head, boring deeper and deeper into your hangover. Armand is calling to give you the rundown of the morning's catastrophes, for there are always catastrophes. "What?" you say.

"I have news."

"Hit me."

"Charlie Rose wants to interview you. They think there's something going on because of the film. The Muslim girl who died. They want to talk about her, how you found her, the process of making the film, et cetera. They're going to have on a terrorist expert."

A wave of nausea. "That's good news," you manage. "I have to go. Can you let Harold know before he leaves?"

"You okay? You don't sound too good."

"Russian jet lag. It sure as hell looked like water."

"Poor baby. Should I cancel your lunch?"

"What lunch?"

"Mary Gage? Harold wants her for *First Chair*."

"Shit. No, it's all right. I'll go."

"Drive safe."

Outside, the light is sharp, vicious. It slams a nail into your brain.

A man emerges from the darkness of the garage. At first you don't recognize him. He is tall, wearing a dark suit. He looks like a Bible salesman, you think, although you have never met a Bible salesman, but if you had this is what he would look like. Then it hits you: He was at Bruno's party. "Good morning, Ms. Chase." He smiles like a cartoon hyena.

"What?" You think back to the night before—when he'd opened the door to Bruno's office. Bruno had assumed he was looking for the bathroom. Thinking back on it now, you're not certain that Bruno even knew this man. He could have come with somebody else; he could have been somebody's date.

"I wonder if I could have a moment."

"I'm late," you say. "Whatever you're selling—"

"I'm not selling anything, Ms. Chase. I just want to talk."

"What about?"

"I'm Hugh Waters."

Vaguely, the name rings a bell. You shake your head, you cough.

"I'm Hugh Waters," he says again, as if he's surprised you don't remember him. *The Adjuster?*"

That awful Cory Rogers script, the one Harold set fire to when you'd threatened to quit. A dull throbbing spreads inside your skull. Your tongue grows fur. This is the absolutely last thing you feel like dealing with. This . . . this person . . . this odd ball . . . this *loser*—it is entirely inappropriate for him to be here now, on *your* property—*what fucking balls*—it's an invasion of privacy, that's what it is!

"You didn't return any of my calls."

Yeah, that's right; I don't return calls to lunatics. "Look, call my office. I'll make sure to fit you in." Instead, you'll notify studio security and have this creep banned from the lot.

"I read that letter you wrote. You said some horrible things about me."

You don't recall what you said in the letter—you had dictated something to Armand. You admit, sometimes Armand takes liberties.

"I just want to talk."

"It's not possible." You bustle toward the car, but he grabs your arm, hard. It comes to you rather swiftly that no is not the answer he wants to hear.

"Look, I've come all this way."

That's when you feel the gun in your back. *This is it,* you think. You have known all along that this would eventually happen, a kind of psychic premonition. They say if you think about something enough you are actually channeling the universe to make it happen. One of the reasons that you didn't want to make a film like his in the first place.

"We'll go inside and have our meeting. And then I'll go."

You nod to let him know that you're okay with this even though you are most definitely *not* okay, and you don't want this creep, this psychopath in your house. But there's a gun in the small of your back. Somehow he gets you up the stairs of your porch. Your body begins to respond, your adrenaline fires up, but not exactly in the way you would like. Instead of becoming stronger, you feel enervated, weak. Breathless. You feel like you're going to be sick. Maybe if you throw up he'll become disgusted and leave you alone. If only you could bring up that vodka, the muddy coffee you drank earlier.

"Give me your keys."

"This is ridiculous," you say, groping around in your bag for your keys. "This isn't happening." But there's that gun again. You try to stall, hoping to encounter the keypad of your BlackBerry—you will dial 911 and they will send the cops and take this asshole away. But he grabs your bag and shakes out the keys. Your thirty-dollar lipstick slips through the wooden slats and disappears in the dirt. He unlocks the door and yanks you inside. He pushes you, jams the gun into your back. "Pour us some coffee."

He stands behind you, too close. You can smell him; a strong smell like tar or dead skunk. Trembling, you take down two cups. Your movements are slow, methodical. You worry you may drop the cups. It is as if you are on some slow-motion drug. It's strange being here, in your own house, and feeling so threatened. He's the one in control, not you.

He takes your hand and maneuvers it onto the coffeepot, just in case you are thinking of throwing it at him, which, you admit, occurred to you a second ago. Outside, your neighbor is having an argument with his brother. If only you could get their attention, but they turn and move around toward the front of the house. Their mother is inside, an old woman who speaks no English. A chainsaw rattles the air.

"Bring the coffee," he says, flapping the pistol in the air; you pray it doesn't go off because it is pointing right at you. The coffee spills over the top of the cups, burning your fingers, but you set them down, making small puddles on the surface of the table. You wonder what it will be like being dead.

"Sit." Using the gun, he points to the chair.

You sit, a force of gravity draining into your feet. "Look," you attempt to ingratiate him. "I'm sorry about what happened, all right? It's not like it's a big deal, it happens all the time. Rogers and I had different ideas. We had different ideas about things. Anyway, he's dead."

"And you're in charge."

"That's right."

"We had a deal," he says.

You realize you are going to have to attempt to mollify him in some way. You are going to have to negotiate very carefully in order to get him to see things your way. You talk to him in your *baby the actor* voice, a tone you use with difficult actors who don't always get what they want. You speak as if there is a sleeping child in the room.

Gently, you break the news to him about his script. The ending is the problem, you tell him, the scenes at the airport. "I had a hard time believing that nobody heard her."

"She was in the trunk."

"Screaming!"

"Your point?"

You explain how the device of the trunk is overused.

Everyone has one, he argues. Then smiles and says how ironic it is. The smile upsets you immeasurably. The phone rings. You make a move to answer it, but he raises his gun.

Your machine picks up. The two of you sit there, listening to Armand's message.

You consider running to the door. It's a risk; he could shoot you. He could kill you and vanish. Nobody would ever know.

Nobody would know.

He gets up and takes the phone off the hook. You admit that the sound is terrifying. Somewhat feebly, you press on. "You don't understand my boss. He gets insulted if I'm even a second late. He takes it personally." Now your cell phone begins to vibrate inside your pocketbook. "Look, I really need to get to work."

"You're not going to work today."

"Look," you say, speaking very slowly, deliberately, as if he is a foreigner who does not speak your language. "You need to go. We've had our meeting. There's nothing more to say. You said you would go."

He explains that he wants to do an experiment. To see who's right about his ending. You are too afraid to consider what that means, exactly. There were a lot of terrible things that happened at the end of his script, none of which you want to be part of. He opens his hand, shows you some pills.

"It's just some Valium," he tells you, "to calm you down."

"I don't want to be calm." You get up and start for the door, but he's on you, tackling you down to the floor. He's on top of you, a disturbing weight, and you try not to look at his face. He holds you down, hard, with such force that it hurts. He is trying to decide if he wants to rape you, but he doesn't. He pulls you up, his hand slowly brushing your thigh. It is a gesture of power, you realize; a threat.

"You're going to have to calm down." He pushes you down into the chair. "Take the pills."

There is no way in hell that you're taking those pills.

"Look." He smiles a little, nods as if he understands something about you, something highly personal—something that even you don't understand. "Either you take the pills, or I shoot you. You decide."

"You're going to shoot me over *this*?"

"I'm not myself. I'm feeling very unbalanced."

"You're not going to kill me," you say in the most patronizing voice you can muster. "Even I know that."

But then he puts the gun to your head. "Are you sure?"

Within seconds you lose your resolve. Your courage drains out of you like blood. "I don't know what you want. I don't understand what you want from me."

"Make me happy." He opens his hand. "Take these."

But you can't seem to move. This is what they call being paralyzed with fear.

"Don't make me shoot you, because I will."

Maybe they are Valium, you think. Maybe he is going to rape you. Maybe he will rape you and leave and you find yourself hoping that this is his plan—as if it isn't everything. As if it isn't enough to ruin your life.

You think of Fatima. You think of her mother's poor friend. What it must have felt like taking those stones, being surrounded by people you've known all your life—people you've trusted, who've watched you grow up—who have watched from afar as you grew hips and breasts and the countenance of a woman—people who suddenly hate you—the betrayal of that—who want you dead. You think of all the women you know who have found themselves in this kind of situation. And you are thinking of the next woman. You are thinking of her too.

He nods at the pills. "Please."

You take the pills, drinking down the entire glass of water as if the water might dilute their effect. "You're dead," you tell him. "You'll never work in this town." You have never been so sure of anything in your life. If you survive this, you will stop at nothing to destroy him.

"All right. If you say so."

He sits there watching you, a satisfied expression on his face. His little plan is working. "That wasn't so bad, was it?"

But you won't give him the satisfaction. "I'm not afraid of you."

"I'm glad. I'm not a very scary person." He laughs.

"You realize this is a mistake."

"Perhaps."

"What were you doing at Bruno's party?"

"Watching you."

"You think you know me. You've made assumptions about me. You think I'm this horrible person, right?" He shrugs, seemingly disarmed by your clarity, your honesty. "But you don't know me. You don't know anything about me."

"I know enough. I know that you're very sad."

For some reason the comment upsets you. Tears spring to your eyes. It occurs to you that he's right. And you've been sad for a long time. You just haven't figured out what to do about it.

Your legs and arms begin to tingle and you realize that you are losing sensation. The idea of it terrifies you beyond description.

"I want to tell meaningful stories. I want to make people feel better about things, not worse . . . I want to make people feel . . ." But you cannot go on. All of a sudden your voice, your mouth, even your teeth don't work.

"Feel what, Ms. Chase?"

And still, you try . . . but you can't push out the words. You watch the kitchen turn on its side and when you hit the floor you don't even feel it.

14

Waking in the darkness, you realize two things. First that you desperately need water and second that you must figure out a way to free your hands. The first few moments of consciousness are worse than any you have ever experienced. Swiftly, you come to the conclusion that you are in very grave danger, that this place—this tomb—that contains your body—your collapsed limbs, your mind, your thoughts, your entire history as Hedda Beatrice Chastowsky—is exceptionally small and hot and smells strongly of tar and gasoline. Under your head you discern that you are moving. It occurs to you that this passage from one place to the next may in fact constitute your very last hours alive.

It is raining. You can hear the rain on the roof. And you are assuming that it is night because the space around you is completely dark. At least he didn't blindfold you; you don't think you could have dealt with that, but your mouth is taped, which presents a problem. And your hands are taped too.

The car stops and you hear the muffled sound of voices. A male and female voice. They talk briefly, and then they're driving again and the radio is on, some pulsing rap tune. Your body jerks with the motion of the car, a jumble of something at your back, something that makes a sound so familiar and particular that you are certain you can identify it, and yet the words and pictures refuse to come. When the car stops again your stomach clenches. Will they be opening the trunk, pulling you out? You can only imagine their plans for you. You must prepare yourself. And in your terror, instead of gaining strength, your muscles go flaccid as jelly.

The doors open then close with a dull finality. You brace yourself, expecting them to open the trunk, but they don't. And you hear their footsteps fade. Now it is quiet. The car waits. Sweat runs down your limbs, your back, and it makes you cold, it makes you feel ill. In the distance, you hear other voices, the sound of a crowded place. And very faintly too there is the sound of music.

In the minutes and hours that follow, it becomes increasingly clear to you that you are going to die. You try to remember when you last had something to drink, food. Many hours have passed. It is impossible for you to tell. Your pants are damp, you realize you have peed—you don't recall doing it, you don't recall anything, really, except for the fact that that awful man came to your house with a gun. You try to picture him now, but your brain won't allow it.

Time slips by. The minutes vanish, one after the other. You must become a version of Houdini. You are too smart for this. And yet, getting out seems impossible. There's a feeling in your head, the profound knowledge that you've been trapped, contained. That someone else is in charge of your destiny. That someone else has power over you. That you are at their mercy.

You assess the situation. You're in a fetal position, your hands bound behind your back, your ankles bound, gaffer's tape in your mouth. You twist your wrists, trying to stretch the tape, to loosen it. It burns, but that is of no consequence to you. You will continue to do it until you have no more strength. At intervals, you rest. You inch along the floor, hoping to encounter something sharp; nothing. Once, you had seen a program about a girl who'd been kidnapped and put into a trunk. The trunk had an emergency release—but that was a newer car. This is your car, you realize. Of course it is. There are no emergency releases in this car. This car is old. It was built during more civilized times, when people knew how to behave. They didn't put people in the trunks of cars. That sort of thing was reserved for thugs in the Mafia, not for ordinary people like you.

You regret buying it now. You are beginning to regret so many things.

If this was a scene in one of your movies, how would the girl get out?

You rock your body back and forth, feeling the car shake. You scream with all your might, but only a muffled terrible sound comes out. Still, you scream and you scream and it sounds like a dying cow. You hear a dog barking in the distance. Maybe the dog can hear you, you think. Now your throat is sore. Even your ears hurt, the back of your neck. You think of your parents, how terrible this will be for them, when they hear about it. It will be the sort of news that could kill them. They are old now; fragile. News like this will make them sick.

You think about the way things are. The world out there. The big awful world. It has always been awful, you realize, accessing scraps from history. There have always been wars. Wars fought by men! Beowulf. Great epic battles. Fields of blood and carnage. Terrible methods of torture and death. Beheadings. Hangings. Burnings at the stake. *Stonings.* Crucifixions. Suffocation. Drowning. Stabbing. Arrows. Bullets. Swords. Daggers. Drugs. Abuse. Neglect. Many have suffered. And the reasons are never good enough. The reasons are stupid. Even the good reasons, when you come right down to it, are stupid.

You conclude: The way things are now is the way they have always been.

No difference.

People are ugly and cruel. They are relentless. They will stop at nothing to get what they want.

Darkness envelops you—a horror so pernicious you fear it will kill you. And then, almost as suddenly as it came, it lifts, and what you need to do next becomes clear. First, you must refuse to die. You must focus on what is left that is good, the shallow breath pushing through your nostrils, the vivid clarity inside your head. You must concentrate very hard. You twist your wrists once more, jiggling your hands. Your arms prickle and burn as if they are crammed with bees. The tape's sharp edge cuts your skin, opening a wound. No matter. You must keep trying. For some reason you think of Jesus. You think of nails through His wrists. The blood. You picture His face, the famous tilt of His head, His crown of thorns. Only now can you

fully appreciate His suffering. Even as a Jew you are not above praying to
Him now—in fact, any God will do—the idea of God—of being saved—
preoccupies your thoughts.

Death, intimate as love, so impossibly near.

You will have none of it!

You must concentrate. Think. But your thirst is too great. You are sick with
thirst, desperate—and there's that jumble at your back. You rock against it,
trying to decipher the sound it makes. Almost instinctively, with a certainty
reserved for those who refuse to die, you know it's a plastic bag, and the bag
contains something you need. That the sound it made before and the sound
it is making now is the crinkle of plastic, the ruckus of dented tin, the tine
of glass against glass—your collection of deposit bottles to return to the
market—your favorite organic root beer, Orangina, the fancy water from
Sweden. You can almost taste the pulpy sweetness, imagining the dregs of
liquid you left behind—so careless—so wasteful. Furious, you begin again,
twisting and twisting, feeling the blood dripping down your wrists. No matter. You are willing to suffer now, you are willing to bleed. There will be time
to heal later. Once the tape is off. Once you're out.

They're coming back. You hear the girl crying. "You didn't have to do
that," she's saying, her voice squealing. "He's nice; he wasn't a creep like the
others."

"Get in the car," he says.

"No."

"Daisy, get in the fucking car."

"You're crazy, you know that?

"I'm just trying to protect you."

"He looked fucking *dead*."

"Not even close. Now get in."

"What if I don't want to?"

"Come on, you know you want to. You don't want to stay here with these
people."

Then you hear the unmistakable sound of someone vomiting.

"What's wrong with you?"

"I'm sick." Again, she vomits.

"You drank too much."

"You don't know me," she says.

"I want to know you."

The door opens and you can feel the car adjusting to their weight. The doors close.

"You don't know anything about me!"

"Start talking. It's a long way to Nevada. I should know you real good by the time we get there."

15

Ida had not answered his calls. He felt somewhat at a loss. He supposed he'd been pretty rough on her. She hadn't liked what he'd done to her, more than once she'd cried out, begging him to stop—but you never knew with women what they really wanted, and it had felt so good he wasn't able to. It was a powerful feeling, as though he had gotten to the very core of her, as though he had tapped into her soul—a dirty place, a dark place—the place that most defined her—and he possessed that part of her now. It was for him and nobody else. And she'd never get it back.

It had been selfish, he understood that now. She had decided not to forgive him. And he had decided that it was all right with him. Maybe he didn't care. Then again, she was in his thoughts. He thought about her constantly.

He sat on the edge of the unmade bed, watching the people down on the street. A crowd emerged from the old stucco church and the bells were ringing in the tower. He liked the sound they made. It was hot that morning, the sun white on a white sky, and there was talk of a heat wave. As usual, the little dog across the street was yapping at the window. Out in front, its oblivious owner was shoveling a hole in the grass, wearing a house dress, her hair in curlers, her husband in a lawn chair on the red-painted stoop, shielding his eyes with a newspaper. It was a strange house, Hugh thought, and they seemed a strange couple. All the while the dog went on barking.

He had gotten a call earlier from Marion's lawyer, a man who was once a personal friend. Hugh thought he could hear Marion in the background and wondered if the lawyer and his wife had become lovers. He wanted an address. She was suing him for divorce. The lawyer had mentioned that his position at Equitable Life had been terminated.

Hugh dressed and went to get something to eat. At the coffee shop, he sat at the counter and ordered a turkey sandwich. It was the same waitress. She brought him the meatloaf instead then disappeared. He sat there looking at the plate. He got up and went to the men's room and saw her smoking in the back, talking to somebody on her cell phone. In the sunlight, he saw that her hair was red.

He spoke through the screen, "I didn't order that. You brought me the wrong thing."

She looked up, confused. "What? I can't hear you?"

"That meal. It wasn't what I ordered."

"I'm on my break." She turned her back on him, muttering into the phone.

When he returned to the counter he picked up the plate of meatloaf and dropped it on the floor. It made a loud sound and everybody stopped what they were doing and looked at him. He stood there a moment, gathering his thoughts. He walked out without paying, jerking the door, shaking up the sleigh bells along the side of it.

When he got back to the motel he saw a FOR RENT sign on the front lawn across the street. On an impulse, Hugh went over and rang the bell. The dog started to bark and growl as if it smelled something on Hugh it didn't like. The woman answered the door in her housecoat, unfazed, holding the dog like a parcel she wanted to mail without a return address. Now the dog was grimacing, baring its teeth, nudging him with its pointy wet snout. The woman had curlers in her hair, secured under a plastic shower cap. Thick tortoiseshell glasses rested on her rather prominent nose. Under the housecoat she wore support stockings and orthopedic shoes. As they walked past an open doorway Hugh saw the woman's husband sitting at a table having a meal, watching some routine catastrophe on TV. The woman took Hugh up the red-carpeted stairs to see the room. It was a furnished efficiency with the same red carpet and a Murphy bed and it smelled a little like bug spray. Still, it might work, he thought. For a little while anyway, "I'll take it," he told her.

That afternoon he went out and bought a computer and a printer, charging the items on his credit card, then stopped in a bookstore and bought the Leo Zaklos tapes to see what all the fuss was about. When he returned to the apartment he could hear his landlords bickering and the little dog torpedoed up the stairs after him and ran around his apartment in circles, yapping and shrieking with delight as Hugh tried in vain to catch it. Then it came in again and urinated on the carpet. Hugh was so incensed that he kicked it out into the hall. The landlord scooped the whimpering, mop-headed creature into her arms and gave Hugh a dirty look.

He set up his desk near the window and dug out his old screenplay, *The Adjuster*, determined to revise it. Going over the script, making notes in the margins with a number two pencil, he felt like a real writer, and he quickly concluded that the script he had sold to Cory Rogers wasn't any good, it had been beyond miraculous that he had sold it in the first place. Hedda Chase had been right. Philosophically, he understood that the thing he had done to her had been wrong, the result of some tragic compulsive neurosis or, even worse, some deep, unfounded sadness. And yet, he didn't really feel that bad about it. It was like something that had happened to him in a dream, not in real life, and when he thought about it from time to time, he tried to understand the lesson in it, tried to fathom the impending consequences, but he could not.

As the sun gently descended the façade of the motel across the street, Hugh poured his first drink. It was his little ritual. He had bought the whiskey around the corner from an Indian with a glass eye who made his wife work the register while he roamed the filthy linoleum floors, helping customers. The wife's eyes were green and spectacular, Hugh thought, although she had met his gaze only once and by accident. She only dressed in saris, some red, some green, gold. Hugh wondered if the owner and his wife thought he was an alcoholic; since his arrival in Los Angeles he'd made frequent visits to their shop, and he imagined the two of them discussing Hugh at home, trying to understand why he drank so much. Sometimes, Hugh felt guilty going in there, and he'd make up an excuse about why, again, he needed a bottle of whiskey, claiming that he was having a party. The wife would smile a little if her husband wasn't around. If you were a good customer, they lowered their eyes whenever they saw you, as though you were committing a royal sin. The wife would lower the bottle into the paper bag, symbolically, he thought, and try not to look at him when she handed him his change. Sometimes he would ask her a question so that she'd have to acknowledge him, something about the weather or the time, and he'd get a brief flash of recognition.

He took the drink to his desk and sat there, staring at the computer screen, at the words waiting for him. Something about the alcohol made him able to focus on his work. The images flushed into his mind like fresh cold water. After an hour of intense work, he felt drained, and lay on his bed, counting the tiny cracks in the ceiling. He thought about his days in the insurance business, what it had been like sitting at that desk with his boss looming over his shoulder. Then he thought about Hedda Chase, alone in the darkness of the trunk. Coming to terms with his crime was not easy for him. If she was dead, he thought, then she was haunting him, he sensed her presence everywhere he went.

He fell into a drowsy stupor and dreamed that the bed was floating. In the dream he sat up and looked down at the carpet, which had turned into a sea of blood. He woke in a cold sweat, hearing the bells of evening Mass, and ran into the bathroom, heaving into the toilet.

Maybe he was drinking too much after all.

Hugh called Tom Foster on his cell phone and asked if he could see him. "I need to talk to you about something."

"Sure, Hugh." Tom told him he was at an editing room in Burbank, with his friend Bruno Morelli. "Come on by," he said, and gave him directions.

It was a nondescript building with narrow corridors lit with long fluorescent tubes. Hugh roamed the hallways, poking his head through doors that were ajar, hearing the backward squeal of rewinding sound tape. Most of the editors looked sleepy, he thought. He found Tom in room number eleven, having a chopped corned beef sandwich that looked delicious. Bruno and the editor were watching something on the small screen. From what he could see of it, a woman wrapped in white cloth was being buried in sand up to her waist. She looked distraught. There were men standing around her, watching her with disgust, their hands curled in fists.

Hugh knocked lightly and Tom put down his sandwich, wiped his hands on a napkin, took a sip of his water, and came out into the hall.

"I thought you'd gone back east by now."

"I decided to stay for a while. I'm working on something with Ida Kent," he lied.

"Good for you," Tom said. "What's on your mind?"

"I've been thinking about Hedda. Any word?"

Tom shook his head. "They haven't found her car yet."

Hugh coughed. "I've been worried. I've really been worried sick."

"They're on it, my friend. They're all over it." Tom patted him on the back. "Appreciate your concern."

Hugh nodded. "Do they have any idea what happened?"

Tom nodded, gravely. "They think it has something to do with our film." He motioned over his shoulder into the editing room. "The previews went well, but we changed the ending. Now that she's gone missing. We want it to be accurate. We did it for her—for Fatima Kassim too."

"Who?"

"The girl who died in the fire. People should know," he said. "People should know what goes on."

Later that night a story about Chase's disappearance appeared on the news. Hugh flipped the channels, only to discover that every station was covering it. Suddenly, the whole town was talking about the missing producer, speculating what might have happened to her. Anyone who knew Chase was considered newsworthy and had been scrounged up for a two-minute interview on prime time. There was Armand, her supercilious, flounder-boned assistant in his tidy Arthur Gluck shirts, and the far less well-dressed

Harold Unger, who, like a recalcitrant turtle shrugged at the camera, gulping out each word as if he had swallowed a spoon. There were the people who called themselves her friends, who were interviewed on couches, in offices, kitchens, or outside with their dogs. Even Bruno Morelli, the famous director, was questioned on his terrace with his quartet of notorious bulldogs. It seemed like every time Hugh turned on the television there was some sort of story on the Chase Disappearance. Everyone had an opinion about what had happened to her; her car had not been found. They had pictures of the house on Lomita Avenue, roped off with police tape, the cops going through it. There was an interview with her neighbor, Mr. Romeo, standing on her lawn, he hadn't seen or heard anything. "She's a real nice lady, keeps to herself." Shaking his head, arms crossed over his chest. "This is a good neighborhood, quiet. We don't have any trouble here."

Like the complicated choreography of a dance, Hugh reviewed his actions inside her house, both on the occasion of the abduction and the second time, with Tom Foster. Foolishly, he'd drunk from a glass upon which he'd left behind his prints. Well, if they came to inquire he'd tell them that, yes, he'd been there. Of course he had. He and Tom had had a few drinks, waiting for Hedda to get home. They were all friends; what did they expect?

Hedda's parents were interviewed. They came from New Jersey, two elderly academics in Thanksgiving colors, they'd had their daughter late in life, they were now in their eighties. Psychiatrists by profession each had segued into teaching, the father a professor emeritus at Rutgers. Hedda, born Hedda Chastowsky, had grown up an only child in a wealthy suburb—of course he already knew all this. Her mother had named her after a character in a Henrik Ibsen play.

A day later, after the premiere of her film at Cannes, a rumor began to circulate that Chase had been abducted by Shiite terrorists. The film had instigated a protest. During the scene he had glimpsed in Bruno Morelli's editing room in which a woman—an adulteress—is stoned to death, people in the audience had thrown their programs at the screen. The FBI had been called. Charlie Rose did a show about the Muslim student, Fatima Kassim, who had, months before, brought the story on which the film was based to Tom Foster. The girl had been found dead in her dorm room. On the program, Tom and Bruno sat around the famous wooden table. They showed pictures of the girl when she was little, growing up in Iraq. They showed pictures of Baghdad before the invasion, and afterward. They showed pictures of the girl's mother, who had been killed in a car bombing on a street near her home. They interviewed the girl's aunt in Syria, who cried into a handkerchief. Hugh supposed it was possible—that what had happened to Hedda Chase was a form of political retaliation for her film. The fact that she was a woman—an extremely powerful woman—who'd been abruptly silenced, sent a certain message to people, one that, in this country anyway, inspired rage.

But it wasn't the truth.

And yet maybe the truth didn't matter anymore.

On Monday afternoon his cell phone rang. It was Tom. "You never told me about your script," he said.

"What?"

"The script you wrote. *The Adjuster.*"

Hugh hesitated. At length he said, "What about it?"

"I'm over in her office, poking around. Digging through stuff. Imagine my surprise finding it there."

"That old piece of crap? I'd forgotten I'd even sent it. Where'd you find it?"

"Buried in some file." Hugh could hear Tom flipping through the script. "What's it about?"

"It's about some asshole in the insurance business. It's crap. It's fucking embarrassing. Do me a favor, Tom. Trash it for me, will you? I don't want anyone seeing that garbage."

"I hear you," Tom said and hung up.

Hugh turned on the TV. He needed to think. So what he had found the script? It didn't prove anything.

He sat there staring at the screen. Another show was on about Hedda Chase and the film. Experts on Middle East relations were giving their opinions, and yet they were perplexed that none of the terrorist organizations had claimed responsibility for her disappearance, nor for the death of the girl, Fatima Kassim. Watching the coverage gave Hugh pause. It got him thinking.

He roared out loud with laughter. He roared and roared. The situation couldn't have been more perfect.

It came to him that he needed to start thinking like a terrorist.

The realization prompted Hugh to become an observer of life. He walked the sidewalks with his head down, his hands clasped behind his back. To imagine that he was partially responsible for all this hoopla thrilled him unspeakably; he felt superior. He had to wonder: What was it like fighting for something that was more important than your own survival? He found the subject compelling. To be willing to risk everything to make a political statement that would affect millions of lives. To sacrifice yourself in that way.

He found it awesome and inspiring.

As a result, he took a keener interest in the world around him. He had to stretch his mind beyond its usual mental boundaries. Watching things closely, analytically—scrutinizing the way people talked to one another in the street, the way they walked, their gestures. He became critical of the culture—the enormous billboards on Sunset Boulevard with their underwear ads—the way women dressed on the streets—the carelessness exhibited by the tourists. In a bar he lingered over a glass of beer, watching CNN on the television, images of the wars in Iraq and Afghanistan. He eavesdropped on a drunken couple who had begun to kiss, their sloppy tongues flashing. On a whim, he picked up a prostitute. He let her blow him in his car, in a supermarket parking lot. He put his head back against the seat, straining as if he were in pain. He shoved her head down. He held her there, hard, and threw the money at her afterward. She ran away from him, crying. *You'd better run,* he thought. He sought out a local mosque and attended a service. He removed his shoes and lingered in the back of the enormous space. It was interesting to him, hearing the chanting of prayer, watching the men fall to their knees all at once.

The public library had a row of computers with Internet access. You had forty minutes at a time. Hugh discovered a profusion of information about terrorism on the Web. Of course their methods were predictable, easy to simulate. What he realized about terrorism was simple; it was useful because it played on the worst fears of ordinary people. Fears that people had and didn't discuss. Fears that had become as routine as brushing your teeth. The fear of getting on a plane, because nobody really understood why it stayed up in the sky in the first place and there was always the very real possibility that it might crash, planes crashed all the time. The fear of getting into a taxi, that the driver might take you somewhere else and kill you. Every time you pulled out of your driveway there were certain odds that you'd get into an accident. Driving anywhere, on any road, at any time of the day or night could lead to your demise. Anyone you happened to meet, any stranger, could end up being your killer. You could step onto a bus, having left the dishes unwashed in your sink, and never see your apartment again. The more he thought about it, the more it made sense. Fear was the essential ingredient. And life, survival, became an arbitrary concept, like a squirrel crossing the road. Therefore, it would not be difficult to terrorize Bruno Morelli—the next logical target. It would not even be the slightest bit challenging to make it look like the work of some extremist Muslim organization, the members of which had the same fundamental beliefs as any honorable patriot: a devotion to their country and their God.

Just before midnight, he drove over to Ida Kent's and knocked on her door. "What do you want?" she asked, without opening it.

"Can't we talk?"

She seemed to hesitate, but then let him in. The TV droned in the other room, another report about Chase; he caught a glimpse of her publicity photograph, the same one they used every time. Ida stood there waiting to see what he had to say.

"I'm sorry about the other night," he said. "I wasn't myself. I was thinking it might have had something to do with hitting my head at Foster's party. Those painkillers maybe."

"Is it better?"

"What?"

"Your head."

"It still hurts."

"Let me see it." He sat down in a chair and she stood over him, looking at his head like a mother, gently pushing the hair aside to see the wound, her breasts grazing his chin.

"I'm getting divorced," he told her.

"Should we celebrate?"

She opened a bottle of wine and they sat at her tiny kitchen table drinking it. She smoked a cigarette, tapping the ashes into a clamshell.

"I didn't know you smoked."

"There's a lot you don't know about me."

"Did I tell you I play the piano?"

"I think you may have mentioned it. Are you any good?"

He nodded, suddenly distressed.

She reached out and took his hand. "My neighbor has one. Do you feel like showing me?"

She took him next door to her neighbor's apartment. The neighbor was away performing an opera somewhere; Ida was feeding her cat. "There."

The upright piano was in a small alcove, piled up with books of music. He sat down at the piano and began to play. First he played a nocturne. But really Brahms was the only thing to play at a time like this. He played a section from the Rhapsody in B Minor, something he'd been practicing before he'd left home. He could feel the chords coming up through his fingers, the dark vibration rushing up his wrists. The whole time he could feel Ida's presence, watching him. Maybe she would understand something new about him, he thought. Maybe she would forgive him for all that he was not. At least he hoped she would. At one point he realized that his hands were wet. He hadn't even realized he was crying. That was all right, he supposed, a little water wouldn't hurt the keys.

She let him sleep there. She held him in her arms. "Let me hold you," she said in a soothing voice, as though he were ill. She held him with great care and tenderness. He didn't deserve it. Her affection rendered him useless.

In the morning, he left without waking her. He drove out to the beach and lay in the sand, under the shy white sun. It came to him that he had lost everything: his wife, his home, his job, his dignity. On the other hand, he had nothing left to lose. Nothing at all.

PART FIVE

FINALE

16

"We lived in her car," Daisy says, her voice groggy, a little drunk. "It broke down a lot."

The road is dark, no streetlamps, and the moon is low. Nothing out there but sand.

"What kind of car was it?"

"Some piece of crap. All rusted out. We didn't have much. My mother was an escape artist."

"What do you mean?"

"She could steal something right off your body, you wouldn't even know it."

"That's a talent."

"People were nice to us. She didn't even care. She'd take anything that wasn't nailed down."

He doesn't know what to say to this.

"I used to get my shoes from the church. They had this bin of shoes they'd put out on Sundays. You had to sit there first for the service. You shoulda seen people goin' through those shoes. Sometimes they fit, sometimes they didn't. Sometimes I got blisters."

"Where's your mother at now?"

"Don't know."

"Why'd you leave?"

"She got a boyfriend. I used to call him Mr. Slick. He used to put this cream on his hair, stunk up the whole car. He was vain as a woman. Anyway,

206 | ELIZABETH BRUNDAGE

he tried to touch me, you know?" She goes real quiet. Tears roll down her cheeks. Then she clams up, twists away, looks out at the darkness.

He reaches over and puts his hand on her back and her eyes close again. For a moment he watches her sleep, capturing a dream, and he feels content. He's tired too, but he can't sleep now. That would be a mistake. They have to keep moving. Just as soon as he can he needs to open that trunk and deal with what's inside.

One way or another, he'll figure it out. You'd get this feeling in the war, like you can deal with things. Just about anything. You have to, you have no choice. Either deal with it, or be done. This part now, this part *right now* is just a brief period of time. It's going to end pretty soon and the leading up part doesn't matter all that much, just so long as he can be with her. That's all he wants. There's an ending in sight and he knows it, he has come to terms with it.

Ten minutes to five and it's still dark, as if the sky's been filled in with pencil. A strange time, he thinks, neither day nor night, but somewhere in between. Like the way he feels in his life an awful lot of the time. Like he's waiting, been waiting a long time. If he didn't know any better, he'd think he was back in Iraq. The same two-lane highway splitting the desert in half. The same dull fear in his belly. Once, he'd seen some Bedouin women danc-ing in a circle, braiding the open space with their legs and arms, but it had been very hot that day and he thought he may have imagined the dancing and singing, the joy. The heat could play tricks on you. You saw things and wondered if they were real.

He had said some things to Daisy about the war, what it had done to him. Nobody ever wanted to hear his stories, but she just sat there, listening. She was someone you could cry with. She didn't make any judgments. She had said, "You're wearing that war like a favorite shirt. Maybe it's about time you took it off."

Wise beyond her years, that's how he would describe her. Plays the har-monica, says her grandpa taught her when she was little, before things went wrong. She's pretty good at it, too. Even knows some Bob Dylan. She let him try it once, the metal still warm from her lips only he sounded like a car horn or a sick goose. She just laughed and showed him how It felt good, blowing into something that made music come out, but it reminded him of something else, too—the day Ross died and he'd tried to give him mouth to mouth. *Take my breath, man, breathe!*

But it hadn't done any good. He could deal out his ghosts like a hand of cards, a losing hand. He tries not to think about it because it doesn't make them go away. The memories are scary. They make his eyes tear. Sometimes, she'll look over at him and asks him what's wrong, and he just says, "Nothing." Because what's the point? Sometimes, he gets a feeling. Like God is right there. *What do You want from me now?* he thinks. *Prepare to be deployed to the gates of Hell!* If there's one thing he knows it's this: No matter how good a soldier he was over there, no matter how justified, no matter that he was just following orders, he's still going to hell when he dies. There's no getting around it. 'Cause killing is against the rules.

"What's that noise?"

"What noise?"

"That."

"I don't hear anything," he says, lamely.

"Listen. *That.*"

He glances over at her. She's sitting up tall in her seat, listening intently. "I think there's something in there."

"What?"

"An animal or something. I *hear* something."

It's too late to lie so he says, "I know. I hear it too."

"What is it?"

He looks over at her and can see her fear.

She says, as if she already knows, as if his answer doesn't matter, "There's somebody in there, isn't there?"

"It's not what you're thinking."

All at once, she moves toward the door and gathers her things. "Stop the car."

"What?"

"Stop this car right now."

He pulls over. Before he's even come to a stop she's out, holding her bag, walking alongside the empty road with her thumb out. Not that there are any cars at this hour, Sunday at the crack of dawn.

"Daisy! What the hell are you doing?"

"Leave me alone."

"Daisy!"

"I'm going back to L.A."

"What?"

"I knew this was a mistake."

"Honey, wait. I can explain."

"I trusted you."

He catches up to her, takes her hand. "Good, you should. You should trust me."

"What's in there?"

"I swear I don't know." He raises his hand like a pledge.

"It's your car, isn't it?"

"Actually, no. No, it's not."

"It's not your car?"

He shakes his head, apologetically. "I stole it."

"You stole that car?"

"Yes, ma'am. I'm sorry I lied. I didn't think you'd go with me if I told you."

She mulls this over. "You stole a car with a body in it?"

"I think so." He looks at her. "Just my luck."

"What are we gonna do now?"

"Get 'em out. Only the lock's busted. You don't got a knife, do you?"

"No."

"We need a crowbar, then."

"We better hurry up and find one."

Back on the road she gets quiet. He can see the child in her face. She doesn't trust him now. Trust is the whole deal in life, he thinks. Something he learned in the war. Without it you have nothing. Trusting somebody with your life is a big deal.

"Hey," he says, and she looks at him and smiles and he is grateful for the smile.

This is the desert. The road is empty. Nothing on it. No strip malls, no gas even. They are like the last people on the planet. Just the sand, the distant canyons. The gritty light. Daisy puts her hand on his leg and he feels like the bad thoughts from before have disappeared.

About ten miles from Death Valley, a cop pulls out behind them. Except for a couple of semis screaming past there's nobody else on the road.

"Fuck."

Daisy turns around. "He's coming. He's got his lights on." Her voice is screechy, like a violin. "What do you think he wants?"

"I have to stop." He glances at her. "Stay cool."

"I'm sorry about before. Okay?"

He nods at her with his heart beating. It makes him sick and a little crazy, how much he loves her right now. "Yeah, okay."

He pulls onto the shoulder and rolls down the window. The cop gets out, saunters up. Denny watches him in the side mirror as he adjusts his hat. The cop leans over, looking into the car. "License and registration."

Denny takes out his wallet. Everything seems real slow. He can feel them both watching him, the cop and Daisy. She sits there ready to spring like a boney stray cat. He takes out his license and opens the glove box and sifts around in the junk. "It's not here," he tells the cop. "I must have misplaced it, officer."

"Is the car insured?"

"Yes, sir," Denny tells him.

"Sure is a nice car," the cop says leisurely. "She's real fine."

"Yes, sir."

The cop stands back up, squinting at something in the distance. D follows his gaze and sees the empty road, the wavering heat, the su bright sunshine. The cop glances at Denny's license, then steps away from the car and starts walking around it, taking a good look at Daisy as he rounds her side. She shifts her hips, pulling her dress down over her thighs. Then the cop gives him a look, trying to figure out how some lowlife hood like Denny fits into this picture.

"Fuck," Denny mutters, watching the cop walk back toward the trunk. "This isn't good." The cop stands there, looking down at the trunk with a curious expression on his face. *Fuck, this is it. Fuck.*

The cop comes back to his window. "What all are you carrying?"

"Sir?"

"In your trunk."

"Nothing special."

"Step out of the car for me."

"What?"

"Get out."

The cop is middle-aged, around the same age as his uncle Hector. Denny figures he has a wife and kids at home. Pulling him over was a mistake, but the cop doesn't know it yet.

"Go," she whispers.

"I'm going." He gets out.

The cop leans backward on his heels, listening again to what's coming from the trunk. "Step over here." He motions him over to the trunk. "Do you hear that?"

"Yes, sir. I hear it, sir."

"Would you mind telling me what that is?"

"It sounds like somebody's in there."

"Yes, it does, doesn't it? Do you want to tell me what somebody is doing in your trunk?"

"No, sir."

"You want to be smart with me, boy?"

"I'm not sure, is what I meant to say. It's not my car."

"Whose car is it?"

"I don't know, sir."

"Are you saying you stole it?"

"I borrowed it."

"Who's the girl?"

Denny thinks for a minute. "My sister."

But the cop frowns, dissatisfied. "I'm gonna have to ask you to put your hands on the car." He pats the roof of the car and steps behind Denny to search him. Denny weighs his options. No way in hell he's going anywhere with this cop. It's not like he wants to hurt him, but he doesn't see he has any other choice. Muscle memory kicks in and his body starts to move. He is a well-trained soldier, a *warrior*. He is not to be fucked with. He whirls around so fast the cop doesn't have time to get his face out of the way. The cop reels back and staggers, blood gushing out of his nose, doubling over. "Son of a bitch."

Moving quick, Denny opens the door of the cruiser and rips out the cop's radio; just fucking yanks it right out of the dash. Then he gets back into his car and pulls out. In his rearview mirror, he sees the cop hobbling to the cruiser, his hands full of blood. Denny's a good five hundred yards ahead, but the cop pulls out quick to catch up, turning on his siren. Maybe the buzzards hear it, Denny thinks, flooring the pedal, thinking how you couldn't drive fast in the war, it wasn't possible. They drove in convoys slow as elephants. Dump trucks; tanks; Humvees; heavy diesel trucks. The tanks were sluggish and dumb. You didn't get out of any place in a hurry. But this car is fast—it's a machine. Watching the needle hit 120 fills him with a mad excitement. He's never driven this fast before and it's like a fucking airplane, like they're about to take off. Daisy is laughing nervously, clutching the seat, leaning back like a kid on a roller coaster. The cop has balls, he has to admit, and the next time Denny looks in the mirror the cruiser's up on his tail. It smacks into his bumper, draws back, then rams up and does it again. Denny hits the gas, but the car won't go any faster, and there's something about the physics of the situation that pulls the cars together. The cruiser hits him again and the trunk flies open. It flaps up and down like the wing of some enormous bi

There's a stop sign up ahead. No way in hell he's stopping. Instead, he twists the wheel and drives off the road, onto the sand—a whole ocean of it—and the cop turns too. The cars stir up the dirt and sand, clouds of it, and he can't see very well, and he would bet the cop can't see either. Sweat rolls off his forehead, into his eyes. It burns. He wipes it on his arm, but it just keeps coming. The car heaves and lurches over low brush, shrubs. Jackrabbits flee and scatter. Not too far ahead is a barn, a trailer off to the side, a pickup truck. Some bad thoughts find their way into his head. Like sometimes when they killed civilians. There was never any point except you were already there, collateral damage and whatnot. To finish things off and make everything quiet. He just wishes things were quiet now.

A glare cuts across the windshield. Through the dust a barn materializes. Someone's shirts on the line, bouncing like ghosts. He drives right through them, heading straight for the barn.

"You're gonna crash, Denny, you're gonna hit that barn!"

At the last second he veers off to the side of it, scraping the corner of the barn with his rear fender, creating just enough of an angle to send the cruiser headlong into it, timbers falling across its hood. Dust and smoke. Feathers.

Daisy screams, jumping around in her seat. Denny pulls the car behind the barn, where no one will see it from the road, and cuts the engine. "Just hold on now," he says, gently. "Just stay calm."

Slow motion, like he's under water, like nothing's real. He reaches under the seat for his gun, loads the clip. The sight of the gun frightens her. She shouldn't be here, he thinks, not now. Another mistake that's going to catch up with you. Just like everything else catches up. After a while there's no escape, you've been designated by the higher powers, you're fucking toast. His throat goes tight and he sucks in some air. Stay cool, soldier. "Wait here," he tells her, and she curls up on the seat, shaking, and nods. He gets out. Slowly, he sidles up to the barn, listening. Silence. Dead chickens. Splattered chicken blood. More feathers. The cop is bent over the wheel, blood pour-ng out from some place. Could be dead, Denny thinks. Just slap another felony on, see if I care. Let them come looking. Doesn't matter now. It's not like he meant to kill this fucking guy. "Fuck, this is one hell of a mess." He moves up close to the car. Cop's not moving, but he's breathing. "You'll live," he whispers.

At least he isn't dead. Knocked out pretty good, but not dead. Big difference.

Distantly, he remembers the dead in Iraq. You have to respect the dead, even the ones you kill. During an invasion, death is intoxicating. For a period of time, you subsist on it like some freak drug in your bloodstream. It's a hard thing to explain. Primal maybe. This mission to kill. You get this energy inside you, like a thousand volts. It's not something you can talk to people about. Nobody wants to hear it. But then afterward. The intense quiet. The aftermath of a massacre—an almost immaculate silence. And the orderly blessings for the dead that follow. It brings about a change. The whole mess of it over and done with. And then you're out, and everything's different, your body, your volume, your weight, the light, sounds—everything—just different.

But the cop—he's alive. Time to go.

By now Daisy has gotten out of the car and is bent over the trunk looking at what's in it. "She's alive, Denny."

It's a woman, a scrawny thing, reaching out for him. "Holy fucking Christ."

The woman's eyes flare with terror.

"It's all right. I ain't gonna hurt you."

"Someone's coming."

Across the dirt yard, a man in coveralls comes out of the trailer with a rifle. He calls out, "Hey! Whatchu doin' on my land?"

Denny's leg starts to hurt. The ghost hole, he calls it. Let him come, he thinks, examining her bloody wrists, pulling the tape off her ankles. "I'll tell you what," he says gently, "you are one brave lady." She's trembling all over, glistening with sweat, burning up with fever. He lifts her out of the trunk and tries to set her down, but she goes limp as a rag doll and passes out. "C

that door," he tells Daisy, and, glad to be useful, she does what he asks. With
some effort, he eases the woman onto the seat, walks around to the other side,
opens the opposite door and pulls her flat. "She needs water."

Daisy hands him her water bottle and he cradles the woman's head and
tries to get her to drink, but she's out of it and it just drips down her chin.
"She's in bad shape. We need to get her to a doctor."

"You ain't goin' no place." The old man addresses them from behind his
rifle. "Get your hands where I can see 'em."

"Simmer down, old man."

"Whatchu all doin' out here on my land? Ain't you seen that no trespass-
ing sign?"

"We had an accident is all. You might want to call an ambulance. There's
a wounded man in your barn. Get in the car, darlin'." He watches the girl get
in the car. "It would be a real friendly gesture if you'd lower your rifle."

"Get your hands up in the air." The old man has a wormy face and mean
little eyes. Denny ignores him and gets into the car and starts the engine. "I
said: *Hold it right there!*"

Denny shifts into drive and pulls out toward the road. They need to put
some distance in before that cop wakes up. Next thing he knows there's a
sound—*loud*—and the car lurches. The old fucker's blown out a tire. Before
he can do anything to stop him, he blows out another. And another after
that. Now Denny's pissed; he slams into park and gets out. "What in hell
are you doing?"

The old man fires again. Denny feels the bullet whizzing past his shoulder. He's been shot once, it's not gonna happen a second time, especially
not here, not now. He lunges at the man, gets him on the ground. They roll
around in the dirt and it's like wrestling with a rabid cat, the old man's fragile bones, brittle whiskers—only takes one punch to knock him out. Old
geezer's not so tough after all. Denny hands Daisy the rifle. "Hold onto this
[fo]r me, darlin'."

[N]ext he drags the old man over to the trailer, up the steps, pulls him inside
[t]he linoleum floor. The old man moans, starts to come around. Denny

hits him again, out cold. He looks around the place. To his surprise, there's a woman in the bed, sleeping, hooked up to an oxygen tank. Sick. Something grips his belly, remorse. He yanks opens drawers, looking for some rope, finds an extension cord, uses that. Ties up the old man. He ain't goin' nowhere. Then he stands over the wife a moment, listening to her snore. Pills on the night stand, drugs, sleeping pills, syringes for insulin. White hair scrambled on the pillow. A shriveled sickly thing, yellow as an onion. Taped to the oxygen tank is some extra tubing. That'll do just fine, he thinks, and takes it, grabs a handful of syringes. Next he opens the fridge, looks around. Not much there. Christ, what do these people eat? But he finds what he needs: baking soda, a bottle of Coke, and in the cabinets some sugar and salt. He dumps out the Coke in the sink and washes out the bottle. Only thing else he needs is sterile water. None here. No telling where there's a pharmacy around. He finds a pot, fills it with water, turns on the stove.

"What the hell are you doing in there?" Daisy asks, coming inside, looking around with alarm. "You didn't shoot him, did you?"

"No, I didn't shoot him. The most he'll have is a headache. A bad one."

"What's on the stove?"

"Boiling some water."

"What for?"

"Sterile water. For the woman. She'll die if we don't get some fluid into her. Do me a favor, will you? Keep your eye on that pot. Boil it good. Then put it in the fridge to cool. I'll be back in a minute."

"What'll I do if he wakes up?"

"Hit him with something."

On his way out, he takes the keys to the old man's pickup.

On its one good tire, Denny drives the BMW back around behind the barn where it was before. He takes out the keys, the old rabbit's foot, and puts them in his pocket. He's going to miss this damn car.

The woman in the back isn't moving and if he didn't know any better he'd think she was dead.

Moving quickly, he runs back over to the old man's truck and gets in and pulls it around to behind the barn and up alongside the car, then goes around and opens the passenger door. Then he gets the woman out of the car and carries her over to the truck and sets her down real gentle on the seat. "You're gonna be all right," he tells her. "I'm gonna fix you up. You ain't dying on my watch, so don't get any ideas."

This one time a car had exploded on a Baghdad street, a young girl had been hit. She lay there, unconscious, but he could see she was alive—a sniper someplace shooting at anything that moved. Still, he couldn't leave her there. So he ran in and got her just seconds before some asshole tossed a mortar, blew the shit out of the whole street.

He didn't like to brag, but saving that girl had made his day.

Out on the road, an eighteen-wheeler roars past, reminding him to hurry up.

He gets back in the truck, drives up to the trailer, and goes back inside. Like a good little nurse, Daisy takes the pot out of the fridge. He adds the salt and sugar, the baking soda, and pours the mix into the Coke bottle, seals it tight with the cap. Then he pours the remaining liquid into some freezer bags to take along for the ride. Using the extra tubing he found, he attaches a syringe to either end of it, then pierces the bottle with the needle, fashioning an IV. "It'll have to do."

They go out to the truck. The woman's wearing a skirt, which makes it easy. He pushes the needle into her thigh and tapes it down with some masking tape. They stand there a moment, watching the fluid slowly drain down. Satisfied, he tells Daisy to get into the truck. The girl climbs up onto the seat and he hands her the bottle. "I got it," she says importantly, holding it up.

"You sure you can hold it?"

"Yeah, I can hold it."

"Keep a little pressure on it."

"Okay."

Finally, they can leave this place—and none too soon. Through his rearview mirror, he sees the cop staggering out of the barn into the light, wiping the blood out of his eyes.

Denny drives the truck across the desert, back up to the road. The heat is dense and thick, the air wobbles. Dust engulfs the truck like the smoke of a grenade. He pulls through it and in a few seconds the whole place is in a big cloud of dirt—the trailer, the barn—it all disappears behind them and he can almost believe it doesn't even exist.

17

In a barber's chair on Olympic Boulevard, Hugh catches the news about Bruno Morelli. An airport employee had found him in an American Airlines cargo bin earlier that morning, bound at the hands and feet, with a burlap sack over his head tied around the neck with a piece of rope—the employee described Morelli's condition when he'd taken off the sack as "barely breathing." *The victim, a film director whose controversial film* Oath of Allegiance *has just been released in theaters, was rushed to Cedars Sinai Hospital where he remains in stable condition.*

Talk about exaggeration. Hugh had chosen the burlap so Bruno *wouldn't* have trouble breathing. The famous director had been a big weepy baby and had shit his pants—they didn't tell you *that* on CNN.

Hugh admits that using the knife had been a little excessive. And *he'd* been the one having trouble breathing. He'd been sweating bullets in that ski mask. Hugh had been waiting for him outside the garage of his Laurel Canyon home. When Bruno's car had pulled in, and the electric garage door opened like a curtain on a stage, Hugh had ducked inside. When Morelli got out of his car, Hugh had assaulted him with a gardening shovel. He guessed he'd beat him up pretty badly. Once he'd disabled him, it was easy for Hugh to carry out the rest of his plan. Right there in the garage, he'd tied Morelli's hands and feet, and covered his head with a shroud he'd sewn himself out of burlap, purchased at a fabric store on Sepulveda.

Miles Beck had suggested the restaurant, what Hugh construed as a hole-in-the-wall Cuban café in Culver City. When he'd called Beck's office and left a message with the secretary that he was in town and wanted to meet, Beck's secretary had him spell his name twice, giving the impression that she didn't remember who he was even though they both knew she did. Hugh takes a booth near the window. The booths are crummy red vinyl. Hugh's seat is slashed and the foam guts are bursting out. Beck is late. It's raining. People come in, shaking off the rain, fussing with their umbrellas. He watches the people at the tables. A group of women who might be secretaries. Two men in suits, their cell phones vibrating on the table, making the salt and pepper shakers shimmy. At last the agent appears in a long, sloppy raincoat. He's older than Hugh had pictured, late sixties, built stout around the middle, with short arms and legs. On his feet is a pair of rubber galoshes, the old-fashioned kind his own father used to wear. Hugh stands up and shakes his hand and they sit down and rifle through their menus. The agent glances around the small café like he's already bored. His expression seems to say: *There's nobody important here.* Hugh has brought his notes for his new script, *Company Man.* In truth, he is rather proud of it. It is a story about a man who works at an insurance agency who makes a pass at a girl who is so desperate for his job that she unjustly accuses him of sexual harassment. The whole ordeal plays havoc on the man's life, his marriage. His wife leaves him. Desperate for work, he takes a job as an orderly in a hospital, where he comes to understand, firsthand, the destruction of the health care industry. He falls in love with a young woman who suffers from a rare disease, the cure for which is not covered by her insurance provider—his old company. The person in charge of her benefits is the woman who'd stolen his job; eventually she gets fired. In the end, he convinces his old company to give the woman the operation, but it is too late, she dies. The dead woman's mother sues the agency for millions of dollars and wins.

Beck is pleasantly surprised by the pitch and tells Hugh to send the script as soon as it's ready. For a few lovely moments, Hugh feels like things are looking up, and he can almost believe he will find success. But when he gets back to the apartment, Tom Foster is waiting for him outside the building, wearing an outsized raincoat like a man in disguise. Tom isn't himself.

Disheveled and unshaven, he could be mistaken for a street person. "You don't look so good, Tom."

"I need a favor," he says.

"Of course."

They go up to the apartment. The rain comes down hard and it makes a nice sound. "Sorry, the place is a mess. It's only temporary."

Tom looks around uneasily, but says, "I used to live in a place like this."

"It's pretty basic, I guess."

"I think I'm being followed. I don't know, maybe I'm paranoid, but after what happened to Bruno I can't be sure. First Hedda, now Bruno. I'm next. I sent my wife back to Rome today. Did I tell you she's pregnant?"

"No. That's good news, Tom. Congratulations."

"I was wondering: Can I stay here? Nobody knows you," he says, then adds apologetically, "I mean, nobody knows about this place."

"Sure, Tom." *Don't worry, I'm not insulted. I know I'm a nobody. It's all right; I'm used to it.* "Of course, you can stay here."

"Just for a few days. I'll make it up to you."

"It's no problem at all," Hugh says. "Make yourself at home."

They get drunk together and watch *The Battle of Algiers* on Hugh's DVD player, Gillo Pontecorvo's 1966 classic about the Algerian War of Independence. He had borrowed the film from the library.

"No different than today," Tom remarks. "How strange is that?"

Hugh drinks in the grainy images. He is inspired by the passion of the Arabs fighting for their independence—their violent tactics no different from the insurgents in Iraq. Even the women have an impact, replacing their robes with Western dresses, filling their pretty pocketbooks with bombs to leave in European cafes. There are checkpoints and curfews, random bombings. Murders in the street. It is all too familiar, he thinks. Again, he wonders what it would feel like to care about something so deeply. To have the courage to risk everything for freedom, even your own life. With pride, he thinks of his convincing charade with Bruno Morelli and laughs a little out loud. These Hollywood people aren't as smart as they think.

"What's so funny?" Tom asks.

"Nothing," Hugh apologizes. "Nothing at all."

When they run out of whiskey, Hugh takes Tom to the store around the corner. The Indian woman flashes her eyes at Tom. Hugh can tell she's glad to see them, glad he has brought his friend. Tom buys the whiskey. "Come again," the woman says in broken English, handing Tom the bag.

They walk in the rain. The rain comes down hard. The little dog barks inside the landlord's apartment, sniffing and growling behind the door. The smell of the landlady's cooking seeps out. It is a strong, familial smell. It reminds him of his grandmother's cooking, when he'd been made to live with her for that year after his mother's breakdown.

Inside the apartment, Hugh turns on the TV and pours the drinks. The rain hammers on the roof. There are mudslides in Malibu. People's homes are at risk. A story comes on about Bruno Morelli, the famous director who'd been abducted by terrorists. "This whole thing is really getting out of hand," Tom says. "I'm not sure I would have written the script if I'd known this would happen."

"You wrote it because you wanted people to know. Because you thought it was wrong."

"Yes," he said. "Yes, that's true. But it's only one side of it. It's only one story. You can't possibly cover the whole war, from all points of view. Like the Algiers film. You side with the Arabs. They are portrayed as peaceful people in a desperate situation. It all depends on how the information is presented. I suppose we could even make a film that makes stoning a woman to death look like a reasonable punishment. It all depends on whose side you're on and what you're trying to accomplish."

"Film as propaganda," Hugh says. "Is that what you're saying?"

"To some degree, all media is a form of propaganda—films, the news, even advertising. It can't be helped."

"But your film is doing well." *Thanks to me.* Hugh can't help feeling a little responsible for the film's success. His "terrorist" acts have boosted ticket sales.

"I don't give a damn about the film," Tom shouts. He puts his face in his hands. "I'm sorry—I just can't stop thinking about her, wondering where she is, what's happened to her, if she's all right—if she's even alive. I don't sleep, I don't eat. We were close. I was in love with her." He shakes his head, wipes his tears. "I feel responsible. I feel like it's my fault."

"Have faith," he hears himself say. "Faith is important at times like these."

They have another drink. Slurring, Tom apologizes for shouting earlier.

"I understand," Hugh assures him. "You're under enormous stress."

Hugh turns off the TV and pulls down the Murphy bed. They remove their street clothes and climb onto the crummy mattress in their undershorts and T-shirts. Like brothers, they lie side by side. Tom lights a cigarette; Hugh wishes he wouldn't smoke in bed, but doesn't say anything.

"My wife filed for divorce," he shares the news with Tom, eager for a little sympathy.

"I'm sorry to hear that. It's what you wanted, though, isn't it?"

Hugh nods, but he's not really sure what he wants anymore; he's not sure about anything at all. "I was involved with Ida Kent."

"That writer?" Tom snickers. "I hear she gets around."

"What?"

"She's seeing Leo now."

The news comes as a surprise.

"They met at my party."

"Zaklos is a slob," Hugh says.

"A well-connected one," Tom clarifies. "In this town that makes all the difference."

Hugh looks over at him, a soggy feeling in his stomach. He feels like he's been punched. It's weird having Tom here, sharing the bed. At length he says, "Can you sleep? I'm sorry there's just this one bed."

"Yeah, I can sleep."

"Good night, then."

"Good night."

But Hugh is wide awake. He looks over at Tom's sleeping face. It's raining again and shadows spill down his face, his wide lips, his square chin, and across the sheets. Tom's face is rugged, used-up, battered. He is a man who has experienced life, Hugh thinks, a man who has seen the edge.

Unbelievably, he feels himself getting aroused.

Unable to fall back to sleep, he retreats to the bathroom and sits on the edge of the tub and begins to weep. He doesn't understand why he's weeping. He thinks of Ida Kent and feels betrayed. He had felt something for her. Something deep and complex. That night in the motel, they'd crossed the line. They'd gone to another place. The unseen barrier between them had come down. They were just two bodies, two human beings; one male, one female. He'd had control of her. It was brutal; animalistic. Even though she'd complained, he'd sensed she wanted it; she'd wanted to be possessed. Women lie, they can't help themselves, it's in their DNA. Every last fucking one of them lies. You never really know what they're thinking, but they've always got a plan. Calculating bitches. Whores! He touches himself a little bit and then more and more. Just as he's about to come, he hears the door of the apartment gently closing. Had Tom seen him? No, the bathroom door is shut. No, he couldn't possibly have seen. Still, he feels intensely embarrassed. His penis throbs. He pulls on his robe and hurries out into the hallway where Tom has started down the stairs. The dog begins to bark. "Tom," he says, and Tom turns, a strange, perplexed expression on his face. "What's wrong? Where are you going?"

"I have to go. I'm sorry."

"In this weather?"

"I'm afraid it can't be helped."

"Okay," Hugh says gently, a little hurt. "But come back if you need anything."

Tom hurries out through the front vestibule. The landlady steps out into the hallway and looks up at Hugh with a confused expression. "Lovers' quarrel?" she says, and laughs her awful laugh. Back in his apartment, Hugh glances out the window and sees Tom, wrapped in the raincoat, rushing down the sidewalk on his cell phone. Soon he is obscured by the falling rain, the glaring streetlights. Hugh sits on the edge of his bed, feeling a rush of self-loathing. On the desk, the clock reads 3:20 a.m. That's when he notices the letter. He'd fished it out of his file before his meeting with Miles Beck and had forgotten to put it back. It was the letter Beck's secretary had faxed to him, the letter Hedda Chase had written on Gladiator letterhead explaining why they were dumping his movie. There were other things there too about Hedda, the information he'd found about her online that he'd copied and put into his file. And there was a picture that he'd taken of her through the window of her house.

Leaving the file on the desk had been a foolish mistake. It's likely Tom had seen it.

Perhaps the cops will come, he thinks, glancing at the clock. The sky is dark. The rain falls hard. He knows he should go—just to be safe—pack his things and get out, but for some reason he doesn't. He doesn't really feel like going anywhere. So what that Tom saw the letter, it doesn't mean anything really. There are probably dozens of disgruntled writers out there who despise Hedda Chase. And as far as his little file on her goes, they're "friends"—why shouldn't he have a photo of her? Was it so unusual that he'd copied a few articles about her career off the Internet? No, he doesn't think so. It's not something they can condemn him for.

He looks at himself in the mirror, dissatisfied by his reflection, the stubble on his cheeks. Presentation is everything right now, he realizes. A certain degree of professionalism is required, the same sort of generic, weary banality that he'd projected on the floors of Equitable Life. As he shaves, he listens to the radio. Remotely, he hears the end of the news: *Chase's car was found at a small ranch a few miles from Death Valley National Park in Nevada. The producer, whose film opens nationwide this week, has not yet been found. Local authorities are investigating the car and the surrounding area.*

Blood splatters in the sink and he feels a sting of pain. He dabs the cut with tissue and tosses the razor into the sink.

The rain continues to fall. The rain is glorious. Its reckless beauty floods the streets. It makes people honest, Hugh thinks, it stirs them sober. The road up the canyon is slippery. Mud runs down the hills into the street. The house juts out, a glistening cube of wet glass. A light burns in the window. The sight of Tom's jeep parked in the carport fills him with relief. They'll talk to each other like civilized men, he thinks. They'll figure it out.

Hugh parks and gets out. The rain pummels his back, a cold rain bleeding through his shirt, making him shiver. He peers through the glass door. Suitcases in the hall. Tom's raincoat draped over the couch. Tom comes around the corner, something rolled up in his hand. A script, Hugh realizes. Tom glares at him, tosses the script on the counter. Hugh knocks on the glass.

Tom frowns, shakes his head, but the door is open and Hugh walks in.

"Not now, Hugh."

"Look," he says, "we need to talk."

"It's too late."

"Calm down, Tom. We can talk about this. You've got the wrong idea. I can explain."

"Tell it to the police."

"I thought we were friends, Tom."

Tom grins unhappily, shaking his head, and mutters, "God, you're sick."

"What did you say?"

"It didn't actually make sense until I saw Hedda's letter. Then I came back here and read your script." Tom puts on his raincoat. He shakes his head. "They found her car; you'd better hope she's still alive."

Hugh stands there a moment, trying to think. "I don't know what you're talking about."

"I'm talking about the woman I love." Tom looks at him, his eyes grim with disapproval. "Now if you'll excuse me I have a plane to catch."

Hugh takes out his gun, the same gun he'd used on Hedda Chase, only this time it's loaded. "You're not going anywhere." He grabs Tom's arm and pulls him outside.

"What are you going to do, kill me now?"

"Outside."

"This is a mistake," Tom says. "You shouldn't be doing this."

"Move."

They step out into the rain. It is just getting light, the sky white, bleak. The world is a dazzling blur. Tom walks ahead of him. He's a big man, walking slowly. Methodically. Trying to stall, Hugh thinks. As they cross the pool deck Tom swings around and hits him in the face, jerks back Hugh's arm. Hugh drops the gun and it skids across the stones. He loses his balance and falls back and Tom goes down on top of him. Tom's weight is powerful. They roll around on the ground, hitting each other, the rain beating down on their backs, their faces, making it impossible to grasp one another.

Tom hits him in the face—Hugh rams Tom's forehead—Tom shoves him down toward the pool, the black water inches from his head. Hugh smells the chlorine, blinks the rain out of his eyes. He needs to cough, but Tom is choking him, his hands around his throat. Tom is going to kill him unless he does something. Some deeper strength is required, some kind of power that he doesn't know he has—something from deep inside of him that has always been there, waiting for a moment like this, some primal force, and he rips Tom's hands off his throat and shoves his knee into his groin. Now the air pulses through him, the sweet wet air, and he gains the upper hand. Tom may be bigger, stronger, but he is less agile, clumsy even, and Hugh rolls him onto his back and straddles him, pushing his head under the water, pushing his head down with both hands, pushing it deeper as Tom weakens, and holding it there until he no longer resists.

Hugh stands up, looking down at the man who has suddenly become a complete stranger to him. Unable to stand the sight of him, the strangely serene expression on his face, he pulls Tom out of the pool and turns him over. Staggering, Hugh picks up his gun then goes into the house to change his shirt. In the closet, Tom's heavy smell overwhelms him and he feels a little sick. He chooses an oxford shirt, buttons it up, and heads for the door. Tom's keys beckon him on the table and Hugh thinks: Why not?

Hugh has always admired the Bronco, the rugged image it gave Tom, an image he envied. Plus, the jeep is good in weather like this. Tom will be with him in spirit, he thinks, brightening a little, the way they used to be, when they were friends.

The rain renews its vigor. The freeway is jammed, he slogs through traffic. Nobody knows how to handle weather out here, not like he does. He's driven through snowstorms, hail, hurricanes. This is nothing. The cars crawl along with trepidation. He doesn't know what he'll do to her when he finds her. He has the next five hours to figure it out.

18

They're at a gas station buying some food and drinks when Denny sees himself on CNN. The TV is up in the corner, over the cashier's head. Mindlessly, she bags their items: some cheese and crackers and a jar of peanut butter and a carton of milk and a bar of chocolate and some bottled water. He pays the woman while his fate unfolds up on the screen.

They show the car at the old man's farm; they show the empty trunk. They have Denny on camera, driving the BMW out of the airport parking lot. They have his army ID picture, the one they'd taken when he enlisted. They say he was allegedly involved in the gang rape of a thirteen-year-old Iraqi girl. They say he's been treated for PTSD. They make it sound like he's a psychopathic killer, like he has an ax to grind with the army, the administration, over the war. The woman out in the pickup is a movie producer, he learns. She made a film about the war that pissed people off. Now they are trying to connect the dots.

Back outside he gets the feeling Daisy wants to run. She twists away when he tries to touch her. Just then a cruiser pulls in and parks. Two cops get out and go inside. He waits till the doors close to ask her what's wrong.

"Is that true, what they're saying?"

"Some of it, not all."

"You raped someone?"

"No. No, I didn't. They've got that wrong."

"I don't know. I don't know anymore."

"You think it's true? You think I'd do something like that? You think I put that woman in the trunk?"

She whirls around, her eyes bright with rage. "What if it is? Where does that leave me?"

"Daisy, look at me," he whispers urgently. "I think you know me better than that."

Through the glass doors Denny sees the cops paying for their coffee, joking around with the cashier.

"Well, if you want to go, now's your chance. They're right there. They can send you back to your mother. Maybe that's where you belong. Just hurry up and make up your mind."

She gets into the truck, slides over into the middle, and resumes her position, holding up the old Coke bottle. But he can tell she still has her doubts. The woman's head lolls on her chest. He waits for the cruiser to pull out. He watches it disappear in his rearview mirror. Then he starts up the truck and drives the other way.

The tricky thing about war is you have to make decisions without having all the facts. It's something you get used to over there. But here, he doesn't have the excuse of war. The woman's life is in his hands. If she dies it'll be his fault. He doesn't know where a clinic is. Could be ten minutes away or two hours. In these parts you don't know. He feels the same anticipation he'd felt in Iraq, driving along in the convoy—anything could happen at any time. Anyone could be aiming at you, easing back the trigger. It didn't take much effort to end someone's life.

The desert is enormous. It stretches for miles on either side of the road. You don't see anyone, no people, no houses even. Nothing. Just that wobbly heat in the distance.

Both Daisy and the woman have fallen asleep, leaning against each other. At another time, he'd be proud of himself for taking such good care of them. But right now he feels at a loss. Pretty soon every cop within a hundred-mile radius will be looking for him, if they aren't already. And at this rate, it won't be long before they find him.

He drives another half hour with the sun beating down on the truck. Even with the windows open it feels like a furnace. Sweat runs out of him, down his back, his arms, his fingers even. Up ahead, maybe a half mile or less, they've blocked off the road. He can see some cops standing there, checking cars.

Waiting for him, he thinks.

Off to the right, beyond fields of desert grass, he notices a cluster of houses, a development of some sort, set back from the road. He turns down the private driveway past a sign that says Rolling Hills Development, only the sign is faded and weather-whipped. As he gets deeper in, he sees that the streets are vacant, the place is deserted. A kind of ghost town. Only the houses aren't old, they're new. Half-built houses lined up along the street, one after another, with unseeded, dirt yards. Open squares for windows, no glass. The roofs are intact, and the sides are wrapped in Tyvek, but no siding installed. A bunch of unrealized dreams, he thinks, imagining all the sad families who never got to live here. It comes to him that something started and unfinished is just as bad as something finished and torn apart, like the houses they'd ruined all over Iraq. Whole neighborhoods taken out, nothing left but dust and blood.

"What's this place?" Daisy says.

"Some kind of development. Looks like they ran out of money."

He pulls the truck up alongside a house. It's the farthest house on the cul-de-sac; he doubts it can be seen from the road. The woman is asleep, her head resting against the door. "Help me get her out."

They bring the woman in and lay her down on the floor and set up the IV, suspending the bottle of fluid with rope from one of the rafters. He feels her forehead, it's cooler. "It's working," he tells Daisy. "She's getting better."

He covers the woman with his jacket. She stirs a little and opens her eyes. "You feelin' better?"

She nods, but doesn't speak.

"That's okay, you don't have to talk. You just rest. We'll get you to a doctor as soon as we can."

She reaches for his hand, squeezes it with considerable strength. "Thank you."

"Don't mention it."

It's just the frame of a house, an empty dwelling. Floors of poured cement. It's plumbed, but no fixtures, no sink or toilets. Windows without glass. "It's nice," Daisy says. "It's nice here, Denny."

"It'll do for a while. I'm not sure how long."

"Look at all this space," she says, twirling around with her arms spread out. "This is our living room. And over here, this is our kitchen."

"We could put a table right here," he says, indulging for a moment in her fantasy.

"Look at the view." She peers out the open window, a little wind going through her hair. Then she starts up the stairs. "This place is amazing."

"Be careful."

"It's nice up here. Come up."

On the second-floor landing she looks at him, shy, and he pulls her close. "I'm sorry about before," she says. "I know that's not you."

He nods at her, appreciatively. "You should think about it, though. You should know what we're up against."

"The truth is the only thing that really matters."

"You're right." He looks away, a little scared of her.

"You want to tell me what happened?"

He shakes his head. "Things happen over there. It's war. You can't predict how you'll react. Everybody gets a little fucked up. People do things they might not have otherwise done, ugly things. I'm not saying it's forgivable; it's not. But the situation makes you different."

She puts her hand on his face like a mother. "It hurt you, didn't it?"

"Yes," he says softly. "It still hurts."

"Put your head here," she whispers.

They stand there a moment, holding each other.

"One day, I'll give you a house," he tells her. "A real house just like this, only finished."

She smiles and closes her eyes like she's making a wish. Her face is shaped like a heart. He touches her cheek.

"We can just pretend," she says, opening her eyes. "That's almost just as good."

He kisses her slowly, carefully. "Welcome home."

They feast on crackers and peanut butter and chocolate. Then they walk up the incline behind the house to look over the ridge. The sun is setting. They stand there a while, looking down at a valley. In the distance there are horses, a whole herd crossing the plain. Denny feels the earth trembling under his feet. It is something to see, the way they all run together, their shadows following behind, quick as clouds.

"You're not afraid of anything, are you?" she says.

"No, I'm not. I've already been through the worst of it. Can't get much worse than that."

When they get back the rooms are dark. The woman is muttering something, steeped in dreams. They kneel down beside her.

"Is she okay?" Daisy says.

"She's feverish."

"She's dreaming."

"She's been though a lot. She needs a hospital."

"Who would do that?"

"Some crazy person."

"It's sad."

"I know."

"It frightens me."

"Me too. Can you sleep?"

"Maybe. No. Not yet anyway."

"You should rest. Do you want to count sheep?"

"Some people count sheep, I say the pledge."

"The Pledge of Allegiance?"

"I still remember the whole thing. I don't know why. It's kind of stupid."

"Let me hear it."

She says the pledge, standing there with her hand on her heart like a third grader.

"When was the last time you were in school?"

"I made it through tenth grade."

"What was your favorite subject?"

"Art, I guess. What about you?"

"History. I liked all the stories. I enlisted the day I graduated."

"Why?"

"I don't know why, really. I thought it would be a good experience."

She laughs.

"I swear. I really did."

"You're crazy, Denny. You know that?"

"Come over here."

"I'm scared to."

"Why?"

"I'm too in love."

"Come over here. Let me hold you."

She comes to sit with him and he pulls her back against his front, making a chair for her, keeping her warm. She smells like peanut butter.

"I said I'd take care of you."

"I know."

"Where's that harmonica?"

She takes it out of her pocket and plays a slow, sad song that he doesn't recognize. It comes to him that there are things about her, things she's experienced, that she will never tell him. And on his side things he won't tell her. Maybe that's all right, he decides. Maybe you don't have to know everything about the person you love.

Finally, when she has exhausted herself, she curls up next to him on the floor and falls asleep. He stays up for a long while, keeping watch, hearing the wind outside rattling the Tyvek, the loose boards of the house, and the distant trucks on the highway barreling through the night.

19

The man and the girl come back, rattling a grocery bag. You are sitting up, something dripping into your thigh. You rest your head on the seat. It still hurts a little where they stuck the needle in. It is the thorn of a rose, you realize. The truck starts to move. The world smears past. The light is very stark. The light is cruel, it wants to bite you. The white sand, the white sky. You are lace; you are paper, you are a clear voice singing. You feel close to God and it terrifies you. Deep inside your head, in the muddy orbit of your brain, someone is whispering.

The truck slows down. The moon is rising, the stars twist and blur.

"Where are we?" the girl says. "What's this place?"

Their voices fade and wander. They leave you alone. You feel as if you're falling. You have fallen into a black pool, a black abyss.

In a little while you hear them again. Vaguely, you realize he is carrying you. You can smell his sweat. It is the smell that comes after lovemaking, the scent you wear all day to remind you. Who is it that you love—you can't remember now. Gently, you descend to the floor. He looks into your eyes, but you cannot return his gaze. You see things there, things he doesn't even know. In your state, you are a privileged spectator. The floor is cold. But it is good to be lying down. He fixes the needle on your thigh and you remember that you are wearing your favorite Marc Jacobs skirt. You had been dressed for work. You'd had a lunch date scheduled. Parker's, you remember, suddenly cognizant, suddenly remembering that you are a woman of some influence. The last time you went to Parker's you'd complained so viciously about the service that you'd reduced the waitress to tears. The manager had fired her on the spot. And you'd been satisfied. What you jokingly refer to as a satisfied customer.

You were running late that morning. He had come out of your garage.

Shivering, your body runs with sweat. It is the thick, painted on sweat of a fever. If it had a color it would be green. It is the green tongue of death, you think.

The idea sickens you and you lean over and retch. Whatever's inside you must come out. You need to be empty. Pure.

He wipes your head, your mouth, with a wet cloth.

You drift and sleep. When you wake it is dark and there are candles. You wonder distantly if you have died, If this is your funeral. Where is everybody, you wonder? And then you remember that you have no friends. What a shame, you think, what a sad thing. You hear the sound of a harmonica. It is a gentle sleepy sound. You imagine that you are a cowgirl around a campfire, but there is no fire here and you have begun to shake. You are shivering with cold and yet you can feel the sweat running out of you like a very slow leak. Eventually, it will all run out. There will be nothing left.

You drift, you need water and yet you are still unable to drink. There is a place you want to go to inside your head. A weary light taunting you like someone walking through a dark field with a lantern. There are people there, waiting on the ridge. You don't know any of them, but still they wait for you. What is that smell: roses. No: they are the flowers on your coffin.

Someone is coming with a black cloth. It is a shroud, you think. A shroud for the dead. But no, it is not a shroud. You are mistaken. The sun is bright. There are two of them, two women in the distance, coming toward you through sand. They hold the cloth between them like a banner. They hold it up over their heads. They are proud and strong; victorious. It catches the wind, it billows up on the blue sky. They too are in black. Long black robes. *Abayas*, you remember the word. They are Arabs, their dark eyes glittering. They have secrets for you. You shake your head. You don't want their secrets. They show you the cloth. For you, they say. *You are so beautiful.* You try to explain. You don't wear these. You are an American woman. You have different ideas, different customs. *But you must, for your own protection. To keep the worms off you.* They giggle, as if you are trying to amuse them, and they catch you in their arms and wrap you up. The cloth is tight, it constricts you. You try to move, but you are trapped. You have no arms, no legs. You have no face. No name. *Don't worry,* the women tell you, *where you are going you don't need a name.*

His name is Denny, short for Dennis, you suppose. He is the one who saved you. He is the one who pulled you from the trunk and carried you in his arms and made you better. His skin is damp, red from the sun, and he smells of sweat and dirt. His hands are large, square, graceful as birds. He has been to war. You can see the war in his eyes. It sits there, crouching in his pupils like a lost child. He walks with a slight limp, but he's muscular, strong, his arms beautifully formed. The rest of him too. Strong, powerful. His hair is dark, his eyes shaped like fish, the way a child might draw them, with extra long lashes, pretty and feminine, but dark eyes that penetrate. Eyes that don't lie. He can't. He doesn't know how. He is young, open. Sad. Terrified.

The girl is very young. In the truck, her blond hair tickles your arm. She should be home with her parents, but she is here, with him. Maybe it's all right. She is like sunlight, always moving. Never still. Or maybe she is a shadow. She is never without his gaze. She wears his love like a veil.

"Who are you?" he asks, when you open your eyes.

I am nobody; I don't exist. "I don't know."

"You mean you can't remember."

You shake your head, but it isn't true. You know exactly who you are. When you picture yourself, in your old life, your eyes burn and you have to stop. There are sharp rocks inside your head. Your thirst is unquenchable. It is time to drink. It is time to recover from this ordeal.

The girl is lighting candles. "Make a wish."

The small flames dance in the wind.

His breath smells of chocolate. "You didn't tell me you were famous."

"What?"

"We saw you on TV."

"He's famous too," the girl says.

"Famous for what," you ask.

"He's a war hero," the girl says.

But even in your state you can tell it's not the whole story.

"What happened to you?" he asks.

"Someone came to my house," you say, trying not to remember. A man appeared one morning, wearing an awful smile.

It was dark in the trunk, it was terrifying. You didn't think you would survive. You were hot; you were baking. Your mouth so dry you couldn't swallow. There was a chase, you rolled around like a watermelon. "What happened to the cop? Did you shoot him?"

"No, ma'am. We had an accident."

"He was going to accuse you of something."

"Yes."

"They're looking for you now, the cops?"

"I stole your car. I didn't know you were in it."

"You stole my car—why?"

"For kicks," he says.

"No. There was a reason."

He shakes his head. "You always ask all these questions?"

"I make movies," she admits. "It's what we do. Things have to make sense."

"Life doesn't always make sense."

"You can tell me."

He just looks at you and you understand at once that he doesn't want to talk about it in front of the girl. The girl crouches at your side like your own child—the child you will never have. She watches you, curious, as if you are some fallen angel. With tenderness, she smoothes your hair from your face, runs a damp cloth over your skin. The gesture, so honest and kind, makes your eyes tear. "This is Denny," she says. "And I'm Daisy. What's your name?"

I don't remember. "Hedda?"

"That's a funny name."

"My mother named me after a character in a play. *Hedda Gabler.*"

"Never heard of it," the girl says.

"You were in Iraq?" You see his tags, the dark hairs on his chest.

"Yes, ma'am."

"What was it like?"

"Hot."

"Tell me about it."

"It was hard."

"That's all you can say?"

He nods quietly; he doesn't want to talk about it.

Abruptly, you start to cry. Tears stream down your cheeks. "I'm sorry."

He puts his hand on your head. "It's just a fever," he says. "We need to get you to a hospital."

"It's too much of a risk," she says. "If they find you . . ."

He looks at you and you can see in his eyes that he is prepared to die.

"I'm thirsty," you say.

"Good. Let me help you up."

He comes behind you and pulls you up and leans you against the wall. He pours some water into a cup and brings it to your lips. The water tastes like the sky. He hands you a cracker. "Try one of these."

Your mouth waters for it. You put it into your mouth and consume it ravenously. The salt unzips your hunger. Out of all of the food you have eaten in your life, the fancy meals, this is by far the best. This single perfect cracker.

"Good for you," he says, handing you the box. You are sitting, you are a person. Now you can see this place, this broken house.

"You saved my life."

He smiles, nods. You can see his pride.

"You're a hero. You're the real thing."

"No."

"But you are. I've never met one before."

"No, ma am. I'm no liar."

"To me you are."

"I'm nothing," he admits. "I'm no one."

"Why do you say that?"

"I have no soul."

"What happened to it?"

"A buzzard came and stole it."

"I lost mine too."

"How?"

"That man took it."

"You'll get it back."

"We both will."

20

Hugh stops at a gas station in Death Valley and uses the toilet. There's a mirror over the urinal, and he can't help watching his face as he relieves himself. It's a strange place to hang a mirror, he thinks, and he doesn't really feel like looking at himself right now. A bruise floats over his eye like a jellyfish. It occurs to him that he's probably wanted for murder. Before he'd come out to Los Angeles, he never would have predicted that his life would change, that he would become a criminal wanted by the law. But that's what he is now. Just like in *Breathless*, when Belmondo kills the cop on a half-assed jocular impulse. He's misunderstood; a man who makes a single, fatal mistake. Just like him, he thinks. Only he doesn't really *feel* guilty. If they catch him and send him to prison, he doesn't think he'll be able to survive. But lots of people go to jail and make it through somehow. The idea of it terrifies him more than anything else, even death. By now they've probably gone through his apartment. They've seen the file he'd made on Hedda Chase. And chances are they'd found her pocketbook in the back of his closet. Somehow, he hadn't wanted to part with it. He'd even used that famous black soap of hers; it had made his skin peel. And her undergarments had been expensive. He's never been with a woman who had underwear like that. From time to time, when he was drunk or depressed, he'd take all of the things out of her bag and examine them carefully, like the souvenirs of a trip.

He buys some coffee and a buttered roll. The cashier is a redhead with buck teeth.

"I'm looking for a friend of mine," he says, and shows her a picture of Hedda Chase. "She's my girlfriend."

The girl shakes her head, shrugs. "Sorry. Haven't seen anyone like that."

"She's the one from Hollywood who went missing." He gives her a pleading look. "They found her car down here some place."

"Oh, that." Now her eyes light up. "Just down the road. Old man Wheeler's place."

"Thank you," he says. "I appreciate your help."

About a mile down the road he comes to a small ranch. A wood sign that says Wheeler on it. There's a trailer at the end of a long drive. An old cowboy comes to the door. "What now?"

"I got your name from someone down the road," Hugh says.

"I thought I got rid of all you reporters last night."

Hugh said, "Do I need to resort to money?"

"Wouldn't hurt."

"How's twenty bucks?"

"Twenty bucks a question and we got a deal." The old man lets him in. The man's wife is in bed, staring up at the ceiling.

"Don't mind her," the man says.

"What's the matter with her?"

"You gonna waste your money on her?"

Hugh looks around. "I heard he stole your truck."

"Yes, sir. Cleaned me out of house and home while he was at it."

"What color is it?"

"Red."

"Any idea where they might be at?"

The old man holds out his hand and Hugh obliges him.

"I have no idea." He grins at him, enjoying his little game. "I would doubt they'd gotten very far, though. Now that it's been on the TV and all."

Hugh glances around at the distant canyons. "You wouldn't have a pair of binoculars I could use?"

"For a small price you can have anything you want. Even her." He gestures to the old woman. Hugh contemplates her deeply lined face, her ragged breath.

"Maybe I'll take you up on that," he hears himself say.

The old man looks over at his wife.

"What's wrong with her?"

"She had a stroke." His eyes mist up a moment and he catches himself. "We get along all right." The old man fishes his binoculars out of a drawer. "Now, look. There's a road just down yonder—you don't even have to drive into the park—it'll take you up past Monarch Canyon, give you a real nice view of the valley."

"That would be fine," Hugh says, and the old man draws him a map.

"We can settle up when you bring those back."

Hugh thanks him and gets back into Tom Foster's jeep and drives down where the old man showed him and turns up the road into the canyon. The road is rough and deserted and he's grateful for the jeep. He goes up about eight miles to the top of a peak then pulls the jeep off to the side and parks. He gets out and looks through the binoculars across the valley. The sun is lower now, a white disc. The sand is golden white, studded with sagebrush and cactus flower. It is the most beautiful thing he has ever seen and it makes him melancholy that his life has come to this.

He switches direction to the west and comes upon a herd of horses. They are running together across the plain, dark browns and bays and paints and palominos. Abruptly, the landscape changes to a cluster of houses in the shape of a horseshoe. There isn't anyone around, no people or anything, except for this one truck parked alongside a house. A red Chevy pickup.

21

Hedda had thrown up the crackers and water. When he feels her head it's hot. Her fever has returned. The Coke bottle had drained out and he'd removed the needle from her thigh. Now her skin has a pasty, yellow color to it, and her eyes are glassy as a drug addict's. It is dusk; time to find a doctor; time to get the hell out of this place. He lifts the woman off the floor and carries her out to the truck. The air is cooler, and a swift wind blows. Daisy is picking wild flowers along the side of the house. There is beauty everywhere, he thinks, you just gotta know where to look for it. "Daisy," he calls. "Let's go."

He sets the woman down on the seat. She's flushed, enervated, and when she speaks it's in a raspy whisper. "There's something I want to say to you," she says. "Before we go."

"Yes, ma'am," he says gently. "What is it?"

"It's about whatever it was you did. What the army wants you for."

Avoiding her eyes, he looks around the empty cul-de-sac. Tumbleweed. Dead houses. A red sky.

"You can't run forever." She takes his hand and holds it tight. "You're a good man. You're not a man who runs away."

He nods to let her know he understands, but he's of a different opinion. She is a woman of dreams, not reality. And dreamers don't make the laws.

Faintly, he hears Daisy singing. And then it goes quiet. Eerie quiet. He walks around back to look for her, but she's disappeared. With his heart clanking he goes back into the house. "Daisy?" But the house is empty, like they'd never even been there. A chill washes over him.

Maybe she's waiting in the truck, he thinks, and walks back around to the front to check, but it's just the woman in the truck, no sign of her. And then he sees her coming round the corner of the house, only she's not alone. There's someone with her, holding her around her neck. Someone he recognizes. And he has a gun.

"I had to get stitches because of you," he says, holding up the gun.

Denny thinks of his gun in the truck, under the seat.

"Get down on the ground. Go on. Do it now."

Daisy squirms and he grips her hard.

"At least let her go," Denny says. "You don't want her getting hurt."

"She's already been hurt," the man says. "It's not right. It's not right what happens in this world. She's just a girl. She shouldn't be here, with you. You should have known better. She needs a home, her parents."

You can smell evil on people, Denny thinks. And this asshole reeks of it.

"Down on your knees. Put your hands behind your head."

They had made their prisoners do it in Iraq. They'd lined them up on the side of the road. Denny could remember the look in their eyes. The bitterness. The hate. When you come to a point and you know it's over and there's nothing you can do about it. He doesn't guess there's anything worse than that.

"No, please," Daisy cries. "Let him up."

"It's all right, honey," Denny tells her, even though it's not. Not even close. The ground is warm; it smells of dirt and life and death, too. It smells of everything he never did, or forgot to do. As a boy he'd wanted to go to medical school, something he's never told anyone. But he wasn't very good at school. And his aunt and uncle didn't have the money to send him to any college. Still, he could have done it; he could have worked harder. Maybe taken classes someplace. One step and then another, that's all it takes. He'd been distracted by stupid things, that was the truth. Thought he wasn't smart enough; wasn't good enough. It's why he'd enlisted, he realized. He thought the army would be good for him. Make a man out of him and all that nonsense just like the commercials said they would. And the army was good; there were good things about it. But not the war. Nobody deserved to go to war. Nobody.

The man walks over to him and steps on his head.

If he survives this, he thinks, he's going to turn himself in. He's going to tell his version of the truth and hope for the best. The woman was right about him, he realizes. He's not a man who runs.

22

It's your turn, you think, your turn to make things right. You owe it to Denny. The gun feels heavy in your hand. Still, you are all right. You can make it. You get out, feel the ground beneath your feet. Your legs are shaking and your back aches, your kidneys, but it is of no consequence now. You have other things to worry about. The man's name is Hugh Waters. It comes into your head, clear as a bullet. As you come around the front of the truck he sees you. Something registers on his face, a weary dissatisfaction, as though you have disappointed him somehow. "Drop your gun," you say, because there is nothing else to say at a time like this, and you have thought about these sorts of scenes a million times, the fact that they never quite make sense, the fact that when there are two guns involved somebody has to fire first. And somebody has to die. You raise the gun, but you are shaking so miserably you're not sure you can even fire it. Sweat burns your eyes, blurs your vision. Your heart pounds inside your chest.

He laughs abruptly. "So you were right after all."

"Right about what?"

"The ending. You got out. You were saved."

"That's right. I was saved."

"Kind of a shame about your boyfriend, though."

"What?" You move a little closer.

"Tom Foster. Not much of a fighter."

You stand there shaking, thinking about Tom. "What did you do?"

"It's not like you were married to the guy."

246

You don't know how to fire a gun, that's your trouble. You don't know anything about guns. You assume there's a safety release, but you can't find it; maybe you just need to pull the trigger. Could it really be that easy? You're afraid to do it. You've never been so frightened in your life. Tears stream down your face. You stagger closer to him, trying to get a better aim. That's the whole problem with your life, you think, right there in a nutshell. Not having all the facts. Not being totally prepared. You're so damn smart you get by with just a little effort. But where's your commitment? Never really been committed to anyone, have you? Nope. True love and all that. Not for you. You're way too cynical to buy into that crap.

If only you could see straight, you think. If only the world weren't spinning.

"Put that thing down before you hurt yourself," he says, and the line is familiar to you. It's familiar because you've heard it in a thousand different movies, only this time it's not a movie, it's real, and he is not some endearing cowboy, but a man who wants to kill you. You want to tell him what a stupid line it is, but it's too late. Your finger squeezes the trigger. And just before you pass out, you watch him fall.

23

In Foster's jeep, they have no trouble getting through the check-point. The town's a tiny grid. The clinic is on Irving Street. They spend some time trying to find it. It's a small square building with a few parking spots out front. Denny pulls right up. He and Daisy get out and they walk around and open the door for Hedda. He pulls the woman into his arms.

"I'm getting kind of used to this service," she says.

"Don't get too used to it."

"I guess we're even now."

"That's right. Fair and square. Thanks."

"Don't mention it." Her eyes shine.

People in the army used to say once you stood at death's border you never came back all the way. You left something behind. Hocus pocus, he thinks now. Still, he feels something for this woman. Something profound. And she feels it too. And he doesn't think either of them will ever forget it.

He brings her inside and raps on the shaded glass. The little door slides open and a nurse looks out and gets up right away and opens the door and tells him to bring Hedda inside and put her down on the gurney. Other people come over and get busy hooking her up. Denny identifies her as the missing woman from Los Angeles, the one on the news.

A doctor comes over to examine her and notices the bruise on her thigh.

"I had to make an IV," Denny explains. "She was dehydrated. She's been through a lot."

"Lucky you did. I doubt she would have made it otherwise." The doctor puts his hand on Denny's shoulder, heavy and sure. "Good work, son."

Denny backs out the door and his eyes go damp with pride. His work is done here. Plus he doesn't want any more questions. Somehow he knows it's the last time he'll ever see her.

Daisy waits for him on the steps, the sun on her face. Sirens, fast approaching, fill the air. "She okay?"

"She'll be fine."

"What's it like to be a hero?"

He shakes his head, about to deny it, but she's waiting for his answer, her arms crossed over her chest with expectation.

"What's it like? It feels pretty good. Now tell me this: What's it like to be so beautiful?"

She just grins at him.

An ambulance pulls up in front of the clinic. "We better get going. There's a bus station around the corner."

"What about Tom's jeep?"

"We'll leave it. They'll think we're still here someplace." He takes her hand. "You're not scared, are you?"

He knows she is but won't admit to it. Instead, she asks, "Are you?"

"I got you to protect me, don't I?"

She smiles, humbly.

"Of course I'm scared. But being scared's a whole lot better than being dead. Anyway, two scared people are better than one, that's what I always say."

The EMS attendants pull Hugh Waters out on a stretcher. As they pass, Waters gives Denny a look that leaves him cold. It's the look of a man who's already dead, but somehow, out of spite maybe, keeps on living, determined to drag the rest of the world down with him.

"Don't look at that, it'll hurt your eyes." Denny puts his arm around the girl and pulls her close. "Come on, darlin'. Let's get the hell out of here."

Just seconds after they turn the corner the cruisers pull up in front of the clinic, the whole place crawling with cops. They catch the next bus to Vegas and sit crammed together, holding hands. The bus is full of gamblers and servants. People trying to change their luck. Just now he is one and the same as them.

Daisy rests her head on his shoulder and he watches out the window as the little town fades behind them and the golden plains spread out, studded with sagebrush and cactus and Joshua trees. They pass shacks and ransacked pickup trucks and clotheslines strung up with sheets billowing and a flag-pole in the middle of goddamn nowhere, its flag snapping in the wind. *Let freedom fucking ring,* he thinks.

He closes his eyes for a moment and says a prayer for him and Daisy, then opens them with confidence, having negotiated their fate with the man upstairs.

24

You wake in a strange room, hearing a familiar voice. Tom.

"Son of a bitch almost killed me," he explains to the nurse, a humorless woman with fastidious hands who is writing notes in a chart. "I guess I got lucky." You feel him take your hand. "I guess we both did." He looks at you. "Good morning, gorgeous. Feeling better?"

You don't answer because you don't feel better. You feel weak and sad. And you don't want to talk. Not yet anyway. You study his face, the bruises and welts, his swollen hand.

The nurse opens the curtains, an assault of sunlight. You shut your eyes, sprouting tears, hearing her say, in an uncharacteristic tone of frivolity, "Oops, you lost one." She bends to retrieve something off the floor and drops it into Tom's palm, the petal of a rose.

Inez, you think.

"For you," he says, arranging the sprawling bouquet in a vase. He kisses your forehead. "You'll be all right, Hed. Get better so we can go home."

Home. You don't remember what that means. The image of your rental house comes back to you—that awful day—no, you refuse to remember it and shake your head with anguish.

"Not there," he says. "The villa."

Yes, your villa. But you shake your head again. You don't know; you don't know if you can go back.

"You'll be all right, Hed," he says again, as if he were trying to reassure himself. "Just give it time."

It isn't until later, after you've had some water, some apple juice, a small bite of toast that you remember you might have killed someone. The idea of it fills you with unspeakable dread. And yet when that bullet flew out, there was nothing you wanted more than to kill. It was basic; primitive. The man you shot had gone down.

But now you are not so sure. There are cops in the hall. One sits on a squeaky chair outside your door. Later, one comes to take your statement. He sits in the green vinyl chair by the window, writing down what you say, his eyes dim with accusation. Vaguely, you wonder if you are in some sort of trouble. After he leaves, you weep like a woman condemned.

Left alone, you watch the day drop to its knees. The hours drift. The sky is very pale now, almost lavender, and you sense that it may rain, but the nurse shakes her head and says it never rains in the desert. Still, all through the night, the sky howls with something like loss.

In the morning Tom comes—this man who claims to love you, who has promised to leave his wife for you. He wants to start again, he says. "For the rest of our lives."

He brings you little presents and dumps them out on the end of the bed in a frenzy of willful deliverance. Magazines, a tin of lemon drops, comics, even whiskey, which he conceals inside a rolled-up newspaper. When the nurse disappears, you let the liquid slide over your tongue. It tastes of straw, remorse. None of it interests you, not really. His eyes are guilty, impatient; greedy. You look at him and think: *You are too late.*

You sleep and wake to their whispering—hissing whispers like the buzzing of trapped flies. Their words sting your ears: trauma; stress; denial. The nurse admonishes Tom's impatience, *She's going to be all right, I promise*—but you are not really sure if you will be all right. The nurse insists, "You'll be back to your old self in no time." But you know it is a lie. Because your old self has already gone.

She has taken your marvelous car and left this place, driving the open highway with the windows down, the wind roaring in her ears. You can picture her there in the seat in her white blouse, the heavy beads around her neck, her hair unconfined in the wind as she drives, barefoot, as fast as she can.

There is something beautiful about a woman making her escape, you think. Something beautiful as she crosses the desert, a fearless pioneer. Heading west. Straight into the sun.

ACKNOWLEDGMENTS

I would like to acknowledge the men and women of the military who have risked their lives for our country. I am especially grateful to a very special marine named Sean who shared his experiences in Iraq with me. The marvelous book *War and the Soul: Healing Our Nation's Veterans from Post-Traumatic Stress Disorder* by Edward Tick, PhD, served as a reference point for the creation of Denny Rios. Had it not been for the courageous and excellent reporting of several journalists I would not have been able to fully understand the war in Iraq and its ultimate effect on the country, our soldiers and their families.

I am indebted to my editor, Carole DeSanti, for both her critical judgment and ideological support, as well as to my agent, Linda Chester, for her sustained belief in my work. My deep thanks also to Clare Ferraro, Kristin Spang, Christopher Russell and Gary Jaffe.

Special thanks to Susie Landau Finch, Rafael Papaleo, MD, Marilyn Mendell, Will Taylor of Bavarian Autosport, Joe Aberdale of A & J Gun Shop in Housatonic, Massachusetts, Scott Morris, MD, Betty Sigoloff, Pat Van Gorp, Harris Appelman, Anita Straussberg, Vivian Friedman, Beth Pine, Stewart and Susan Kampel, Helen Beck, Janice Denburg, Gloria Winston, Grace Dugan, Beth Appelman, Lynn Hidek, Ginny La Juene, Becky Marvin, Matthew Tallow, Jeff Jacobus, Cheryl Kravetz, Paula Lippman, Gladys Cook, Toby Cooperman and Killara Burn of Hampshire College. Finally, I would like to thank my parents, Joan and Lyle Brundage, and my aunt Dorothy Rosenberg, for their incredible support and guidance.

Also by
Elizabeth Brundage

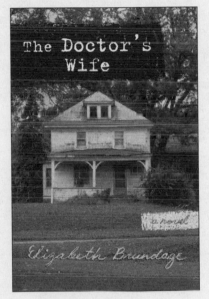

ISBN 978-0-452-28691-7

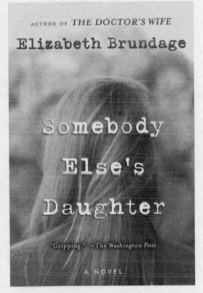

ISBN 978-0-452-29537-7

Visit www.elizabethbrundage.com

Available wherever books are sold.

 Plume
A member of Penguin Group (USA) Inc.
www.penguin.com